Shadows Wake

By Aiki Flinthart

To all the authors out there – both published and aspiring – don't give up.

Thank you to my husband for his unfailing support and willing services as beta-reader. Thanks also to everyone who has encouraged and assisted me along this very challenging journey called authorship. Often, it sucks, and only the kindness of friends and strangers keeps you going.

Shadows Wake

Cover artwork by Harper by Design
Copyright © 2018 Aiki Flinthart

A Cataloging-in-Publications entry for this title is available from the National Library of Australia.

ISBN-13: 978-0-6482878-0-3 (Trade Paperback)
ISBN-13: 978-0-9945660-9-6 (e-book)
Computing Advantages & Training P/L
PO Box 3388, Darra
QLD 4076, Australia

NOTE: This book is written with AUSTRALIAN SPELLINGS, not USA spellings.

Discover other titles by Aiki Flinthart at:
www.aikiflinthart.com
Including:
The 80AD series (YA Adventure/Fantasy)
80AD Book 1: *The Jewel of Asgard*
80AD Book 2: *The Hammer of Thor*
80AD Book 3: *The Tekhen of Anuket*
80AD Book 4: *The Sudarshana*
80AD Book 5: *The Yu Dragon*

The Kalima Chronicles (YA Adventure/Fantasy)
IRON – Book one in the Kalima Chronicles

Sold! (Contemporary Romance/Adventure)

Short Story Anthologies
Return
Like a Woman

Shadows Wake

Aiki Flinthart 2018

ONE

If they find you, run. Surviving is more important than proving yourself. So, promise me, Rowan? Just run.

My father's last words whispered in my head and I backed up the aisle between the pews, edging away from the two men and their reassuring smiles.

Just run? Easy for Dad to say. He wasn't here. Sometimes running wasn't possible. And sometimes it wasn't right. If I ran, sure, I'd survive. I was small for my age, but fast. Sarah was plump, soft, and slow. I had to protect her. She'd brought me here, but she wasn't part of this.

Why had I gone along with her suggestion to come into the cathedral? Why had I been stupid enough to leave the safety of my class tour group behind? Now we were both in danger. Thoughtless. Careless. Everything my mother had trained me not to be. How did I get us out of this?

'Carly?' Sarah's voice was tight, her face pale.

'We'll be ok, Sarah,' I whispered. 'Just follow my lead.' If only I believed my own words.

I pulled at her arm, dragging her towards a doorway about twenty steps behind. My boot heels tapped on the diamond-tiled floor. Around us the cathedral waited, dark and almost silent. Huge, white pillars and arches marched down either side of the central aisle. Sunshine poured through the rose window high in the west wall. A patch of the floor glowed in a blurred rainbow of colours. Dust danced in the beams; tiny angels floating in God's brilliance. My quick breaths disturbed them, set them swirling in the light. If only I believed in Him, maybe praying would help. Doubtful.

The two men moved towards us, their solid bodies and hands relaxed. Their faces were calm, eyes hidden by caps and sunglasses. They were dressed as tourists, complete with water bottles and backpacks. But their broad shoulders and sure strides seemed too arrogant. Whatever they wanted, it wasn't selfies with the stained glass window.

Fear and anger churned in my stomach. I swallowed them.

My mother, Anna, always said fear was just my imagination telling stories about how things might go. I couldn't listen. And anger screwed up my thinking and made me do horrible things. I couldn't afford that, either. She also said, *only when you're tested do you know who you truly are.* Anna thought I was a better person than I am. She also thought I was ready.

Then again, she wasn't here, either.

My mind wouldn't settle on a plan. It jumped about, playing with the fear-stories. I couldn't concentrate with my heart pounding so loud, my mouth dry.

'What do you want?' The quaver in my voice betrayed fear and I ground my teeth. Sarah whimpered.

'We represent an interested party who wishes to speak to you, Carly.' One of the men held out an empty, upturned palm. His tone was friendly. His mouth shifted into a wide smile. 'Come with us. You won't be harmed.'

'Riiight,' I said. 'I've seen enough movies to know that no-one ever means that.'

Who were these men? How did they know where to find me?

'You've got a smart mouth for a kid,' one of them replied coolly.

'Is there an age limit for having a smart mouth?' I shot back. 'I'd've thought thirteen would put me in the right bracket, actually. Teenager and all.'

The taller of the two men actually stifled a laugh.

Sarah gasped and tugged free of my hand.

I shuffled a few more steps backwards. Could I buy enough time for someone else to come into the cathedral and prevent this…whatever this was from happening?

'Go, Sarah,' I muttered. 'Run. I'll keep them busy.'

Her eyes widened and she bit her lip. The sound of our classmates' chatter faded and a door slammed. Thick wood blocked out the hum of traffic circling outside. Our school group had moved on. Sarah edged in the direction they'd taken.

'Who do you work for?' I glared at the men. 'What do they want?' I searched for other exits as my mouth bought time to reach them.

'Just to talk about...you.' Came the calm reply. 'And the *ocair*. You tell us where the *ocair* is and everything will be fine. '

'*Ocair*? What's th—' I shut my mouth. No point in even talking to these thugs. They probably didn't know either. It didn't matter, anyway. They stank of deceit.

'Run, Sarah,' I urged. 'I've got this.'

'Yes, Sarah.' The second man switched his gaze to her. 'You can go. You've done well. Speak to no-one or you know what will happen.'

I gasped. Sarah's brown eyes, usually narrowed and glittering with mischief, were wide and haunted. She swallowed hard.

'I'm sorry, Carly,' she whispered, moving further from me. 'I'm sorry. They said they'd take my sister if I didn't bring you.'

I had no words. They lodged in my throat behind the sick lump of betrayal. How could she? I gulped down tears and steeled myself. It was my own fault for trusting her. I should have known. Why else would she suddenly start being friends with me today?

With one more terrified look at my face, Sarah fled. Her sneakers made barely a sound on the hard tiles but her sobs echoed, almost like laughter.

I looked back at the men and squared my shoulders. I had this. Eight years of training had prepared me for this. They wouldn't expect a kid to fight. Staying calm was the key. I shuffled back, lifting my feet so my heels wouldn't catch. Behind, my fingers touched cool stone: the doorway arch.

I turned and ran into the half-lit space beneath the spire; on tiptoes to stop the echo. An open door cast a deep shadow. I slipped behind. Blood roared in my ears. My throat closed on a cry. Calling out was useless. The cathedral was empty. Besides, this was my problem. A witness would just make it harder to do what was needed.

Shadows shifted and slid across the walls, into my mind. My head throbbed. I leaned against the cold stone and stared into the darkness within.

Not again. Not now. Suddenly fighting seemed like a terrible option, but there was nowhere left to run.

Feet scuffed on stone. Red-hot blackness pressed against my thoughts. I bit my lip to prevent a cry; dug nails into my palms to distract from the pain. Tears made the dark space shimmer.

Strong fingers clamped onto my hand, grinding fine bones together. Images flickered and I knew his intent. But I froze, afraid to act, afraid of the result. Spikes of pain drove through my flesh and nerves. Into the prison holding blackness fast inside.

Something broke in my head. Darkness billowed out.

A gargling scream. The man dropped to his knees. He clutched his wrist, which dangled, broken. I lashed a kick at his head. He collapsed. A rustle of cloth gave warning. The second man grabbed for me. I ducked, turned, grabbed, twisted. Drove home an elbow then a knee. His blood warmed my skin.

Sickened, I stared down at the two men. One lay unconscious. The other groaned, holding his face. Scarlet seeped between his fingers. The scent of blood hung heavy in the cold air. My hands shook and I gulped for air in the still, hushed gloom.

The conscious man squinted up at me, sunglasses gone, eyes pained and astonished.

Fearful. Of me.

What should I do? Both men knew what I looked like.

What did they want with me? What was this *ocair* thing?

As I stood there, unsure, pain flowered in my head. An aching expectation gripped my chest and the metallic taste of ozone caught in my throat. The skin on the back of my head tightened. I rubbed it and looked around, searching for a new threat.

Strong fingers grasped mine again. The ground trembled. Low and soft at first, it rose through my feet into my chest until my body shook in time with the bones of the Earth. From somewhere outside, a scream floated, faint through the thick, grey walls. Stone cracked.

The man at my feet staggered upright.

'You're coming with me,' he snarled, and pulled at me.

The darkness surged forth again as the walls shuddered. Ozone and blood danced on the back of my tongue. My attacker fell back to his knees, eyes wide. His face twisted into agony and his eyes rolled up in his head. His skin crumpled to brittle paper. On my wrist, his fingers withered to brown, mummified sticks.

I burned from within. He was mine. The world was mine.

The room imploded.

Darkness...dust...a scream of despair...dust...a roar of unending, thundering destruction...blackness...nothingness…

I coughed through lips crusted in grit. My eyelashes were clogged as I opened them and saw...little dust-angels dancing in beams of sunlight. Sunlight? I'd been dreaming of forests, soft in silver-shadowed moonlight, keeping me safe from darkness and fire. Sunlight stabbed through the comforting scraps of my dream and blinded me. My head pounded.

Through a haze, inside my head and out, I squinted up. Blue sky arched above where before were shadows and stone. Why?

Voices called. Was it my name? Who was I supposed to be at the moment? Whoever called, they mustn't find me. Run. I had to run, like my father said.

I reached up to wipe my eyes but my fingers were bonedust-white. Brushing them on my shirt made no difference. With the inside of a collar, I rubbed most of the dust away. I struggled upright, leaning heavily on the gritty stone wall.

I licked my lips and spat out dirt. Of my attackers, nothing remained but a pile of broken stone and timber where they had lain, some ten metres away. How had I ended up so far away?

The church spire had collapsed. They couldn't possibly have escaped. A twisted, stick-like arm protruded from the stones, unmoving, dusted ghost-white. What had I done? I closed my eyes and clung to the wall, weak and trembling. Only the distant wail of sirens and screams of survivors broke the shivering silence.

Whoever wanted me, they had come too close this time. If it weren't for the earthquake I'd be in their hands now. Or maybe not, if what I thought I'd done was true. I didn't want it to be true. Either way, I'd been lucky to get out alive. I might not get a second chance.

I staggered a few steps and stopped, trying to think. I needed to get out of the building, find my mother and protect her. Hopefully they hadn't connected her to me yet and didn't know she existed. If she was safe we could get out of Christchurch, out of New Zealand entirely; make a new start under a new name. Leave it all behind.

Again.

Crap.

I yanked off the short blonde wig that made me Carly Edmonds and jammed it into my pocket. I wiped sweat from my forehead. My fingers came away red. Blood dripped into my eyes. Tears dripped from them. No. Crying wouldn't help. I tore a strip from my shirt and bound the gash by touch.

Voices screamed and called in a confused babble of wordless sound. I had to leave before anyone found me. Between me and safety lay a treacherous pile of broken timber and masonry. By the time I reached level ground again, my hands, knees and elbows all bled from deep grazes. I stumbled out the ruined square, mingling as one more frightened victim. The sun beat on my head and the stench of blood and pee rose from the ground, mingling with dust, catching in my throat as I picked my way through broken concrete and brick.

Huddled in the middle of the open square, my school group clung to each other as the teachers counted heads over and over. Off to one side, Sarah sat on the ground, staring in blank horror at the collapsed church spire and damaged cathedral. Tears left pink tracks down her white-dusted cheeks.

She looked around dully. Her eyes caught mine. She bit her bottom lip and glanced at our teacher. Sarah's mouth opened. I shook my head. She nodded and mouthed 'Go'. I slipped behind a car and hid myself from view.

In the midst of frantic people running, sirens, and the wails of the injured and lost, a moment of stillness stood out. Across the square: a man wearing almost the same "tourist" clothing as my dead attackers. He watched me. His bony face was hard and calm, his dark eyes thoughtful. A mocking smile curved thin lips.

They'd sent three.

After a quick check around the square he lifted his arms. A coat hid his right hand, but the hollow end of a pistol or tube was just visible in the shadow.

I froze. My legs refused to move and I trembled, awaiting death.

Darkness stirred again, rattling its cage.

Something plinked off the stone wall next to me. Liquid splashed onto my arm, bright sparkles glittering in the air like fireworks. A needle tinkled to the cobbles at my feet.

Darts. Some sort of drug?

He took aim again.

A black-windowed Hummer drove up, bouncing over debris to stop in front of him.

The ground rumbled. Dust shivered in the air and the screams took on new notes of terror as walls swayed and stone clattered off stone.

The shaking eased. I forced my feet to move and used the moment to slip out of sight. Hiding behind a half-destroyed building, I peeked around the corner at the rubble-strewn square.

He was gone.

Why did they want me? And what was this *ocair* thing? If I could find that out, it might answer a lot of questions. If they wanted the *ocair* badly enough, I might be able to use it as a bargaining tool to keep my mother and me safe.

Sick and sweating, I fled. Well-meaning emergency workers tried to stop me. I dodged them, uneasy as the world saw my real face, Rowan Gilmore's face.

I pushed down, into darkness, the memory of my attacker's wasted body. He'd been dead before the building fell on him. His light had burned within me. I tasted the remnants of it, still; lightning on my tongue. Whatever lay inside me had taken over and I hadn't been able to stop it.

Never again. I would be so careful from now on. I had to keep it under control; had to stay out of sight of these people, whoever they were. People weren't safe around me and I wasn't safe around them.

I wouldn't trust anyone. No one would ever find out. Ever. Because if I lost control completely…

I shuddered and ran on.

'Rowan! Rowan? Where are you?!'

I froze, then turned towards the voice. My mother stood at the edge of the cordon being erected by emergency workers. Her red hair danced in the breeze and she squinted against the sun.

I stumbled to her side. 'Anna!'

'Oh, God!' Her arms engulfed me and I was home. I sobbed into her shoulder as she stroked my back and held me tight against her softness.

Finally, we parted and she studied my face, her blue eyes anxious. 'Are you hurt? I was on my way to pick you up when the quake hit.' She lifted the bloodied cloth on my forehead. 'Not too bad. Anything else?' Her hands roamed over me, seeking assurance, giving it.

I shook my head and the words tumbled out: the men, the earthquake, the dartgun. She paled and glanced at the mad collapse of civilisation around us.

'You're sure you're ok? And they were definitely after you?' When I nodded, her jaw hardened and her eyes glittered as she swept the square with a piercing look. 'Damn!'

'What do we do?' I whispered. 'How did they find me?'

She stroked my sweat-matted hair back and smiled determinedly. 'It'll be alright, Rowan. We'll leave today. You'll be safe, I promise.' She kissed my cheek and gathered me close again, but her heart beat a rapid staccato under my ear and her breath came fast and shallow.

'You'll be safe,' she repeated.

We tell ourselves stories, inside our heads, about who we are. Usually they're stories about how special and important we are or would be. Usually they're wrong and we're depressingly-ordinary. But only when we're tested is the truth revealed.

So what happens if, just once, they turn out to be right?

Ordinary was my dream.

My truth lay elsewhere.

TWO

Five years later…

They aren't looking for us. They aren't even aware we're in the city.

<Who then?>

Not sure. They must be close to taking whoever it is, though. They're excited, but hiding it well. I just can't pinpoint who they're watching.

<One of ours?>

Reasonable assumption. Possible they aren't certain or they would have moved in already.

<Keep watch. If you can intervene without discovery, do it. If not, we can't jeopardise our mission. Be careful.>

Understood.

'Dammit!' I closed my eyes against the sight of the body sprawled at my feet. 'You're an idiot, Rowan Gilmore.' A quick check showed I was, at least, still out of sight of the security cameras.

The high, whitewashed walls of the MJE Enterprises employee gym echoed emptiness back at me. The big overhead lights were off, but city lights slanted through upper windows, illuminating the empty boxing ring and gym equipment in a sick, grey glow. Impossibly-perfect bodies and faces, plastered to every vertical surface, smirked down at me.

I tasted the faint smell of old sweat and antiseptic, and released it on a shuddering exhale. One moment. All it took was one moment of unguarded idiocy to undo everything. I hadn't made this sort of mistake since I was thirteen. What was wrong with me these days?

I'd broken someone. Already.

I rubbed at the back of my neck, trying to erase the uneasiness prickling there.

What was he doing sneaking up on me anyway? Who was he? Building security? No. No uniform and he looked only about my age of eighteen. Had he seen anything?

Blue rubber jigsaw mats underfoot absorbed sound as the guy on the floor groaned. At least he was alive and coming to. How injured was he? Any minute he'd open his eyes and the game would be up. Did I cut and run now? Everything was ready.

He blinked vaguely up at me and shook his head, comically dazed. I suppressed a laugh that had more to do with relief than humour. He groaned and pressed his temple before rising clumsily to his feet.

I stood back, my hands safely tucked behind me.

'You OK? That was some fall.' I tried to sound bluff and encouraging with a hint of concern. Not too concerned though. Not like I'd been worried, seconds before, that I'd killed him. Would he remember what had happened?

He staggered and squinted down at me. His handsome face firmed to good humour. Now he looked familiar. His blond hair was barely mussed and his white t-shirt and cargo pants were tailored and still crisp.

'What the hell happened?' He grimaced and pinched a neck muscle between lean fingers. 'I was just trying to get your attention and then...I have no bloody idea. What'd you do? I feel like I've been hit by a truck.'

'Nothing. You tripped on the edge of the mat and just about broke your neck. Scared the crap out of me.' I held his gaze with practiced innocence. He glanced down at the mat. I'd lifted the corner moments before, while he was still out.

'Huh. Well that was dumb. Good thing I learned how to fall in judo.'

'Yeah.' I smiled weakly. 'Sure you're ok?'

He grinned. 'No worries. Just don't tell anyone what a klutz I am.'

'Your secret is safe.'

'What're you doing here, anyway? I was on my way up to meet my dad.' He jerked a thumb at the ceiling. 'He's at a meeting. Saw you and thought I'd come introduce myself. We're seniors at the same school, y'know?'

Ah, now I recognised him. I'd seen him around the halls of Cairns High and already decided he was a good person to avoid. Anyone who attracted that amount of attention was trouble. Not that he'd ever notice me. Compared to the flashy cream-skinned beauty of the girls he hung with, my current look of long, dark-brown hair and grey-blue eyes faded into the background.

Being ignored was the point. I was good at it. Being invisible at school was practically my super-power. Well, one of them.

On the wall above, the clock ticked in loud, dragging clunks, nearing six o'clock, filling the silence I left in the wake of his question.

He cleared his throat and shuffled his feet, his smile sliding to the determined. He stuck out a hand.

'I'm Paul. Paul Eisen. We sit next to each other in History.' He grinned wryly. 'But you might not have noticed today. Looked like you fell asleep when Fraser was droning on about Vikings invading

England.' He chuckled. He had a nice laugh. It made his blue eyes crinkle at the corners and showed off even, white teeth.

He'd been watching me in History?

'Ah.' I cleared my throat. Conversation. Always tricky. 'Yes, who'd have thought the people who gave us elves and dwarves could be taught in such a dull way?'

He kept his hand out long enough that it became awkward and I had to respond. I grasped his carefully. I much preferred the Asian custom of bowing. Nothing stirred; nothing bled through. Thank God. Hopefully that meant these gloves worked.

'Meghan Greene.' I wasn't thrilled with my new name. My turn to choose next time. Anna always chose colours for some reason. Last time I'd been Leanne Ochre for chrissake!

'Yeah, I know.' He inspected my thin, grey, fingerless gloves, and raised his eyebrows. They were ordinary gloves, not gym-workout style. It must look strange. 'Wait, what? Elves?'

I retrieved my hand and fiddled with a loose hair over my ear. Catching myself at the nervous gesture I stuffed my fist deep into the pocket of my baggy gym shorts.

'And dwarves. Straight from Viking mythology to you via Lord of the Rings.' Serious nerd-stuff. If that didn't send him running, nothing would.

'Huh.' Paul cocked his head. 'They were good movies. I don't see you around school much. Where do you hang at lunch?'

'Library.'

'How come?' He sent me a look laced with curiosity and just a hint of scorn – though that could have been my imagination. 'You don't have to. You've only been here what, two or three weeks? Get out and make friends.' He waved at himself and gave an exaggerated leer. 'We don't bite. Much.'

'But I do,' I said, dead-pan.

Paul blinked at me and I relented.

'Sorry. Dumb joke. Library's quieter.' Truth be told, libraries and the internet were the source of far more of my education, and ongoing research, than schools were. If my mother'd let me I'd do all my schooling that way. Friends were the last thing I needed.

I glanced around the silent gym. I'd come here after hours on a Friday precisely to avoid encounters with people. Most of the MJE staff bolted straight after work, home to families, friends, beers, and the beginning of the weekend.

'What're you doing here?' He sounded more curious than belligerent. 'This isn't a public gym, y'know.'

'Safer than the public gyms. I have an employee card,' I said, concerned he might report me to security. 'I did some data analysis work for Anna Morgan after school. Thought I'd get some training in after sitting around all day. I like it when it's not so busy.'

'Oh?' His blue eyes turned thoughtful. 'You're working with Anna? That new change management consultant?' He chuckled. 'Everyone's scared shitless of her.'

I nodded and stepped off the mat, drawing him away from the memory of being slammed into the ground. He paced beside me, moving quietly for such a tall guy. He had a gym-built physique that would quickly succumb to gravity if he stopped training.

'Hey, I've got to meet Dad upstairs for a few minutes but after that I'm free. Wanna come to the movies tonight? A few of us are going to see the latest Marvel movie – if you're into that sorta thing?' He shrugged, his charming smile undiminished by my lack of immediate enthusiasm.

'Thanks, but I can't tonight…or at all this weekend,' I added as he opened his mouth again. 'Sorry.' I offered a faint, false moue of regret.

He hesitated, looking aggrieved for a moment before grinning carelessly. 'Whatever. Some other time then?'

I shrugged once more, temporising this time. Paul seemed to take it as assent and launched into a description of his friends, the movie and his plans for the weekend. I regarded him beneath my lashes with a mixture of regret and hope. Catching myself, I pressed my lips together. I picked up my gym bag and flung it onto my shoulder with more force than necessary.

Hope? Really? Hadn't I learned my lesson yet?

Paul frowned at me, turning his head this way and that. 'Hey, are you and Anna related? You just…well you look a bit alike.' He pointed at my long, dark-brown wig. 'Apart from the hair, that is.'

I groaned inwardly. As hard as we tried to hide my existence from the world, in small towns like Cairns it was difficult. We did look enough alike that our relationship was obvious to people who saw us together. Paul was too sharp for comfort.

There was no point in denying it, so I nodded. 'My mother.'

'Well that's great! I just thought,' he added, eager again, 'y'know, since you'll be here a bit if you're working for Anna, and I'm here a lot helping my Dad, we could hang. Dad'll be cool about it.'

I shrugged just one shoulder this time and turned aside. So *that's* what this was about. Very occasionally, someone made the connection between the new kid at school and the woman hired to drag some local business into the modern world. Then, inevitably, they thought I could influence Anna on who to fire and who to keep. If nothing else occurred to make things worse for me, the badgering would go on for a few months, until we moved.

Private though the gym here was, coming to the building where she worked had been stupid and, as it turned out, a waste of time.

'Meghan.' Paul touched my arm and halted. I pulled my wrist away as gently as I could. He still looked affronted.

This had to stop. Whatever he was doing, I couldn't afford to buy into it and there was no point in torturing myself with the possibility of normality happening. He was just sucking up to me because his dad's job was at stake. I had to keep that in mind.

'Look, you seem like a nice guy Paul.'

He raised one brow. 'I hear a "but" coming.'

I lifted a shoulder. 'I just don't think it's smart to get too friendly with anyone connected to MJE. It complicates things for my mother.'

He stared down at me, a mixture of disbelief and annoyance in those clear blue eyes. 'You're dodging me because our parents work together? That has to be the most bass-ackward thing I've ever heard.'

'I'm flattered but I'm just not the kind of girl you want to be friends with. My life's complicated and I'm only in town for a little while. We'll be moving on as soon as Anna's job is done. I can't get tied down here. Sorry.'

He tilted his head and sent me a shrewd look that belied his cheerful, open countenance.

'But don't you get lonely, doing all that travelling? You're eighteen. You should be out partying and having fun. You avoid everyone like the plague.' He gave a sympathetic half-smile. 'But you don't really strike me as the loner loser type. What's with you?'

'I'm a cold-hearted bitch who'd rather read than party?'

He laughed and shook his head. 'Nah. I saw the way you stood up for that first year kid in the hall last week.'

When I looked blankly at him, Paul grinned lopsidedly. 'Never seen Adam Burke look so shit-scared. Whatever you said to him, it worked, he hasn't looked sideways at the younger kids and he's stopped groping the girls as well. What did you say?'

I twitched a smile, savouring again the moment the bully had seen the truth in my eyes.

'Just that I'd push his nose into his brain if he tried anything again while I was at the school.'

Paul cocked his head. 'And could you?'

'Probably not,' I lied. 'But he seemed to think I could. I hate bullies. Look, I've really got to go.'

I headed past him, in the direction of the change-rooms. This was hardly the person to bare my soul to, even if I felt so inclined. If I agreed I was friendless, the next thing would be an offer to assuage my loneliness. The truth was: I found him attractive enough that I might even do something dumb, like fall for him. Wishful thinking aside, I did not need that sort of complication right now. I couldn't afford to get close to anyone, physically or emotionally. So I said nothing.

He stepped in my way.

I lifted my chin to keep eye contact, giving him a strait, no-nonsense stare; one that usually kept eager guys at bay. His mouth twisted into a self-assured little smile.

'Don't.' I strode away.

He followed again. He was persistent, I had to give him that. In fact, much more persistent and I'd have to show him what happened to guys who stepped over the fine line between chasing and stalking. But that would mean a hurried departure. And both Anna and I were so over those it wasn't funny.

Stopping outside the door I eyed him pointedly. 'This is the Ladies, Paul.'

He started and actually blushed. 'Oh, right. Well, look, if you change your mind, let me know. What's your number? I'll text you mine.' He waited expectantly, phone ready.

I stared at him, unspeaking.

With a grimace, he shrugged. 'Fine. Here's my number.' He pulled scrap of paper out of his wallet. Using a pen dangling from a nearby exercise record chart, he scribbled a number on it and grinned in unspoken apology. 'It can be just a movie, I promise. If that's all you want.'

'Sure.' I tucked the paper into a pocket, saluted and shouldered the door open, watching to make sure he didn't follow.

Clearly he wasn't used to being told "no". It hadn't fazed him, but he also hadn't taken me seriously; certain of his appeal. I wasn't afraid of him, but if he did get bent out of shape by rejection he could make my life at school very uncomfortable. And if he spread the word about Anna's connection to me, our lives could get very dangerous.

I could live without friends, but I didn't need any more enemies.

Screwing up my nose against a twist of depression, I leaned against the closed door and considered the Exit sign. The little green man on it symbolised my life: forever running, never escaping. Paul was right. I was lonely, but what choice did I have? No-one would understand who I was. Hell, *I* didn't.

I inspected my hands; they had almost killed Paul. I retrieved my gear from the lockers and strode to the sinks and gripped the steel towel rail until my knuckles whitened. I stared at myself in the mirror. It might be just a movie to him, but to me it represented a whole lot more: a life that most people took for granted. Metal creaked and cracked under my palm. I grimaced, released the twisted, snapped rail and wiped my prints off it. Dammit.

I plucked Paul's number out of my pocket and stuffed it deep into my bag, dismissing him and all my stupid, childish dreams.

I changed into street clothes. Gently straight-arming open the door to the foyer, I checked shadows and exits out of habit.

'Paul!' An urbane tenor voice echoed outside, hollow in the vast, glass and marble foyer.

I slid into shadows. From this position I could see Paul, but he couldn't see me. He stood not far away.

'Dad.' Paul folded his arms across chest and lifted his chin.

On the opposite side of the open space, the elevator doors stood open. Mr Eisen stalked across the floor, heels rapping sharply on the marble, arms swinging. His jaw was sharp with tension; his deepset blue eyes snapped with the fire of intelligent impatience. He was an older, more intense version of Paul; his equal in height and slightly broader across the shoulders.

His gaze swept past my hiding place, unseeing, before flicking back to Paul's face, then jumping away again. He stopped a few feet from his son and shoved his hands into his pockets. In the half-darkened foyer, he stood in a pool of sharp light that cast heavy shadows beneath his eyes.

'What are you doing here? You were supposed to meet me in the conference room twenty minutes ago.' He spoke quickly, each word clipped and precise. He checked his watch and looked over Paul's shoulder towards the massive clock hanging above the glass front doors.

'I was catching up with…a friend.' Paul's evasive answer was disappointing. Evidently I wasn't good enough to rate a mention by name.

By the expensive suit and gold watch on Mr Eisen, the family wasn't short of money. He probably wouldn't approve of his son dating the daughter of a single mother who didn't even own a house.

'Obviously someone you don't care to tell me about.' Mr Eisen gave him a cool look. 'Which means I wouldn't approve.'

Bingo.

Paul shrugged and curled a lip. 'You don't approve of any of my friends, so why should I bother trying?'

'Well, if you'd go to St Augustine's, like I asked, I would.'

'That's why I don't go there.'

Mr Eisen's eyes narrowed. Another check of his watch deepened his frown. With quick movements, he scraped long fingers through his short, blond hair, glanced at the darkened sky outside and swore. A smile stretched his lips and disappeared again, leaving his eyes untouched. His face relaxed as he seemed to get his irritation under control.

'You're right. I apologise.' Mr Eisen raised one shoulder in a half-shrug. 'Things are a little…stressful with all the changes Anna Morgan's implementing. We're all working long hours and I'm tired. Sorry I snapped. I just meant that I have big plans for you. Don't get in with the wrong people now.' He grabbed Paul by the elbow and moved him towards the elevator.

By the pained expression on Paul's face, he must have accidentally dug into a pressure point at the joint.

'Anyway. We're late for that meeting,' Mr Eisen added, giving the foyer one last inspection as they reached the lift. 'It's important. We can talk about this later.'

The doors closed, cutting off Paul's indignant reply.

That was…intense. If he was like that all the time I did not envy Paul his home life.

I shifted the weight of the gym bag on my shoulder and headed for the front doors. As they slid open, North Queensland's humidity enveloped me, the air thick and perfumed with greenery and distant rain. Nectar after the thin, cool, staleness inside.

I squared my shoulders, paused and eyed the patterns of shadow and light in the street. Nothing untoward was visible but disquiet fluttered my breath and tightened the back of my neck. Something felt off.

No, I was being paranoid again. That happened a lot.

The MJE office block was a shiny-new monument of blue glass and steel. The gym at the bottom was clean and usefully located, but once in the streets it became a different matter. This wasn't the most wholesome area after hours. It was across from a pub and a park notorious as a hangout for binge-drinkers thrown out by the publican. The combination of that, single female, and Friday night potentially made me a target. Perhaps that was the source of my uneasiness.

Overhead, thick clouds obscured stars and moon and reflected the city lights as an unpleasant orange-grey glow. The sweet scent of frangipani and seawater lingered, heavy in the air. A distant rumble of thunder signified a possible storm. The sky seemed to spill its pent up fury almost every afternoon here; like the sky gods were making a determined effort to wash away the town. Electricity flickered high in the clouds. Ozone caught on the back of my tongue.

I strode to my car. Disquiet slid down my spine, infecting my limbs with the shakes as my body reacted to an unseen threat. I transferred keys to my pocket and bag to my left hand, leaving my right free.

At the car, I flicked the bag into the boot. Tension twisted a thin wire of pain in behind my left eyeball. Dammit. Another migraine? Now? Darkness pushed at my thinking. I thrust it down, stepped back...

THREE

<Anything?>

Possibly. They're about to make contact. A test, by the looks of it.

<Be careful. Don't let them see you. You're more important.>

Don't worry. I won't interfere unless I have to.

… and jammed an elbow into the solar plexus of the man directly behind me.

He folded with a grunt and dropped a wine bottle. It shattered and sprayed cheap red wine onto my ankles. The vinegary smell overpowered the soft scent of distant rain on hot tarmac.

A second man's thick arms wrapped me in a bear hug from behind. I swallowed a scream and crouched. Raising my elbows bought space. I shot straight back up. The hardest part of my head caught him under the chin. I saw stars for a second. My attacker went down like the proverbial sack of potatoes. His head smacked audibly on the road. I stomped on his knee for good measure. Something important snapped with a *crack* that echoed off the buildings.

The first guy regained his breath and pulled out a knife.

I swarmed in faster than he could react or move. Locking his arm straight across my chest cracked the elbow nicely. I dragged the knife from lax fingers. He stifled a shriek. His fingers raked at my arm, ripping off one of my gloves. He staggered back, cradling his arm. Anger blazed in his dark eyes. He straightened, his broken arm dangling, and stalked towards me.

From the corner of my mind, darkness pressed against my adrenalin-soaked thoughts. A thousand needles prickled delicately at my skin from the inside. My hands shook as I struggled for control. Fear mounted. Not of my attacker, for him. Perhaps I should end him with his own knife just to prevent something worse happening.

He grasped at my throat. I turned and wrapped an arm over his, trapping it. The point of my elbow struck his nose. He cried out. Blood spurted. His fingers clutched at me, digging sharp nails into my skin. A foot kicked at my knee.

Darkness surged forth. My bare palm fell onto his forehead. He gasped and dropped to the tarmac, eyes wide, mouth gaping. I burned, gloriously alight from within. I laughed. He fell. His eyes rolled back. His skin tautened.

'No!' I let go the fire, released him, and stumbled a few steps away. My heart hammered. I fought against myself, struggling for calm.

Limp on the ground, he moaned. At least he lived. The knife hilt, thumped into the back of his head, stopped the groaning. His chest rose and fell rhythmically. The darkness retreated, taking the taste of blood and ozone with it.

I watched the two unconscious men a while. Gritting my teeth, I mastered the weakness in my knees and the roiling in my stomach and fumbled for the car keys. If I didn't think about the horror on his face, and the heady fire of his life curling under my skin, I could get through this.

Sharp little diamonds glittered behind my eyelids as I closed them against the overbright streetlights. Adrenalin ebbed, leaving me weak and sick, my mouth full of saliva. Needles drilled behind my eyes.

I thumbed the electronic key and squinted against the flash of the car lights as it unlocked. The knife went into the back seat. Time to get out of here. If the police showed up there would be questions and a report filed with my name on it. I didn't need that.

'Hey!'

I jumped and spun, hands up defensively. A man approached from the back of the car. Even in the muggy evening heat he wore black jeans and a black motorbike jacket. He nudged the two unconscious men with a toe.

There wasn't enough time to get into the car and I didn't want to be caught half-in and vulnerable. How did I not sense him? Was he another attacker?

He moved closer.

I backed away.

Light spilling from the pub opposite illuminated a pair of dark-rimmed, lead-grey eyes, startling against tawny skin. Dark, straight brows snapped together in some emotion I couldn't read.

Why did he seem…familiar? Black hair, short and deliberately untidy, framed a lean face. But not a face I knew.

'What happened? You ok?' He cocked his head. 'Aren't you in…Cairns High? I think I've seen you there.'

What was this, schoolies night downtown? I backed away again, keeping fighting distance. I didn't remember seeing him around the campus, but it was a big school. Maybe that's why he looked familiar.

'What are you doing here? You with them?' I jerked a chin at the two insensible bodies.

'I'm not going to hurt you. I was in the pub across the road.' He pointed. 'Saw those two coming after you. Just thought I could help.'

'The pub. You're too young.'

He shrugged and stepped closer again. 'Drinking age in Australia's eighteen.' An overhead streetlight emphasised high cheekbones, a sharp jaw and narrow nose. He wasn't classically handsome so much as striking; strong.

I stepped back.

He held his palms out in a placating gesture. 'I just want to make sure you're alright. Those guys seemed pretty serious. I'm Fynn Litson. What's your name?'

Checking the unconscious men, I swallowed. There was no evidence of what had almost happened. But what had Fynn seen? Anything? Had I betrayed myself again in another act of stupidity?

'I'm fine. Those two attacked me. I defended myself. Hardly even a fair fight, considering how drunk they are. Now I'm going. Stay out of it.' Tension made me more abrupt than I meant to be.

'But you...' He seemed to reconsider his words. A flicker of something akin to doubt or suspicion crossed his face as he took in the inert forms on the ground.

I should never have come here tonight. I'd nagged Anna until she let me use MJE's secure server to search some otherwise-inaccessible online archives in the hopes of finding a new lead to the *ocair*. It'd been fruitless and now two people had almost exposed me.

Fynn's eyes widened. He muttered something that sounded very much like *'ocair'*.

'What did you say?' I straightened out of a fighting stance.

He cleared his throat. 'I said, "take care". You don't look all that good. Let me drive you home.'

'No! I'm not some damsel in distress. I rescued myself, thanks.' I glared at him. 'Just get out of my way.' One of my attackers stirred and groaned, his fleshy, meaty fingers scrabbling at the warm asphalt. 'Now.'

'Fine.' Fynn yanked up the zip of his motorbike jacket. His jaw clenched. He gave a sharp nod and stalked down the silent, grey-and-orange shadowed street. I half-expected his jacket to have "Hell's Angels", or something like, blazoned across the back. Instead, it bore an intricately-embroidered Celtic symbol of some sort; a stylised silver tree.

He vanished into darkness.

A motorbike engine roared. The red taillight dwindled down the length of a dim street.

He'd lied. He *had* said *ocair*. I was certain of it. But why? How did he even know the word? I was an idiot to let him out of my sight.

I needed to find out. If I'd heard correctly, then he was the first person to even know the word. The first evidence in five years it even *was* a word. I had to find him again. Had to be sure.

I slid into the driver's seat, struggling with the simple act of sliding the key into the ignition. As I pulled into the street, I scrabbled for my phone.

'Anna!' For a relieved moment, I thought she'd answered, but it was her voicemail telling me cheerfully to leave a message. Why wasn't she picking up? Was she alright? Damn. I'd forgotten: she had a meeting until eight at least.

I hung up and kept driving, holding the single red taillight in sight.

Lights and streetlights lashed my eyes, lending strength to the headache that clouded my thoughts and fed on my fears. If I went home and lay down in a dark room, I could probably avoid a brain-fry migraine. I kept driving. My brain could roast over hot coals if it meant finding out who was after me and why.

About twenty minutes north, somewhere around Smithfield, where the road split, I lost him. The red light vanished in a sea of traffic and I couldn't tell if he went left, to the Tablelands, or right to the northern beaches.

A petrol station nearby offered a chance to regroup. I slammed a fist against the steering wheel, swore and closed my eyes. Migraine *and* no answers. Perfect.

What I needed now was somewhere dark and cool to sulk and groan a lot.

I bought a drink and some painkillers. My phone told me the beaches were close. The thought appealed. Dry, cool sand. The sound of waves hissing and sloshing. A huge, golden full moon had risen and shrunk into a silver disc. It would light my way.

Following the moon took me north but the sledgehammers in my head grew too much and I had to stop. Painkillers weren't helping.

I drew to a halt at Ellis beach. The sand lay right in front of me. Glistening water beckoned, cool and inviting. A sign warned of lethal box jellyfish, lurking in the summer-warm waters. What a pain in the ass. Literally. Another warned of estuarine crocodiles. A third of poisonous stonefish. What sort of place was this? Next they'd be telling me drop-bears were real.

With a regretful sigh, I unbuckled the seatbelt. kicked off my shoes and headed for the sand. It crunched and squeaked, cool beneath my toes. A palm tree leaned at the right angle and I sat with my back against it, eyes closed.

Slowly the smell of sand and salt; the soothing ebb and flow of gentle waves lapping on the beach; the breeze whispering through leaves above, all filtered past the blanket of pain. I willed my shoulders to relax. Tension drained away but the migraine stayed, stabbing in behind my left eye.

I thumped my head gently against the tree in a vain effort to beat the pain into submission and tried to think of something else.

Had Fynn spotted me? I'd been mugged before, twice in LA, and successfully defended myself both times without being seen – and without turning life-vampire on anyone. So was it just bad luck this time? What had triggered my self-control breakdown? I'd come so damned close to killing that guy. Frighteningly close. It'd been two years. Why now?

And what had Fynn seen and said? Now I wasn't certain of what I'd heard. Perhaps it was just wishful thinking. Maybe I should just cut my losses and get out of town, just in case. That would be the smart, safe thing to do; the thing I always did.

No. I had to know.

I opened my eyes. The silver-water moon path shimmered at my feet. I was tempted to step onto it and fly away; to dance through the forest on beams of moonlight, leaving the cities behind.

The pain tightened a band around my skull. Nausea churned my stomach. This was worse than normal. I threw up the meagre remains of my afternoon snack into the sand. It didn't help. Now even the glow of the moon hurt my eyes. I wiped my mouth, wished for water and half-heartedly buried the nauseating mess in the sand. Somewhere dark to curl up. Somewhere in the cool rainforest. That was all I wanted now. The future could wait.

A mosquito whined in the dark and settled on my arm, its sharp sting barely registering. I couldn't stay here. I'd be sucked dry by morning. Determined, I struggled up from the sand, leaning heavily on a palm tree.

The first step jarred my head so much tears welled. I bit my lip against the urge to throw up again. Another step brought me to my knees, tears coursing freely down my face. It hurt too much. I couldn't think; couldn't see.

I swore inventively through clenched teeth, despising my weakness.

Strong arms scooped me up and cradled me, like a child, against a broad chest. I protested weakly as each step unsettled my stomach. The arms gripped tighter. I struggled. I wasn't safe. I had to run.

'Stop wiggling or I'll drop you!' an impatient voice muttered in my ear.

He put me down long enough to fumble through my bag for my car keys. I peered up at the dark figure looming over me and heaved a sigh of relief.

Paul Eisen. Hopefully not a threat.

'Come on. Get in,' he said. 'I'll drive you home.'

The drive home barely registered. It was all I could do not to throw up again and humiliate myself in front of Paul. Streetlights stabbed at my brain, even through closed eyelids. I whimpered and swore at my own wretchedness.

'Hey.' His warm hand patted my knee. 'We're almost there. I called your mum and she's waiting. You'll be ok.'

'Thanks.' My voice was a cracked whisper. 'You shouldn't have called her, though. I'll be ok in the morning. I just need to sleep.' I draped an arm across my eyes.

'You get these headaches often? Is it normally this bad? Should we get an ambulance?'

'No,' I muttered. 'No hospitals. This is…a little worse than usual but I can handle it.'

He gave a soft chuckle. 'You're a tough one, I'll give you that.'

His words barely registered and I didn't understand them, anyway. A tough what? Girl? Why did he sound so surprised a girl could be tough? What was tough about surviving a headache. I was a prize idiot. Stories of my pathetic weakness would be all over school on Monday.

Paul pulled into my driveway. My door opened and my mother helped me out. I half-heard her grateful thanks to Paul and his easy assurances in return.

The elevator ride up to the apartment was a blur; my dark, cool room a blessing. I threw the wig aside, sank onto the bed and curled around a pillow. The smooth cotton pillowcase felt rough against my skin.

The mattress sagged. My mother brushed hairs from my forehead.

'Bad?'

'The worst. Just shoot me now.'

'Oh, babe.' Her fingers massaged my temples.

'Where were you? I called. I was worried.'

'Sorry sweetheart. I'm fine. I was at the meeting at work. Didn't hear the phone. Taken anything?' She tugged my shoes off. They thumped into the corner of the room, joining various other bits of discarded clothing and three half-unpacked boxes lurking there. The sum of my life.

'Not helping,' I managed. 'Could only find synthetics.'

'Do I need to call a doctor?'

'You know we can't,' I whispered. 'I'll be ok. Let me sleep.'

She rhythmically stroked my damp hair.

'Anna?' I said.

She made an inquiring noise in response.

'I might have screwed up again.'

'Oh?'

'I think maybe someone saw me.'

There was a long silence and she sighed. 'You sure?'

Right now, with the fire in my head consuming logic, I couldn't be. 'Not really. Maybe not. I don't know. I'll try and find out tomorrow. I don't want us to have to go so soon.'

'Well.' She smoothed my hair again. 'Sleep on it, then we'll discuss it in the morning.'

'I'm sorry.' Tears slipped down my cheeks. 'I'm sorry I keep messing up your life. I try but I can't help it. I'm sorry I ruined your night. I know you like that Mick guy you talk about at work. You deserve someone to look after you.'

'Oh, baby, I know how hard you try and I hate seeing you turning yourself into something you're not. You used to be such a bubbly, happy little thing. You're too young to worry so much.' She wiped the tears away and kissed my forehead. 'If we have to go, we do. It'll be ok. Mick is...well, it doesn't matter. As long as you're safe, it'll be ok.'

'Thanks, Mum.'

She gave a little gasping laugh. 'Now I know you're sick. You haven't called me that since you were six.'

I managed a weak chuckle. 'What, in London, when I was dressed as a boy and you were my aunt? It was easier to call you Anna.'

'I'm surprised you remember.'

'I remember everything – from after Dad left, anyway.' The pain spiked in my head again.

She stroked my cheek. The bed sprang back as she stood.

'I'll let you sleep. Love you. Call if you need anything.'

What I needed was a bullet in the skull. Anything to stop the pain.

What I got were dreams.

One in particular. A recurring dream I hadn't had for months. Inspired by my trip to the beach, perhaps. I rode up silver moonbeams to a forest. Tall, beautiful people, with glittering firefly crowns, greeted me; beckoned to me. When I stepped forward, the ground fell away and I flew, sailing free in the velvet night air.

The stars winked out one by one. Someone flew beside me but I couldn't turn my head to see who. Below us, leaves on the trees withered and died as we passed. The people vanished like mists, leaving brown death where the forests had been. The world burned.

And I knew it was my fault.

A strong brown hand grasped my wrist in a bone-grinding grip. The street was so far below. Warm tropical breezes lifted my hair. The fingers relaxed. I plummeted towards concrete and asphalt.

My eyes flew open, heart hammering, my skin sticky with sweat. Quiet darkness told me it was still early. Thick curtains obscured the windows and hid the world. Faint, pink-gold light crept in around the edges. The clock said five oh two. I swore at it. The readout ticked relentlessly over to five oh three. Living in the tropics might sound appealing, but the heat and early sunrises sucked for a night-person like me.

I closed my eyes and willed myself back to sleep. A flock of parrots picked that moment to squabble outside my window. Clearly it was morning enough that I may as well get up. Lying in bed would make neither headaches nor my current problem disappear for good.

I sat up. My brain didn't explode. Thank God. I wasn't sure I could handle any more like that. Shucking the clothes I'd slept in, still sandy from the beach, I stepped into the white-tiled ensuite and played the age-old game of balance the hot and cold. I stood for ages under the steady stream of water, letting it pound on my shoulders and neck; relaxing muscles made sore by jujitsu and tension.

What to do...

The image of Fynn's suspicion and doubt last night replayed in my head. What had he seen, though? No more than a girl defending herself against two muggers in a carpark.

Unless he was very observant...

Damn! I had to be sure and I had to know if I'd heard him correctly. I couldn't walk away from the first chance I'd had in five years of finding out. If this *ocair* thing was important, I could use it as leverage, get them to leave us alone. Then I could stop living in constant fear of myself and what they might drive me to do.

I groaned. That meant confronting this Fynn guy and there was something unsettling about him. But he was only human. I was perfectly capable of defending myself if he turned out to be some weirdo serial killer.

I left the comforting warmth of the shower and got dressed.

FOUR

I've found their target.

<Who is it?>

No bloody idea. I just met her.

< We need to know who she is. She may lead us to them.>

My thoughts exactly. But she's... Nevermind.

<Where is she now?>

Home. Sleeping. I should have brought her to you.

<You could hardly kidnap her in the open street>

Why not? They tried. We need to know who she is. She has potential.

<Just stay close to her. We know she's who they want and we may be able to use that.>

It was too early to contact Fynn, but the alternative – schoolwork – held zero appeal. I gathered my throwing knives and headed for the living room. I put on the coffee percolator and opened the window that looked out over the sea. The air was already thick and warm, redolent of salt, mud, and frangipani, and noisy with the squawk of brilliant red and green parrots clowning around in the trees outside. Early sunlight glittered off the still ocean. Boats of all sizes left white trails across the blue water. A cruise ship's mournful horn wafted across as the ship inched into port.

Irritatingly picturesque. I closed the window, drew the blinds against the sun and switched on the airconditioner. Anna didn't much like the outdoors and hated the heat, so airconditioning was as essential as coffee for her. I found the lush smell of greenery surrounding Cairns reassuring and welcoming. The nearness of the rainforests pulled at something primal in me. When we had time, I fully intended to go hiking, regardless of Anna's distaste.

In the meantime, I had some thinking to do and throwing knives helped. I gathered the knives and paced four metres from the scarred wooden target I'd built two weeks before, on the first day we'd arrived. The rhythmic *thwack* of metal into wood and the focus required to get the spin right settled my mind. After ten ends I switched to left-handed. After that, I turned my back and spun and threw in one move.

'Couldn't sleep?' My mother, improbably young in blue pyjama shorts and a white t-shirt, with wild, red curls loose to her shoulders and face free of makeup, emerged from her room, yawning. 'Me neither. Feeling better?'

I nodded.

She inspected the close grouping of my latest throws. 'Nice. Four metres with a turn-about? What about six?'

I went back to throwing. 'Not enough space unless I start at the end of the hall. Do you mind being impaled as you come out of your room?'

She chuckled. 'Just wait 'til I go to work. But don't miss. I'd hate to have to replaster the wall again.'

'Hey! That was ten years ago. I was eight. I don't miss.' The rest of her words filtered into my brain. 'Hang on. It's Saturday. You're working today? I thought we were going to the markets later. I have to find you a present for your birthday, on Wednesday, remember?'

The percolator beeped and she poured herself a cup of black coffee. I sniffed the rich scent appreciatively. Her blue eyes watched me speculatively over the rim of the cup.

'Birthdays are overrated. The markets might have to wait. I told the MJE Board we'd be live with all the changes in six months.' She screwed up her nose. 'Means a lot to do.'

Six months. Shorter than many of our stays. But long enough to let me finish senior. There were only three months left.

'Found a new dojo?' Anna sipped at her coffee and leafed through a pile of junkmail on the kitchen counter.

'Two. There's a good kung fu one two blocks away and a jujitsu one about two minutes from school. I'll start on Monday. Hopefully no meatheads. They're harder to resist breaking.'

'Mmmm…' She narrowed her gaze. 'And did you find what you were looking for last night on the work servers?'

Three more knives landed in the target centre before I answered. 'No.' The next knife over-rotated with the vehemence of my throw and bounced off, clattering on the tiled floor. I swore. Gathering all the knives I laid them on the glass coffee table and joined her at the breakfast bench.

'I know you think I'm crazy, chasing after this *ocair* thing,' I said, avoiding her eye, 'but it's the only lead I've ever had. If I can find out what it is, maybe I can give it to them and they'll leave us alone.'

'But in five years,' she said, 'all we've come up with is a similarity to the Celtic word for "key". Nothing else. And we haven't seen any indication that they've found us again – not for two years. I just think there are more important things you should be concentrating on.'

It was an old argument, so I didn't bother responding.

She carefully touched my wrist. I suppressed my automatic retreat and glanced up.

'And last night?' she asked gently. 'What happened?'

I hunched a shoulder. 'Two drunk muggers, that's all.'

'You sure? Nothing else? They didn't hurt you?' Her grip tightened, her eyes anxious on my face.

I shook my head. 'Just lost a glove.'

'But you said something about making a mistake. Was it…like Japan? That bad?'

I shuddered at the memory. The pawing of strong hands on my skin. The beer-sweet breath on my face. The seductive drag at life; the burn of power drawn and savoured. The slowing heartbeat beneath my palm.

I stared at the glittering, white and pink granite countertop. 'No. They weren't trying to…do anything to me, like that. But almost as bad as Christchurch.' I looked up at her. 'I managed to stop it. This time. It's getting more difficult, though.'

The metal chair legs scraped loudly across the floor as I rose. I strode to the huge living room windows and flung the curtains aside to stare out at the bay and the verdant green hills that formed a backdrop to the city.

'Every time something threatens me it gets harder not to…protect myself. I can't help it.'

Anna's light footsteps hastened across the tiles. Her cool hands fell on my shoulders, hair tickling my skin as she rested her head on my back.

'Oh, Rowan.' She sighed. 'I'm sorry. If it was that close, maybe you should pack.'

I groaned and turned around, leaning my cheek on her shoulder, though I stood half a head taller. 'I don't know. They could have just been plain old muggers.'

'No, I don't think we should take the risk.' Her tone firmed. 'It's not worth it.'

'But it just delays things,' I said. 'It's only a matter of time before they track us down again, no matter how careful we are. I just need to find a way to get them off our backs. Then it will get easier to control this. It's my fear that triggers it, I'm sure.'

Her fingers combed through my hair. 'You get better all the time, sweetheart. Remember when you used to break glasses just picking them up? And straight out tell people if you saw their death or an accident when you touched them?' She lifted my chin. Her cheeks were pale, her eyes steady, but with a hint of fear in them that tore at my heart.

'I know. But controlling myself physically isn't what I meant.' I tapped my temple. 'This is what scares me. Last night I wasn't even in that much danger. I'd handled things. But it happened anyway. And this time it was like...' I pressed my palms against my head. 'Something took over completely. Or I became...no. I don't know how to describe it. All I know is that it scares the shit out of me. Like there's something inside me that wants...' I spread my arms wide then dropped them to my sides, helpless. 'Everything.'

I sank on to the white leather couch and rested my forehead on my fists. Anna sat beside me, one arm across my shoulders.

'I know it's hard, sweetheart,' she murmured. 'But I know you. You're tough and smart. You can control it. You go back to Ireland. I'll find another city – somewhere bigger so we can be invisible. After you finish senior we can focus on finding out who's after you, and learning how to hold it together when you're scared.'

'It won't matter.' I stood and paced the white-tiled floor. 'Whether it's here or a bigger city. I hate living like this – constantly running and hiding. Afraid of them – and we don't even know who they are! Afraid of myself. I know you promised Dad you'd protect me, but I need to have a say in this, too. I don't want to run anymore. Not unless we absolutely have to.'

'Yes but—'

'Just give me a chance,' I begged. 'There was a guy last night. He came to help after I'd taken the muggers out. I don't know what he saw. But he seemed a bit strange about it, and I'm sure he said something about the *ocair*. I'm going to try and meet him today and find out for certain.'

'Well.' Anna sounded doubtful, her sandy brows contracted into a straight line. 'I might start getting things ready at work, just in case. Worst case, you can go back to Ireland and I can join you in a couple of weeks. I only need two more weeks to put the bones of the MJE changes in place, then my staff can handle it from there.' She touched my father's heavy gold and emerald signet ring where it rested on my left middle finger. 'You'd be safe at his estate for a couple more weeks.'

I hung my head, twisting the ring. 'I know, but I can't spend my whole life hiding there. That's like being in a cage, like some sort of monster. I just want a normal life.'

'You're not a monster, Rowan. I'm sorry this is so hard on you. I really am. But you know you've always been special.' Anna held me close for a minute and I rested in the balm of her love, breathing in the security of her familiar smell and softness. Then she leaned back and smiled encouragingly.

'I could do without being special, actually,' I said. 'Ordinary would be nice.'

Anna gave a twisted smile. 'Not going all teenager on me now, are you. We've been doing so well.'

I rolled my eyes. 'Pretty sure I'll scrape through one more year without turning into a stereotype.' I frowned. 'But while we're on the subject of special…we've never really discussed me, have we? I mean, I've asked but you've never told me much. I think it's time you did. Maybe it would help me understand what these people want with me.'

She released me and walked into the kitchen. 'I'm not sure what you mean, sweetheart.'

'Yes, you are,' I pressed. 'Why am I different?'

Anna poured herself another coffee, not meeting my gaze. 'Everyone's unique, Rowan.'

'Nope,' I said. 'Not good enough this time. I haven't asked for years because I didn't want to *be* different. But I am.'

Anna sighed. 'Alright. But the truth is: I don't know. Your father was the same, though – different like you, I mean.'

'So...?' I prompted, trying to stay calm when my heart jumped in my chest.

She hesitated, then plucked a photo off the fridge. A photo of a pastel done by a street artist when my parents were in Calais. An image of a younger, happier Anna O'Reilly wrapped contentedly in the arms of a handsome, serious Calain Gilmore. They stood in front of the ocean, wind whipping their hair, her cheeks flushed with love and cold.

'He was...so quick; so strong,' Anna murmured. 'I noticed it the first time we met. He saved me from being run down by a car, you know.'

That story was an old one. Anna told it often at social occasions when asked about her absent husband. It was safer and more romantic than his death.

'At the time, he downplayed it as an adrenalin rush, but it wasn't long before I saw it come out in other, little ways he probably didn't notice.' She smiled reminiscently. 'When he saved me he sort of sighed and said "so it's you."'

'Well, that's a pretty bizarre thing to say.'

She shrugged. 'He was a good man, but there was something about him I could never quite fathom.'

'What, that he was insane?' I asked wryly, trying to hide the fear gnawing at my guts – the fear that maybe he'd passed on more than speed and strength to me; that the darkness in my head was also his.

I regretted the comment immediately but Anna reacted with neither anger nor hurt, just with pensive thoughtfulness.

'No. He always seemed...conflicted, more than anything.' She sipped her coffee, focussed somewhere beyond me. 'It's funny, he was only thirty when we met but he seemed so much older and wiser. He was reluctant to have kids. After three years, he agreed. Said he'd just been delaying so he could have as much time with me as possible.' Her lips twisted and tears sheened her eyes. 'He was so happy when you were born. He looked at you and cried. It was the first time I'd ever seen him so emotional about anything.'

'But that doesn't answer the question of why I'm different.'

'No, I know. I'm sorry.' She swept stray hairs back from her pale, smooth forehead. 'I've been thinking about things he said but he never told me much. I loved him and I was focussed on us and you. I knew you were special from a very early age, though.'

'How so?' I selected a bunch of grapes from a bowl on the bench and ate a few without really tasting them.

Anna looked fondly at me. 'Well, you were saying words by the time you were seven months old. Full sentences by the time you were one.' She threw me a proud smile. 'All my friends told me to get you into a genius child course.' Her expression clouded. 'But your father insisted we move town. That was the first move we made. He seemed afraid when he saw you were like him.'

'How do you mean, "like him"?' My appetite vanished.

Her brow furrowed. 'By the time you were four, you could speak three languages fluently and you were doing written schoolwork at a grade three level. Plus you and your father had a secret language only you two could speak. To me it sounded like gibberish, but he took you seriously. And sometimes the two of you seemed to communicate just by looking at each other.'

'Seriously? I can get by in Japanese and French, but three or four languages? What the hell?'

'I know.' My mother screwed up her nose. 'I can't explain it, either, except that Calain spoke at least twenty I was aware of.' She laughed. 'Including Old Norse, for some bizarre reason. In you, though, it all stopped when he went away. You just...stopped and became a normal four year old. Almost. You were sad your dad was gone, but it was like you'd forgotten how to do everything. I was so distraught at the time I didn't think about it until much later.' She touched my face, her expression wistful. 'But when I asked, you just looked at me blankly and said Daddy told you to stop.'

I gaped at her. 'I have no memory of that, at all.'

She smiled and rinsed her cup. 'I know. And I know that all these years of running, and not having him around, have been hard on you. So, if you're sure those two men last night were just ordinary muggers, maybe we can stay. That's the biggest concern I had.' She gave me a shrewd look. 'We'll plan for both contingencies. But in the last fourteen years since your Dad left, we've only run into serious trouble twice. I'm sure you're right and this is nothing. So why don't you go find this witness of yours. Then we can be sure of our next steps. I trust your judgment.' She kissed my head. 'I'm going to have a shower.'

The burden of my fears was a little lighter after talking to Anna. She had such calm good sense it was impossible to maintain any level of hysteria around her. And she was right. I was being paranoid.

I headed for my room to track Fynn Litson down. I didn't know how to get in touch with him, so that left social media. Booting up my laptop, I logged onto a rarely-used fake Facebook profile. A quick search revealed only one Fynn Litson, whose profile showed a thirty-something hardcore goth in London, so not the one I wanted.

But the members-only section of the school website had his email address listed on the student contact details. At least he really was enrolled there. Now it was just a matter of working out how and when to meet him, and what to say.

I sent a message. Admittedly, it was rather cryptic but hopefully he was smart enough to work out who I was, as I hadn't given him my name last night.

Need to meet you this morning asap. Want to discuss the incident in town last night. Meghan Greene.

It was still early and a Saturday, so I was surprised when an answer popped straight up in my Inbox.

Of course. Coffee Club in town in twenty minutes. FL

I hesitated over replying, not sure what I to say, either now or in twenty minutes. I hit the send button on a simple 'OK' message and logged out.

So what the hell would I say when we met? Ten minutes later, having changed clothes twice to find a comfortable outfit, I left Anna a note and snuck out of the flat, still unsure of the words.

FIVE

She's contacted me. We're meeting.

<If they're watching her, they'll see you.>

Not my real face, though. I'll watch for cameras. If you want her to stay, I have to see her. I get the sense she'll run again if she doesn't hear what she needs to.

<Very well. Be careful.>

I arrived a few minutes early, ordered a latte and sat in a corner booth, breathing in the heady scent of coffee. As my drink arrived, Fynn's motorbike roared into a parking spot outside. He pulled off helmet and gloves and ran stiff fingers through his unruly dark hair.

I paused in mid-sip to watch. Last night I hadn't noticed how hot he was.

He wore faded blue jeans and the silver-tree jacket again, in spite of the heat. Sensible rider, then. Tucking the helmet under one arm, he yanked a baseball cap out of his pocket and flipped it onto his head, tugging it low. Then he swung a long leg off the bike and strode into the coffee shop. His grey eyes scanned the room. When they encountered mine, he nodded acknowledgment and moved to the counter.

He'd had training. He moved smoothly; controlled strength and graceful power; something in him always calm, centred, always aware of his surroundings. After speaking to the girl behind the counter, he strolled over to where I sat. Placing the helmet on the seat and a number on the table, he slid along the cushioned bench.

'You picked my favourite seat,' he said. 'A warrior's spot: back to the wall and both entrances in sight.'

I started. After all these years, I'd done it automatically. It hadn't occurred to me anyone would understand why. I fumbled for an answer.

'Too many action movies. Delusions of being an assassin. Thanks for coming,' I added belatedly.

'Sure.' His grey eyes met mine. His showed nothing but calm distance. Mine, I'm sure, were wary. 'Delusions or hopes?'

'Does anyone hope to be an assassin one day?'

His smile quirked sideways. 'You'd probably be surprised.'

'Definitely.' I slurped froth off my cappuccino. 'Still, people are pretty weird sometimes.'

'Oh,' he said, 'you have no idea.'

'Actually, yes I do.'

He shot me a wry, amused look as his coffee arrived. He sipped it and gave a satisfied sigh. After a swift a survey of the room, he leaned forward, put his elbows on the table and clasped his mug in both hands.

'So what'd you want to talk about?'

I almost choked on my drink. I coughed and snatched at a serviette to cover my mouth. The woman at the table next to us screwed up her nose at me. Around us the bustle and laughter of early morning weekend breakfasters continued unabated; the clink of silverware and babble of talk oblivious to my confusion.

'What? Well...about last night?' I managed. Why the heck was he acting dumb?

Hot morning sunshine streamed through the window, heating the back of my neck, in spite of the airconditioning. My legs stuck to the vinyl bench seat.

Fynn eased out of the riding jacket, his grey t-shirt straining across muscular shoulders. He draped the jacket over his helmet.

'Didn't realise we had anything to talk about. I offered help. You blew me off.' He eyed me coolly, sipping his coffee. 'What'd you want me to say? That I'm impressed you could beat two guys at once? I am, but it's not unusual if you've done martial arts. And you did say they were drunk. I only came in after the fact, so I didn't see much. You ok this morning, by the way?' He eyed me without any apparent concern. 'That sort of encounter usually has some psychological after-effects, even if you came off without any physical damage.'

'I'm fine, but...' I didn't know how to continue.

He raised his brows at me, just a glimmer of amusement lurking in his expression.

I couldn't exactly say "so what did you see me do last night?" or "did you say the word *ocair?*" What if he didn't see anything? What if I'd imagined his suspicion, misheard his words, and was being paranoid? If he knew nothing we could stay - as long as he didn't spread the story around school. The last thing I needed was to be the object of admiration or attention. The only way to stay under the radar in a new town was for me to slide through school totally unnoticed.

'If you're worried about me spreading the story around school, then don't.' His lips twisted into a wry smile. 'I have no interest in making either of us the centre of attention.'

I froze. 'That's bizarre. That's exactly what I was thinking.'

His face lit with such easy, ironic amusement that I almost missed his next words.

'You're pretty transparent, you know. Don't play poker.'

I glowered. I was a damned good poker player and most people found me hard to read. I'd cultivated it on purpose. He was just trying to throw me off balance. Why?

The half-smile he gave me was wry with a hint of "don't-give-a-shit-what-you-think" attitude. Relaxing into his seat he transferred it to the waitress as she delivered a steaming muffin. She dimpled at him in return and cast me a quick, assessing look.

I put my half-empty cup down. The scent of the blueberry muffin made my stomach rumble. I looked away resolutely.

Fynn pushed the plate across the table. 'Want some of my muffin? You look hungry.'

'What?' I repeated, more to buy time that because I didn't understand. Why did it feel like I was missing something important in the subtleties of this conversation? 'No, I don't want your muffin. I want—'

'Hey, there you are!' A cheery, familiar voice interrupted the tension between us. Paul Eisen sent me a quick salute from where he stood at the counter. He sauntered over, blue shirt stretching across a broad chest as he shoved a hand in a pocket of his grey cargo pants. The epitome of cool and charming. Sunlight glinted off his blond hair and slanted through his blue eyes so that, just for an instant, they seemed to glow with an inner light.

'How are you after last night, Meg?' He leaned over our table, all concern and friendliness, but his question made me wince.

I caught Fynn's eyes, expecting to find good humour or at least surprise. Instead, just briefly, something icy and frightening flashed. Then the shutters came down. He slid out of the booth and stood. Face to face, the two men were much of the same height. Fynn, however, was lean and graceful, the muscles in his arm and wrist defined and smooth, the angles of his face sharper. Paul was broader across the shoulders, his power all in bulk and size.

They shook hands and introduced themselves politely but an undercurrent I couldn't quite fathom passed between them. They smiled at each other but it was the smile of competitors, not friends - all tension and teeth.

What a novel concept. I'd never had two guys squabbling over me. No. I had it wrong. This was just a standard alpha-male face off; something stone-age and unrelated to me except that I was the female witnessing it and, presumably, meant to be awed. It annoyed me.

'How'd you find me here?' I broke into their silently-aggressive eye contact.

Paul's face lit with roguish delight. I couldn't help smiling back.

'Called your mother this morning to see how you were. We were pretty late in last night and you weren't well.' He sat down beside me.

A little too close. I scooted a few centimetres away.

After a moment's hesitation Fynn slid back into his seat and picked up his coffee, watching us both enigmatically.

Paul grinned at the waitress as she placed his cup down. 'How's your head this morning?'

'Hangover?' Fynn's dry question was accompanied by an even drier look.

The waitress examined me speculatively, her eyes darting between me and the two men.

I grimaced. 'No, migraine.'

'Yeah,' Paul put in. 'Don't think I've ever seen anyone so bad. She could barely walk. Wouldn't even let me take her to the hospital. Lucky I was there, huh?'

'Yeah,' I agreed reluctantly. 'Thanks again, Paul. Hey, could I ask you a favour, though?' I tried a smile. 'Can you keep it quiet? I hate people treating me like glass or—'

He elbowed me and chuckled. 'Giving you a hard time? Never fear, fair maiden. I shall protect your reputation. One condition, though.'

I winced, not looking in Fynn's direction. He hadn't put any conditions on silence. 'What?'

'You have to go to the movies with me tonight.' He threw Fynn a quick, triumphant grin.

Fynn's face slid further into blankness. His fingertips whitened on his mug.

'Seriously?' I hesitated. This was getting out of hand. Paul was going to ridiculous lengths to ingratiate himself with me and, I assumed, my mother. I didn't want to go out with him on that basis but I certainly didn't want him talking about me behind my back, either.

Paul gave an endearingly sheepish laugh. 'Not just me. Everyone's going. So it's not like a real date or anything. Just get to know some of the guys at school.'

'Fynn's one of the guys at school,' I said.

Paul eyed him narrowly. 'Huh. Never seen you. The *other* guys, then. C'mon. Won't kill you.'

With a sigh, I gave in. 'OK, one movie but that's it. This isn't a date and I'm not going to be blackmailed into a second one. If you don't keep your word...'

Paul held up both hands in surrender. 'I promise!' He swallowed the last of his drink with a quick toss and gulp. 'Gotta go meet up with the old man. He's dragging me off to meet the dude running MJE's anti-aging research team.' He grinned ironically. 'He keeps thinking I want to be a geneticist because I mentioned it, like once, when I was like fourteen. Doesn't get the message and sometimes it's easier not to argue with him. Parents!'

'Anyway.' He shrugged. 'Pick you up around five-thirty.' He jerked his chin at Fynn in reluctant acknowledgement of his existence. 'Mate.' With a jaunty wave aimed at me, he strolled out, apparently oblivious to the admiring looks of our waitress.

As he sauntered away I sighed again and turned back to my cooling cup. Fynn watched Paul leave and flicked me a narrow look. A blush stole into my cheeks. Who was he to judge who I went out with? Surely he could see it was a date under duress anyway.

'I have to go, too.' I pushed my cup away, the coffee turning bitter in my mouth.

Around me the swell of conversation became unbearable as more morning-people filled the busy cafe. The tink of spoons on cups, the wail of a child, the high-pitched laughter of a gaggle of teenage girls; all merged into a din that thrummed against my eardrums.

Fynn extended a hand towards my wrist, then dropped it back to the table when I snatched mine away. His expression was pensive.

'Don't go out with him tonight.'

'Why?' I stared at him. 'What do you care?'

He switched his gaze to where he played idly with a sugar sachet. 'I don't. I just don't trust him.'

With a short laugh, I flicked my long braid back over my shoulder and shuffled around to the edge of the booth.

'I don't trust anyone. Not you, not him, not me, not anyone. I'll be fine.' I collected my bag.

When I straightened he was standing, staring down at me with those searching grey eyes. How had he gotten up so fast? He laid warm fingers on my arm.

'Like you were ok last night? If you were that sick, then you were helpless.'

'And he took care of me, so what? Surely that means I can trust him.' I tried to tug my wrists free.

His grip tightened.

'Let go, Fynn. I don't want to hurt you.'

He chuckled. 'You could find that tricky.' He drew me one step closer. The scent of him filled my nostrils: leather, warmth, mown grass. I froze, anger and fear building. Darkness quivered, straining at its bonds.

'Wanna bet?' I smiled bleakly.

He lifted his brows.

My stomach growled and I laughed.

'Look.' I twisted free and edged towards the exit. 'I don't mean to be rude, but I guess I do need to eat something after all. And I've got homework. I'd better get home.'

His eyes sparkled with secret humour. 'You don't mean that, you're just being polite, for once.'

I glared at him. He was right, of course, I hadn't been particularly polite to him so far. He hadn't exactly been one hundred percent nice, either. He still made me uneasy in a way I couldn't quite define. Maybe the fact he was just so damned cool and sure of himself. Paul, I understood. Fynn, I didn't. It bothered me.

He collected his helmet and jacket. 'Don't worry. I have to go anyway. My mother is expecting me home to babysit my kid sister.'

'You have a family?' Surprise made me blurt out the question without thinking. Of course he had a family. What a dumb thing to say.

He quirked an eyebrow at me. 'Just me, my sister and my mother. They're my aunt and cousin, really. My parents died when I was young. My aunt took me in.'

'I'm sorry.' I shifted uncomfortably.

'Long time ago.' He shrugged and jerked his chin at the door. 'Walk me out?' As we walked, he eyed me. 'You got interrupted before you could tell me what you wanted to talk about.'

I'd had a chance to think about it now. 'I just wanted to know what you thought of those men last night. Did they seem like ordinary muggers to you?'

Fynn tilted his head and stared off into space. 'Yeah. What I saw, anyway. I saw them in the pub before and they looked like they'd been there a while. Why?'

'Oh.' I shifted my bag on my shoulder and flapped a cooling breeze under my shirt as we stepped into the thick, warm air outside. 'Just...not a lot of experience with this sort of thing, I guess,' I lied.

'Well,' he returned, smiling, 'you handled it like a pro - if their groans were anything to judge by.'

The rush of pride I felt at his words annoyed me. At least it sounded like he hadn't seen anything unusual. Now how to ask the other question without sounding weird.

I shaded my face from the already too-warm sun. A few brilliant-white and grey seagulls soared through the hot blue sky. Something larger, a pelican, flapped lazily by. Flies buzzed my face and I waved them away.

We strolled across to where Fynn'd parked his bike and I stood by as he swung a leg over. It was one of the new Honda twelve hundred roadbikes: built for speed; with clean lines and an aerodynamic sleekness in black and silver. In short, it looked dangerous – a lot like Fynn, himself.

'Come for a spin?' He sat back on the saddle.

I shook my head dubiously, wanting to accept, knowing I shouldn't. I'd always been an adrenalin-junkie but circumstances forced me to get my fixes solo. 'No, I don't think so.'

'Coward.' He seemed more amused than bothered.

'No, just not an idiot. I don't know y—' I stopped but the ironic look he gave me said he'd filled in the blank. I lifted my chin.

Fynn gave an ironic chuckle. 'Not a serial killer, in case you were wondering.'

'That's what they all say.'

'Point. Let's start again, shall we?' He bowed formally and gathered my hand in his. 'Hi. I'm Fynn Litson. Now you do know—'

An image flashed into my mind. A thousand pins prickled my palm and the taste of lightning tanged in my mouth. The skin-connection with him was so strong the images blotted out the real world, leaving me blind; knees weak.

I'd forgotten to replace my gloves.

I wrenched free and staggered back. The after-image burned into my eyelids: *a black truck; Fynn's bike; a red car; the tearing of metal; a flying, ragdoll body; a silver Celtic tree glittering in the sunlight.*

'Ro—Meghan!' His strong grip held me upright, digging painfully into my arms.

I fought with myself, struggling against the compulsion to speak; afraid of the result if I did – and if I didn't. Why did I only see death and destruction? I splayed my hands towards Fynn's chest to break free. In the depths of my mind, the darkness emerged. Its hunger for power burned under my skin. I whimpered. There was no threat! Fear stayed my hands. They hovered between us like trapped butterflies. I curled them into fists against my breasts. With gritted teeth, I concentrated on slowing my heart and settling the fears roiling my stomach.

The darkness retreated.

'What?' Fynn let go. 'I didn't hurt you, did I?'

'No.' I shook my head. 'No, it was—' I stopped myself in time and backed away. 'Just go, alright! Leave me alone.'

Fynn opened his mouth, then closed it. Then he drew on one glove and kicked the stand up.

He pulled a small piece of white card out of his pocket and flicked it. I caught it reflexively. It just had his initials and a phone number on it, nothing else. He tugged on the other glove, his expression blank.

'Call if you need help when you're out tonight.'

'Wait!'

He looked at me from beneath dark lashes.

'Which way are you going home?' I asked, my voice breathy.

Fynn jammed his helmet on. 'Gatton Street.'

'Oh.' I nodded. 'Good idea. Anderson Street's always really busy on Saturdays…I hear.' He didn't ask why I'd asked, just gave me a level, ironic look.

The black visor flicked down. He revved the engine. I wrapped my arms around my waist, holding myself together. He roared off down the street without even a wave and disappeared around the corner.

Tucking the card into my bag, I headed home, disturbed by the whole morning.

My self-control was slipping too often.

SIX

Did you see that?

<Yes. This puts a new perspective on things. Perhaps that's why they want her. That skill's rare enough.>

Maybe we should consider—

<No. Just stick to the plan. It's them we want, not her.>

Anna began a careful interrogation as soon as the door to our unit had closed behind me.

'Did Paul find you? He's nice.' She cast me a shrewd look as she buttered bread.

I sat at the table and put together a sub sandwich with the ingredients she'd organised from our rather haphazard fridge selection. It gave me time to think.

'Yes, he found me.' I focussed on my sandwich. 'He asked me out tonight. To the movies.'

She paused with a piece of fetta halfway to her lips. 'Will you go?'

I shrugged one shoulder. 'Kinda have to or he'll blab about my migraine.'

'Chivalrous!'

'He's young.'

'Quoth the greybeard,' Anna said, grinning. Her smile slipped away. 'What about your witness? Did he see you last night?'

I considered Fynn again and shook my head. 'I think...I don't think he'd say anything, even if he had seen me. But I'm pretty sure he didn't. I think we're ok.' I didn't tell her about the vision. If he went home by Gatton Street, it wouldn't come true. My heart stuttered. Should I have said something more direct?

'So, we're staying?'

I nodded.

Anna smiled, the sparkle back in her eyes. 'I'm so glad. But keep an eye on him, just in case. I'm sure everything will be fine. We've been so careful changing names and identities.' She laughed ruefully. 'Lucky I own the business, huh? At least I can keep hiring all my alter-egos. I'm sure whoever those people were that caught you in Christchurch and in Japan have lost our trail now.'

Hopefully she was right.

'But I get to pick the next name,' I said, pointing a stick of celery at her. 'You're getting too predictable with the whole rainbow of colours thing.'

'You just didn't like Ochre.'

'And there was that, too.' I smiled at her. 'It's a revolting colour and a worse name.'

'Fair enough.' She watched me through her lashes. 'Was it Paul? Your witness?'

'No.' My cheeks burned. 'Someone else. Another guy from school, named Fynn.'

She made a mock-impressed face and sipped her orange juice. 'Two boys at once? From famine to flood, huh? That's great. I'm going out tonight with Mick and a few others from work, but that's not an excuse to stay out too late with Paul.'

'You know I won't.'

'I know, but I'm a mother. I can't help worrying.' She gave me a significant glance. 'It's not like you've done a lot of dating.'

'*That*,' I said, 'I'm aware of. Don't panic.' I patted her shoulder condescendingly and grinned. 'I'll be safe, I promise. You too.'

'Rowan!' She pretended shock but her eyes twinkled. 'Just have fun, ok? You're too young to worry so much. At least yours is a real date. Mine'll be all work.'

I applied myself to the sandwich and listened to her shop-talk with half an ear. In truth, I wasn't particularly excited about the date, but I couldn't afford to have him talk about me. When I was young, we'd left too many towns in a hurry because kids at school noticed my strength and speed, no matter how hard I tried to hide.

And I did have questions for Paul. They hadn't occurred to me last night, but now my ingrained suspicion re-emerged. How had Paul known where I was? Had he followed me? Co-incidentally been at the same beach? I might be paranoid in thinking these things, but the only way to be sure was to ask him.

I was also now more certain than ever that Fynn was hiding something; that he knew something about the *ocair*. What made me so certain was a mystery. But I'd learned to trust my instincts about people. I was usually – depressingly – right.

The rest of the afternoon Anna and I spent mostly in silence or desultory conversation as we both worked on our laptops, set up at the dining table. The familiarity of her bent head and frowning concentration gave a comforting sense of security. No matter what happened, I'd have her and she'd have me.

At around three o'clock Anna stretched, yawned, closed her laptop and flopped onto the couch. She flicked on the tv and skimmed the channels. My history assignment on the Viking invasions of Britain complete, I spent half an hour smacking the muk yan jong – the kung fu training dummy I'd found at an op-shop the week before. My hands blurred and the wood cracked ominously. This one wouldn't last long. They never did. When my hands hurt too much to continue, I grabbed a cold drink from the fridge and joined Anna on the couch.

Outside, the sun hovered above the rim of the Great Dividing Range that formed a verdant backdrop to Cairns city. The light mellowed, toning down from the blazing insanity that melted mind and matter throughout the middle of the day. Palm trees and pink bougainvillea glowed in the golden-warm, afternoon light unique to North Queensland. It softened everything and made even me consider taking up painting, bad though I was at it.

Across the road, mothers with small children brought them out to play in the park fringing the shoreline. There wasn't really a beach here, just vast tidal mudflats. Swimming wasn't an option, with or without jellyfish. Which explained the enormous, fake beach-pool complex up the other end of town. Mangroves and mudflats weren't the tropical paradise tourists expected.

Anna's restless channel-surfing ceased and she settled on one showing news.

And our headline again, the cheerful blonde newsreader said, a *five car pileup today on Anderson street in central Cairns has claimed the lives of two people. This footage was taken by a tourist who happened to be on site when a truck lost control and rolled into oncoming traffic.*

The drama unfolded. A black truck out of control; a red car; the tearing of metal; a flying ragdoll body. I swore and sprang from the couch. The drink tin crumpled into a solid ball in my palm.

Ignoring Anna's worried call, I ran to my room and dug in my bag. By the time I found Fynn's card and my phone, my fingers shook so badly I could barely dial. It rang just once and he answered.

'You're ok?' I asked, breathless. Why did it matter? 'On the news. There was an accident. You didn't go down Anderson street?'

'No. Gatton, like I said,' he replied, his tone curt, almost dismissive.

'I...' I didn't know what to say; couldn't explain my call without sounding like a lunatic.

'Look, I can't talk now.' His voice was quiet, practically a whisper. 'Let's meet for lunch tomorrow. I'll tell you what I can about the *ocair,* and—'

'What?'

'You heard me. Meet me tomorrow, same place. But don't go out with Paul Eisen tonight. Stay at home where you're safe.'

'But—' The phone beeped in my ear.

I called him straight back but it went to voicemail. And again. What the hell? He *did* know about the *ocair.* But how? And what was so dangerous about going out with Paul? After last night I felt safe with him. What right did Fynn have to tell me what to do, anyway? He couldn't just order me around, hang up and expect me to sit home waiting for him to dole out information. I had no reason to trust his word or obey him.

I texted him with a demand to pick up the phone. No reply.

Paul might want me to protect his father's job, but he hadn't proven untrustworthy. He hadn't lied to me, as Fynn had.

Paul was also arrogant enough that if I didn't go out with him, he would spread stories about me at school and draw too much attention to my whereabouts. I wasn't going to leave town until I'd spoken with Logan, so I certainly couldn't risk my anonymity by standing Paul up.

'Rowan?' My mother stood in the doorway, sounding worried.

A strident buzzing made me jump. Anna hurried to the security camera screen by the door.

'It's Paul. What do you want me to say?' It was only four-thirty.

'Tell him...' I swept my thumb across the smooth screen of the phone, over the last number dialled. 'Tell him I'll be down in a minute.' I shut my door and dug frantically for a decent outfit that didn't need ironing.

If not for the questions about how Paul found me at the beach, and Fynn's order to stay home, I probably would have found an excuse to get out of this no matter how long Paul camped on my doorstep. But meeting with Paul was my best chance to be a hundred percent sure we were safe here. If a simple date would close his mouth and keep me out of the limelight, I had to do it. I couldn't be driven out by something as dumb as teenage gossip, not with the chance of learning about the *ocair* so close.

'Hey beautiful.' Paul grinned at me as I emerged from the elevator. 'How's the head?'

I shrugged one shoulder and slipped a thin, grey-green overshirt into my bag in case it got cooler later. I'd had to leave my spare pair of gloves at home. It was one thing to wear them as a quirky fashion statement at school, but just plain weird with a dress and strappy flats. I'd just have to be careful.

'Fine. Thanks. What's the deal? You're only like an *hour* early.' I held up my watch significantly.

He chuckled. 'Thought you might bail. Figured I'd come get you early so you'd have no excuses.'

'Wow. And I thought I had trust issues. So where are we going?'

'My Dad's having a barbeque,' he said, then laughed – probably at my horrified expression. 'Don't panic. We're not doing the "meet the parents" thing. Just gotta go home for a sec. Forgot my wallet. Then we'll grab something to eat and meet up with the others to catch a movie. There's that Marvel movie on if you're up for it.'

Relieved, I agreed. Anything but an interminable evening making smalltalk to adults I didn't know. A movie was infinitely better and being with his friends would save me talking about myself.

'I thought you were going to see that last night?'

'My Dad pulled me into a stupid meeting. Then I rescued a damsel in distress.' He sent me a cheeky grin.

'I meant to ask…' I tried to sound casual as we clung to the shade and headed for his car. The heat radiating off the ground made my skin sticky. The air was thick and heavy with moisture. 'How'd you find me?'

Paul shrugged. 'Wasn't looking. I was pissed at my Dad and just went to my favourite beach to relax. There you were.'

Relieved, I laughed back at him. One of my worries lifted, leaving me lighter.

When we reached his car I paused, admiring it. He owned a convertible Porsche. Silver. Gallantly, he opened the passenger door and waved me in. I slid into the leather seat, trying hard not to be impressed. At the touch of a button, the top retracted.

He slid in the other side, turned the engine over, revved the accelerator and grinned wickedly. Rebellion spurted inside me again and I returned a nod, tightened my seatbelt and grabbed hold of the armrest. He floored it and the car leapt from a standing start to sixty in about two seconds. I laughed, holding my long wig in place as it twisted into knots. The adrenalin rush hit my blood and I yelled my exuberance, flinging an arm into the air.

The ride was over too soon. Paul wound his way up into the hills, the prices of the houses most likely going up with every metre as the view improved. At the top of the hill, he pressed a button and a majestic wrought iron gate slowly slid back to reveal an unbelievable house; no, mansion, behind.

I raised my eyebrows at him. 'Seriously?'

Paul laughed, all white teeth, blue eyes and mischief. 'I did tell you my dad worked at MJE Enterprises.'

'The "at" part of that sentence now seems suspicious.'

'He owns it.' He grinned. 'Michael John Eisen Enterprises. Didn't you know?'

'No.' I didn't know what else to say. 'Well, crap.'

Here I'd been afraid he was sucking up to me because my mother had the power to fire his dad, and it was the other way around. Relief flooded in, coloured by a hint of cautious excitement. Maybe he did like me just for who I was. I could relax and enjoy the evening. After all, it wasn't often a girl got taken out in a Porsche. The cautious girl in me asked what Paul would want from me at the end of the evening. The rebel elbowed her aside and urged me to find out.

He pulled the car up before a massive front double door and jumped out. He ran around and opened the passenger door for me, bowing and holding his hand out. 'My lady.'

I hesitated, then took his fingers and clenched my teeth against the expected connection. Nothing happened. I slid out of the car. Brushing at the skirt of my floaty green sun dress, I tried to feel at ease. This sort of place; this sort of money – it spoke of cameras and security records of my face.

Paul grinned. 'Don't worry. If we're lucky we can sneak in and be gone before they know I'm here.'

I gently withdrew, not wanting to risk my luck by holding on too long. He didn't seem to mind. He flexed his arm, picking loose a bandage taped to the inside of the elbow. When he saw me looking he grinned and poked at the small red dot on the skin.

'Dad's into the health-stuff. He insists we both get blood tests every six months.'

'What for?'

Paul shrugged. 'Who the heck knows? His brother died young of some crazy-weird disease. Maybe that's it. I figure if there's anything bad he'll tell me. C'mon. Let's get in and out of here before anyone sees us.' He threw the balled-up bandage into a garden bed and strode away, waving me on.

Instead of going in the front entrance, he led the way around to a smaller door in the side of the house. From there we tiptoed up a narrow flight of stairs to the second floor and into a long, marble-floored hallway. A few steps on carried us past a room that made me stop and gape.

'What?' Paul followed my eyeline. 'The gym?'

'That's not a piddly little home gym,' I blurted, 'that's a full sized training facility and dojo!' I bit my tongue, regretting the hasty words.

Paul didn't seem to notice. 'Yeah, we can come and play some other time when the house isn't full of Dad's friends wanting to dump their daughters onto me.'

The murmur of voices and the clink of glasses and laughter wafted up from the back yard of the property. Soft jazz music floated in. There was a splash, a shout of laughter and a female voice raised in laughing complaint. Apparently someone had gone into the pool. Of course there was a pool. Probably a tennis court, too. And a Jacuzzi.

Paul ducked into the next room and came back out with his wallet. We ran back downstairs, giggling like kids. At the base, Paul skidded to a halt and I barely avoided crashing into him.

'Who's your friend?' A male voice made me peer around Paul's broad shoulders.

Paul dragged me forward and introduced us.

'Dad, Meghan. Meghan, Dad. Or rather: Mr Eisen, I suppose.'

On catching my eye, his father's smile slipped for just a fraction of a second, then switched on again, brighter. His eyes showed a hint thoughtful interest. He held out a hand. I hesitated then grasped it, bracing myself. Nothing.

'Meghan...' Michael Eisen said musingly, 'Meghan Greene. You'd be Anna's daughter then? Call me Mick, please.'

An image flashed into my head, catching me unprepared: a snapshot of him and my mother locked in an embrace. I clenched my jaw to keep words from spilling free. This was the 'Mick' from work my mother had mentioned so often recently. That accounted for the interested inspection. But why had she told him who I was? They'd only known each other two weeks. She wasn't usually that reckless about my safety. Or had Paul told him?

I wasn't comfortable calling him 'Mick'. It was an easy, friendly nickname and I couldn't see him that way. He wasn't an easy, friendly person. He was a Michael, or even a Mr Eisen, formal and distant.

'Nice to meet you, sir. Yes, Anna's my mother,' I said, trying to cover my discomfort.

What did she see in him? Besides the wealth and good looks, of course. His edgy intensity and strength was a far cry from the gentle, patient men my mother was normally attracted to. Maybe she sought security after all the years of uncertainty with me. My heart sank. Of course she did. And why not?

When he released my hand, I unthinkingly wiped it on my hip.

Michael's eyes followed my action, a small crease appearing between his brows for a fraction of a second.

'Your mother is an extraordinary lady,' he said, after an awkward pause. 'She certainly keeps a low profile, though. It wasn't easy finding her.'

'Well.' I cleared my throat, 'I hope she's helping.'

Michael smiled a hundred watts. 'Absolutely. Things were a little stale. She's brought in exactly what I wanted.'

'I'm glad, sir.' I needed a polite way to end the conversation.

Luckily, Paul interrupted by grabbing my wrist and dragging me away.

'Gotta go, Dad. Back after the movies.' He flipped Michael a salute as we dashed out the door.

'Don't be too late in,' his father called. 'We have training in the morning, remember?'

'Sure Dad. Don't stress.'

I glanced back. Michael Eisen stared steadily at me, with just the faintest hint of satisfaction lingering about his mouth.

As we closed the front door Paul let out an exaggerated "whew" and swiped the back of his hand over his forehead. Opening the Porsche door for me, he climbed in his own side and threw me a grin.

'Sorry about that.'

I shrugged. How could I diplomatically ask what I wanted to know? I decided to just go ahead and ask.

'Was your mum home, too?'

Paul grimaced. 'She and Dad split up about ten years ago. Usual crap. She thought his obsession with the whole martial arts thing was a bit weird. She lives in Sydney now.'

'Martial arts thing?' I asked warily. 'What sort of martial arts? Is that what he meant by training?'

'Oh, yeah.' He grinned. 'Forgot you're new in town. Everyone knows he's a nut for it. He likes to train in the old European martial arts styles – boxing, swordfighting and such. I didn't mind so much when I was a kid. Y'know how kids like to hang with their dad. But it's a bit old now. I do it just to humour him.'

I gave a sympathetic grin. 'Parents, what can you do? They all have their hangups, I guess. So is that what got him into owning gyms?'

An MJE emblem, emblazoned on a brochure on the floor of the car, caught my eye. The M and E were in a flowing font, separated by a sharp, straight J that looked more like a sword or a T. Glossy and professional, with a picture of a gleaming blue-and-brushed-steel gym, and two muscular, oiled, grinning models on the front, the brochure presented the ideal everyone supposedly needed to be.

Paul slipped the car into gear and planted his foot. 'Guess so. He's got about a hundred around the world. He's buying a couple more next year.'

'Is that how he makes his money?' I asked. 'Sorry. That was rude. I meant, I thought MJE was more about science r-and-d stuff?'

'Yeah, that was how he got started. Not sure why he got into gyms. Guess it's the health-trend. A lot of his research is about health.' He curled a lip. 'Which is why he wants me to get into genetics – so I can take over the business. I s'pose gyms were sort of a natural next step. He bought his first one about five years ago and he travels a lot buying others. Off to Italy next week. I'm thinking I might go too.'

'Italy...That'd be cool. I haven't been there yet.' I put the thought aside. Maybe next year, when I was free. 'So where are we going?'

'Thought we'd meet some of the guys at that new Thai place down on the Esplanade.'

'Sounds good,' I replied, resigning myself to an evening of testosterone.

SEVEN

<Where is she now?>

Out, with Paul Eisen and his friends. I'm following.

<Stay out of sight.>

I'm just going to keep an eye on her. There's something very strange about her. Whatever happens, you need to see her.

<Stop playing the hero. They'll be watching her and if you get involved they'll see you, too.>

If they're that good, which I doubt, they probably already have. I can take care of myself. She can't. She doesn't know what she's up against.

<Don't underestimate them. Remember what happened to Jonathan.>

As it turned out, the "guys" weren't too bad. Sure, they were full of themselves and their girlfriends were a bit stand-offish to start with but they all loosened up as the night went on. Paul kept them in a ripple of laughter with a series of off-colour comments about people. It was hard not to laugh along, even though the inherent snobbery in his observations made me cringe.

It was pleasant to almost feel part of a group, though. They were all perfectly nice to me, even the girls. Paul also behaved like an absolute gentleman the whole evening, treating me with easy camaraderie in front of his friends; never mentioning the whole headache incident, as promised. I kept the sarcasm to a minimum, listened and smiled encouragingly a lot.

After dinner and a movie we gravitated to a coffee shop. The group broke up around midnight when the girls pestered their boyfriends to take them to a nightclub catering to the under eighteen crowd. I opted out, so Paul drove me home.

He pulled up outside my place, leapt out and opened the door for me again with a sweeping bow. High overhead, our windows were dark. Anna must be either still out, or in bed. I smiled politely at Paul, hoping he would get the message without making too much of a fuss.

'Thanks, Paul. I had a good time.'

He hesitated, then stepped closer, sliding one arm around my waist. His other hand feathered its way up my arm, leaving goosepimples in its wake. My heart sped and my cheeks burned as his gaze fell to my lips.

'Do I at least get a goodnight kiss?'

For a heady moment I was tempted. Just a taste. Just one hiatus in my crazy life. Then I broke free from his embrace and stepped back. I must be mad. Bloody teenage hormones. He might not be trying to influence my mother for his father's job, but I still knew better than to get involved with someone as high-profile as Paul Eisen. There was no way I could slide through six months unnoticed on his arm.

'I'm sorry, Paul. I just can't.' Tonight's normality made the ache of reality all that much worse. But I couldn't keep torturing myself. At least, if I ended it now, it would hurt less.

'What's wrong with a kiss?' He reached for me again.

I stepped back again, hunching my shoulders and half turning away. He gripped my arm. The first inklings of old fear rose up in my throat and I pulled my bag across in front of me. My heart thudded in my ears, my breath harsh and quick. Memories of Japan flickered: flesh-on-flesh, humiliation, fear; life slipping away beneath my hands. Darkness raised its head.

That galvanised me. Fear was just stories. Stories that wouldn't happen this time. I was older, better disciplined. I could control it. I had to.

But if I refused Paul, what would he do? I didn't want to have to hurt him. That would ruin my plan to stay faster than anything. And the collateral damage to Anna's business and her relationship with Michael would be awkward, to say the least. Breaking a guy's arm didn't usually go down well with his dad.

Deliberately, I pressed my palm to Paul's wrist, concentrating on the next few minutes, steeling myself against the flash-images. Pinpricks shifted under my skin. Flickering and jumping like an old film it played out in my head. Warm relief surged. He wasn't the sort to force himself on me. I released his arm.

'I'm not going to sleep with you, so it's not fair to start something – that's what's wrong,' I said.

He stepped closer. I held a fist firm against his chest. He pushed forward then blinked in surprise when he couldn't close the gap between us.

'No one said we had to sleep together tonight. I can wait 'til our next date.'

That effectively doused what remained of my ambivalence. 'Saintly of you, but nope. Not in the market for a boyfriend, Paul, and there won't be any more dates. The deal was one, remember?'

His jaw dropped. 'Seriously? You really don't want to go out with me anymore? Why not? I thought we had a pretty good time and I reckon we'd be good together.'

'It's complicated,' I said. 'I told you I can't get involved with anyone right now. I want to concentrate on senior year. You're a great guy and I'm sure there's heaps of girls at school who'd be happy to hook up with you.' Catching a glimpse of irritation in his expression, I eased off, annoyed to have to placate him at all. 'I'm sorry. I don't mean to offend you, Paul. I did have a good time.'

'Wow.' He moved back. 'You know I think that's the first time any girl's ever said "no" to me. Man! That friggin' blows.'

I bit my tongue, holding in a sharp retort that would do nothing to calm the situation. I waited for his reaction. I'd seen only that he wouldn't resort to violence right now, not what he'd say and not what he'd do tomorrow. He could still make my life miserable at school, and possibly my mother's life at work, if he wanted.

The irony of the reversal of situation wasn't lost on me. It tasted bitter in my mouth.

There was a long silence. I couldn't see his face in the shadows. A motorbike growled past, then a busload of partygoers screaming their drunken delight to the tropical darkness.

'Y'know.' Paul's thoughtful voice made me jump. 'Dad told me you guys were new in town and asked me to make friends with you. I didn't want to because I thought you weren't my type.'

'Ah.' I tried to ignore the flash of hurt. 'That explains a lot.'

He continued. 'When you blew me off at the gym I was pretty pissed. Then I found you at the beach and you were so miserable I couldn't stay mad at you. Then, tonight, you've been one of the coolest girls I've ever talked with, so I thought we could be, y'know, an item. Now you tell me you don't want me? Man, that's harsh. Didn't tonight mean anything to you?'

'Of course it did,' I lied. Amusement flashed, easing my internal tension. He thought I was cool to talk with but I'd barely said a word. I smiled with just the right amount of friendly distance and regret. 'I'm sorry Paul. I don't want to get close to anyone. It would just make leaving too hard. Please understand.'

There was enough truth in that to sound sincere.

'Wow.' He huffed, but at least he didn't seem angry. 'And I thought I was messed up. No, no.' He backed away as I stuttered another apology. 'I get it. Well, friendzone it is, then. I guess I'll get over the blow to my ego with about five years of therapy.' He grinned and the worst was over.

'Thanks, Paul. I'll see you at school on Monday.' I turned to go into the unit complex.

'Hey!' Paul called me back. 'Just so you know... I'll keep my word. I won't tell.' He tapped his forehead significantly.

I smiled and planted a quick kiss on his cheek. 'Thanks. G'night.'

He saluted and strode jauntily away. 'Later.'

His Porsche sped off and I gritted my teeth against the unexpected ache in my chest. It just wasn't fair. What if I'd just rejected the one person who might be able to accept me and love me anyway? How would I ever know who I could trust?

The roar of a motorbike startled me out of childish resentment.

On the rider's back, a silver, Celtic tree glittered in the streetlights.

'Dammit!'

What was Fynn doing checking up on me? I did not need these stupid, soap opera complications. Was he stalking me? Well, time he learned not to.

A quick check showed Paul was well out of sight. I pulled keys out of my bag and headed for my car, parked beneath the apartment building. I skipped down the stairs two at a time, determined to catch up with Fynn. If I was quick I could follow him and have it out.

My hasty footsteps echoed back in slaps off the concrete walls. Two of the lights in the garage were out, leaving my car in a pool of darkness. Luckily, I'd always had good night vision and found the door handle without difficulty.

Something touched my shoulder.

A muscular arm slid across my collarbone, going for the rear choke hold. I tucked in my chin, dropped into a half-crouch and grabbed his wrist and elbow. My attacker gave a grunt and tightened his hold. He tried to counter; tried to pull me upright and back.

I spun to the right, opening his arm and twisting his hand. Yanking his bent elbow forward, I dragged the hand forcibly towards the ground. His shoulder dislocated with a sickening crunch. I dropped his head onto the concrete and his scream cut off into a choked gargle. His eyes rolled back. He twitched once and relaxed.

I scanned the carpark, heart thumping. It couldn't be an attempted robbery. Twice in as many days wasn't co-incidence, it was planning. Where was his partner? There must be another. My cover was definitely blown. By who? Fynn? He was the only suspect at the moment. He'd just been here. Had he pointed me out?

Something pressed into my back.

'Hands behind your head,' a low voice ordered.

I pivoted to one side and smashed my forearm into his. The gun flew free and skittered across concrete. It vanished under my car. I latched onto his wrist and turned back. Folding and twisting dislocated elbow and shoulder. Ligaments popped in his wrist. He screamed and collapsed, swearing. I kicked him in the temple and he sagged to the concrete.

In my head, the blackness threatened, eating at my self-control. I dug my nails into my palms and focussed on that pain. The darkness was so close to the surface. So close. I just had to hang on. The exit was only a few steps away. My phone was in my pocket. A quick call and we'd be packed and gone within the hour.

I hesitated.

If I left, I'd lose my chance to talk with Fynn about what he knew. I'd be forever running, forever afraid of these people, whoever they were. We'd been running since I was four and the gaps between them finding us were shorter each time. And each time they caught me, the results were more horrific. Soon it would come to the point where I lost all control. And I had no idea what would happen.

It had to stop. I had to stop running. I had to find out what the *ocair* was so I could give it to them. Then maybe, just maybe, I could live a close approximation to a normal life. This was my first and only opportunity. I couldn't run this time. Not if I could fix everything.

I glanced down at the two figures at my feet. Here was my chance to find out who they were. Perhaps what, exactly, this *ocair* thing was they wanted.

Patting down the unconscious man turned up nothing of use. No identification in his black cargo pants and plain blue polo shirt. Nothing. The second man woke, groaned and blinked reddened eyes at me as I approached. This carpark was too public. I'd have to take them upstairs to interrogate them further.

A flicker of movement caught my eye. Another man. This one stepped out of the deep shadows, holding some sort of gun. It didn't appear to be a normal pistol. Dart gun? Dammit. That meant he wanted me alive, but sedated. Who *were* these people? Who had these sort of resources?

I raised my arms slowly. If he just came a little bit closer... No, he wasn't going to. He'd seen what I did and wasn't risking himself. A thug with a brain.

He squeezed the trigger.

I twisted, trying to get out of the way…and misjudged. The dart landed in the thickest part of my thigh muscle. I swore, yanked it out and flung it away. It tinkled onto the concrete. Warm lassitude spread like honey through my leg muscle.

The man stayed where he was, watching.

I slid along my car to the driver door, feet numb and steps uncertain. The keys were random lumps of metal in my thick fingers. I drove an elbow through the window. Glass sprayed into the car. The alarm blared, deafening in the concrete carpark. Maybe someone would come. I hauled the door open.

Close behind, my attacker chuckled. 'That won't help. You'll be unconscious in a few seconds. You can't drive.' His voice was mild and cultured. Australian with overtones of English boarding schools and a hint of sinus trouble.

I ignored him and scrabbled beneath the seat, trying to focus through the distortion creeping into my brain. The urge to close my eyes almost overpowered the adrenalin pumping through my blood. At last I came up with what I wanted. Slewing around in the seat I dragged myself upright using the steering wheel.

The gunman moved closer, watching me. Perfect. His face was half-lit, shadowed, angular, deep eyesockets, short, buzzcut, dark hair. I committed it to memory as best I could.

No. It was already there. I'd seen that face five years before. In the ruined square outside the cathedral, after the earthquake.

He'd found me.

The smugness about his thin mouth spoke of amused superiority.

'Laugh at this.' I squeezed and watched in fogged satisfaction as he dropped to the ground, twitching in time with the taser cords sticking out of his chest.

Now I really was done with running. If I woke up alive I'd get Anna to safety, then I'd come back and show these guys who they were dealing with. Enough. I'd had more than enough. I couldn't live in fear like this any longer.

Darkness roared deep in the drugged bonds of my mind.

Too late. The drug took me, and it, into oblivion.

Lights flashed overhead. Voices surged and retreated like waves on the beach. I liked the beach. Maybe I should go again. Maybe I could try parasailing. Or diving. I could use a good rush. Life was way too tense. Wasn't it meant to be at least a bit of fun?

'Meghan?' Something slapped my face gently, chasing away idyllic, forest-rimmed beaches and cold mountain streams overhung by sharp basalt cliffs.

'Meghan, can you hear me?'

I groaned, pushing the hand away feebly, my arm so heavy I could barely move it. 'Hate that name.'

More lights flickered, steadily, rhythmically. Squinting, I twisted my head to try and make sense of it. Not the beach, then. Ah, right: streetlights. Their orange glare flashed and vanished and flashed again, leaving no space for recovery.

I closed my eyes, willing myself not to throw up. This was my car by the sound of it and I would not throw up in it. Why was I lying down in it? Who was driving?

'You ok? Open your eyes,' a vaguely familiar male voice ordered in a tone I found difficult to disobey for some reason. It had no-nonsense harmonics.

I opened my eyes and squinted against the lights at the driver, trying to bring him into focus.

'You? You *are* behind this?'

It was Fynn - all sarcasm and anti-hero dark good looks. Wind from the open driver's window ruffled his hair.

'No. I just happened by at about the time you passed out. Figured you could use a hand.' He checked the rear view mirror, his expression calm, with just a hint of a frown. Did he find young women sedated in the basement carpark, presumably still surrounded by twitching casualties of war, perfectly ordinary?

I closed my eyes again, turning his blithe explanation over in my sluggish brain. Nope. Still didn't make a great deal of sense. There was something about him I had to remember. Something connected to the attack on me. What was it?

'So why are you driving my car? Why didn't you just take me upstairs? Where are you taking me?'

Hopefully he wouldn't offer to let me drive. Right now even the frangipani smell blasting in through the broken window turned my stomach.

'You're welcome.' He cast me an ironic look. 'I didn't know your entry code and your mother isn't home so there's no-one to buzz me in. Plus I didn't fancy carrying you unconscious past the night guard. You should have stayed in tonight, like I asked. I'm taking you somewhere safe.' Another glance in the mirror and his brows knitted tighter.

'My mother!' I clenched my teeth as he changed lanes. 'If they know where I live, they'll find her.'

'She's safe enough while she's with Michael Eisen,' he said coolly. 'He's got security coming out his ears. I sent her a text in your name telling her to stay with him if she wanted. You really should password your phone, you know.'

His long fingers flexed around the steering wheel. Dropping back a gear he accelerated, turning a corner a fraction faster than was wise. I gripped the seat and swallowed again, concentrating on thinking healthy thoughts until he slowed and straightened.

'Well,' I managed, raising a leaden arm to shade my eyes against the lights, 'I'll tell you this: you need to pull over or I'll throw up on you.'

Showing great intelligence, he pulled the car off to the side of the road, under the shadow of a broad tree. He doused the lights and watched the rear view for a few seconds before relaxing.

I peered out. We seemed to be somewhere in the suburbs. Groaning I scrabbled at the seat until I managed to slump half upright against the door. It took some careful thought to operate the seat-back mechanism, but I finally raised it to vertical. The last dregs of the sedative seemed to be wearing off.

With clumsy fingers, I flipped open the glovebox and extracted a small bottle of water. Swallowing the luke-warm, tasteless stuff settled my stomach and wet my cottonwool mouth so I could speak properly. I was pretty confident I wasn't going to chuck.

'What the hell happened and why should I believe whatever you tell me?' I wasn't in the mood to be polite. 'You already lied to me once.'

He ignored that jibe. 'You were mugged again. The groaning bodies suggested you handled it ok – again. I particularly enjoyed seeing the twitching guy, by the way. I was tempted to kill him, but dead bodies bring cops and I'm sure neither of us want that.' He shrugged, slewing in the seat so he faced me. 'As for believing me, well, that's your choice. I can only tell you what I know, which isn't much.' The orange overhead streetlight cast shadows, emphasising strong cheekbones and jaw. 'Twice is a little odd, don't you think? Did you know any of them?'

'A little odd? That's an understatement. No, I don't know them.' I rubbed my thumbs into my temples, pressing against the fuzziness muddling my thoughts. Angular, deep eyesockets, short, dark hair, somewhere in his thirties. 'But I'll recognise the one I tased. The one who darted me.' I took another swallow of water, washing away the bitter taste of anger and fear. 'And when I find him, he'll frigging well regret this.'

My rescuer, if he could be called that, didn't reply. He checked the rear-view mirror again, watching it for long enough that I turned to scan the road behind. Either we weren't followed, or our tail had parked. I couldn't see anyone.

'How do you feel?'

His quiet question retrieved my attention but he wasn't watching me. His eyes were still on the mirror.

'Like I've been beaten with very large, heavy pillows and had my brain replaced with their stuffing. Thanks for asking. How long was I out?'

'About fifteen minutes.' He caught my apprehensive peek out the back window. The suburban street was still dark and quiet. 'We're somewhere on the northside. We weren't followed.'

He held a phone. My phone. Before I could protest, he pulled the battery out of it and dropped it back into my handbag in two parts. I shut my mouth and checked his body language for threat. Disassembling my phone stopped anyone tracking me…and stopped me making calls.

'And now they shouldn't be able to ping you,' he said. 'What about the car gps?'

'I disabled it the day we rented the car. So, who are you again? And who are "they"? And why are you acting like this is perfectly normal?' I scowled at him.

I should be grateful. It was just difficult to work up any emotion other than suspicion at him and anger at my attackers. But my mother had drilled manners into me, so I tried.

'Don't get me wrong, I appreciate you getting me out of there, but why did you do it? And I know the "just happened past" is bullshit. I saw your bike when Paul brought me home. Why did you follow me? Where do you fit into this?'

'Into what?' He raised a brow, just visible in the orange half-light.

'Yes,' I growled. 'Exactly. What?'

EIGHT

I don't think she knows her heritage, or who's after her.

<Not unusual. We've met similar, before. Don't get distracted. She's nothing special.>

I think you could be wrong about that. I don't think they're after her just because of what she is. They haven't been nearly this circumspect with the others. They could easily have killed her both times. I think they want her alive and undamaged. We need to find out why if we're going to have the advantage. I'm going to bring her to you.

I stared out the window, ignoring the cookie cutter rows of houses with curtains flashing blue-white as government-approved, televised brain-junkfood went on behind them. Tugging at my lower lip I re-ran the attack.

Outside MJE must have been a first attempt. They'd upped the ante tonight to make sure I'd go down. Who the hell were those guys? Had the guy who'd been in Christchurch, and darted me tonight, also been in Japan? Maybe I just hadn't seen him?

'Logan.' Fynn extended a hand. I flinched back in non-comprehension. 'My real name is Logan,' he repeated. 'I lied. Twice. Sorry.'

Logan Litson? The comic-book, alliterated hero-name did nothing to ease my suspicions. His *real* name? Why was he living here under a false name? And what prompted him to give me the real one, if it actually was, now? Something was off here. So off it stank.

I kept my hands safely tucked into my folded arms. I didn't want to touch him in case it triggered another reaction. It would be nice to know his intentions but my head was too fuzzy to handle it right now. I might say something and things were already complicated enough.

'What do you want?' It wasn't the friendliest reply but I wasn't feeling inclined to be friendly. It'd been a buzz-wrecking end to a half-decent evening and I disliked being in anyone's debt.

His face hardened. 'I want to know who you are. Do you know?' He mirrored my pose, folding his arms.

Irritation cleared the last dregs of fog. 'That's a stupid question. Of course I do. I was sedated not concussed. I also know I'm not some pathetic princess waiting to be rescued. All I need from you is what you know about the *ocair*. After that, feel free to find the nearest taxi and go back for your bike. Appreciate the help but I'm fine. Thanks.'

He examined me in silence then shifted, moving in until we were eye to eye. I leaned away, head pressed against the window glass. Putting my hands out to fend him off, I encountered warm, smooth muscle barely masked by the thin cloth of his t-shirt. I snatched my hands back. He seemed unmoved. His gaze skimmed the contours of my face. It was unnerving.

His mouth twisted into a grimace. His eyes gleamed with unshared knowledge.

'Interesting. You don't know who you are, do you?' He stared briefly out the front window, his eyes glazing. Then he shrugged. 'Would you like to? And you're not fine, by the way.'

'I do know. No. And I damned well am,' I replied, glad of the distraction. 'I've managed to get along for eighteen ignorant years without your opinions so you can keep them to yourself now. You have no idea who I am. Tell me what I need to know so I can get these bastards off my case, then get out.' I put my hands back on his chest, intending to push him away.

He gripped both my wrists. I twisted against the weakest part of his grip. His fingers tightened and he countered easily, teeth flashing white in the half-shadowed space. What the...?

'Let go, Litson. I don't want to hurt you.' I glared at him, trying to ignore the adrenalin-fuelled racing of my heart. The sedative must be still affecting me. No-one had ever been able to stop me from breaking a grip. No-one.

The tension in his face eased into irony. 'Give it your best shot.'

I pursed my lips and repeated in a no-nonsense tone, 'Let. Go.'

He drew me even closer, until we were just a few centimetres apart.

I ought to feel threatened, but didn't. I ought to be afraid, but wasn't. I froze, breathing in the scent of his skin. The warm, solid strength of him exerted a powerful attraction and, just for one insane moment, I knew an urge to lean against his calm strength and rest. He peered into my eyes intently then touched the centre of my forehead with a fingertip.

A shock snapped into my head, as though he'd built up a static charge and touching me discharged it straight into my brain. My body jerked and sagged. I grabbed at the dashboard for support. Random images popped into my mind like a movie played at an indecipherably high speed. Images of people I'd never seen, places I'd never been. Someone else's life flared behind my eyes. I couldn't hold them and they vanished, leaving a vague feeling that some part of my brain wasn't quite under my control; locked away and inaccessible. I'd always felt that way but had never known what was missing until it was, for the briefest moment, there.

A baseball bat made of pure, thought-killing pain slammed into my head, turning my brain to mush and agony. I pressed my temples in a vain effort to squeeze the pain out. Biting my lip was a distraction at best. I whimpered and tried to resist the urge to curl into a small ball around the hurt and just die.

'Dammit. That wasn't meant to happen.' Logan shifted, gunning the engine. 'You won't want to go to a hospital. I'll get you to someone who can help.'

'No,' I whispered. 'I just need somewhere dark and cool to sleep for a while. Then I'll be ok. If you move the car I'll throw up.' The thought of it made me choke.

He swore and pulled out into the street anyway. Brilliant streetlights stabbed through my closed eyelids and I couldn't help the tears of despair that slipped beneath my lashes, even as I hated myself for such weakness. Every bump in the road sliced like a dagger in the brain. Where was he taking me?

I flailed at his leg. 'Leave me. I'll sleep in the car.'

'Don't be any more stupid than you have to be. You can't stay in a car. Not in this condition. Not even you,' he said. 'You'd suffocate in this heat. I know someone who can help. She's a doctor but not mainstream. Dammit, Rowan, stop!'

That car ride was worse, even, than the drive with Paul, for Logan was far less careful around the corners. Twice he pulled over so I could throw up. At some point we stopped and he lifted me into a different car; bigger, more comfortable, smoother. Helpless, I couldn't even walk, let alone take the chance to run.

'Hang in there, Rowan,' Logan murmured, helping me into the back seat. 'Not far now. We'll be out of town soon, so it should get easier.' He climbed in beside me. I lay on my side, aching head on his leg, his fingers warm on my shoulder. Someone else drove. I didn't care who.

Eventually, the quality of light torturing me changed, becoming cooler and darker, almost soothing. Voices swirled around me, shifting in and out of hearing, sometimes even sounding like they echoed inside my skull. The words made no sense. They spoke a different language, one I almost understood, but not quite. The effort of trying to understand made me retch.

Logan lifted me out of the car. Too-bright lights shone through my closed lids. I groaned and covered my eyes. The lights flicked out and the voices softened to a murmur. Logan deposited me gently on a bed not my own, but I didn't care. The voices stopped. An airconditioner hummed in the silence that followed.

The bed dipped. A cool cloth descended over my aching forehead and eyes and I managed an inarticulate thanks. Seconds later, an arm slid under my back, raising me. Protesting faintly, I tried to push away, but he gripped me tightly.

'I told you not to be stupid. Drink this. It'll help,' Logan's impatient voice ordered. 'Yes, I'll let you sleep when you've drunk it all. It's just herbal tea with clematis and a little willowbark – good for migraines. Synthetic painkillers don't work well do they? No, didn't think so. Drink. Good girl.'

I swallowed the bitter liquid. How did he know about the painkillers? He laid me back on the blessedly soft pillows. Cool fingers stroked my temples, draining the pain as I sank into oblivion.

Just before sleep swamped me, fear resurfaced.

He'd called me 'Rowan'. My real name.

It is remarkably silent this high up – apart from the faint whistling of a warm tropical breeze that steals my breath; breath rushing harshly from my lips. My heart is oddly slow, as though it hasn't yet realised the danger. Wind, breath and the slow, steady pulse of blood in my veins; that's all I can hear. Oh...and the sound of soft, triumphant laughter from the man holding my arm so tightly.

Man? Is it a man, or some sort of ghost? I'm not sure now. Not sure how I got here. Not sure if he'll keep holding on, or if he'll let go. I crane my neck to try and see his face but it's shadowed. All I see is the gleam of a pale eye and the white-tipped fingers of a tanned, strong hand.

I glance down and regret it. The street is a long, long way below.

He lets go.

If only I could fly.

I awoke with a scream of fear strangled in my throat. Sitting up in the half-light, I clutched at the bedclothes, heart racing. I struggled against the remnants of the dream.

A light snapped on. A pair of arms wrapped around me. Weren't they the same tanned, strong hands that held my life over the edge of a building; the same hands that dropped me? I shoved against their binding strength and scrambled away from the bed, staring in suspicion at the man who occupied it.

Tousled and bleary-looking, Logan yawned at me, rubbing his eyes. He swung long, jeans-clad legs off the bed. He only was half-dressed. As was I. He must have taken off my dress, leaving me in underwear and a white, lacy bra.

On a small table nearby, a plate and empty glass spoke of someone's late-night meal. I edged closer and palmed the butter knife, hefting the weight. My handbag sat on a chair not far away. My dress was nowhere to be seen.

'What is it? Your head?' Logan pushed his fingers through his dark hair and glanced at the clock. Red numbers glowed six am. The morning light crept between shutters closed across the window.

'No.' I took another step away, closer to where my handbag rested. 'No, it was just…a dream, I guess.'

I flipped the knife over. Not the most effective edged weapon, but better than nothing.

'Put the knife down,' he said wearily. 'I'm not going to hurt you. If I was, I'd've done it already.'

'I know,' I said reasonably, 'because if you try I'll take your eye out with it.'

He raised one brow and slid off the other side of the bed with his hands up in surrender but no hint of it in his cool, grey eyes. I retreated. A white wicker chair caught the back of my knees and I half-fell into the seat. My head was remarkably pain-free though post-migraine lassitude made my movements clumsy and slow. Now I needed to shake the lingering adrenalin from falling so I could think clearly.

Walking slowly around the bed, Logan then knelt before me, plucked the knife from me and regarded me like a doctor making a diagnosis.

'You know I'm not going to hurt you.' He flipped the butter knife at a wooden board on the far side of the room. It stuck firmly in the timber, leaving one more amongst dozens of similar cuts in the surface.

His distance softened to understanding and his eyes narrowed as he inspected my face. 'Migraine gone? You look better.'

I nodded, leaning away from him. I touched my own hair, short and wildly messy. My wig hung over the back of a nearby chair. Logan's mouth quirked in a slight, wry grin.

He flicked an auburn curl with one fingertip. 'It suits you better than brown, I have to say.'

I remained silent, exposed and vulnerable. No-one but my mother had seen my real hair and eye colour since I was four.

Seeking to change the subject away from myself, I studied the dimly lit room. Timber-slatted window shutters let strips of light fall in patterns of light and shade across the rumpled double-bed. A white ceiling fan turned lazily up near the high ceiling, but the room was cool enough not to need it. The floors were polished timber, the walls tongue-and-groove, white-painted timber, the furnishings a hodge-podge of old colonial and shabby-chic white wicker. Not a motel room.

'Where am I and why are we in the same bed?' My voice came out a little more panicked-sounding than I intended. I quashed fear. It wasn't helpful.

He seemed unfazed. 'You're at our weekend place on up on the Tablelands. You needed to be away from people and town.'

That made no sense and sounded a lot like kidnapping.

'We're not kidnapping you,' he said gently, 'and I didn't want you to freak when you woke up in a strange place so I stayed here with you. There's only three bedrooms, anyway. This is mine.'

I grabbed a cushion, holding it before my body, shivering with more than the pre-dawn cool. 'Who's "we"?'

He jerked his head at the door. 'I told you. I live with my aunt, Maeve, and my cousin, Jennifer. They're still asleep in the other rooms.'

The presence of an aunt and female cousin seemed incongruous for someone with ill intent. Reluctantly, I studied him again, relaxing wariness to allow for the possibility he meant no harm.

'Where's your…um… shirt?' I dragged my eyes away from his smooth latte skin. Annoyed at myself, I gripped the cushion until my knuckles whitened. At least he couldn't hear my heart thumping a mile a minute.

He gave a faint, tolerant grin, his teeth white and even. 'Maeve threw it and your dress in the washing machine. There was blood on them from your attackers. I figured you'd definitely freak if you woke up in bed with a guy not wearing *some* clothes, though.'

I stared at him in horror and his fleeting humour vanished.

'You ok?' He frowned.

'You…you let me go and I fell,' I blurted, still half-caught in the dream, and entangled with other memories I tried to ignore.

His eyes turning stormy. The muscles along his jaw worked.

'In my dream,' I added, although he probably already thought me crazy and we hadn't even started on the issue of why I'd been attacked twice. 'You were holding me at the top of a building and…you let me fall.'

The tension in his jaw vanished and his expression segued into thoughtful consideration. He straightened his back, still balancing on the balls of his feet as he crouched in front of me. The action only served to emphasise the lean beauty of his body. I shifted in the seat and held the pillow tighter.

'Sure it was me?' He seemed to take my dream seriously.

I considered it. 'No? I didn't see his face. Just grey eyes and hands like yours.'

He examined one smooth, strong appendage then gripped one of mine with it. I jumped and pulled free. He grimaced and looked straight into my eyes, serious and intent.

'I won't let you fall, Ruadhán.'

I started again, this time in surprise. He'd spoken my real name, and with the original Celtic softness my father had intended. No-one else said it like that, not even my mother.

'Meghan,' I corrected, half-heartedly.

The ironic smile returned. 'Like the hair: Rowan suits you better. It means "light", you know.'

'Really?' I allowed myself to be distracted. 'What language? I've looked it up and I thought it meant "red-haired" in Gaelic.'

He shrugged and didn't reply. Irritation flashed across his face. It vanished so fast I thought I'd imagined it.

We considered each other; him with calm, cool seriousness, me with wariness born of long caution. The atmosphere between us crackled with a different sort of tension and I swallowed hard against the ridiculous urge to drop the cushion and climb back into bed. That was so out of left field it was a slap in the face. Sitting up, I clutched at the chair arms, aware I was alone in a bedroom with a half-dressed man I barely knew.

Fear leapt. Darkness woke, watchful.

NINE

<Tread carefully, Logan. Back off a little. She's scared. There's a...history there she's hiding. An old fear. She could be dangerous if you frighten her.>

We just need to find out who she is. Why they want her.

<There's something else.>

Yes, I saw it.

<It will have to come down. It's hiding something. I can't tell what, though.>

Will that hurt her?

<...does it matter?>

She's one of ours.

<No. A rogue. Uneducated. Untrained. Impossible to work with as she is. Better to wipe her.>

What about with the impediment cleared?

<...possible. Why?>

There's something about her...

Logan scooted back and sat on the bed again, putting a more comfortable distance between us. Something tight-wound in my stomach relaxed a fraction. Leaning elbows on bent knees and letting his fingers dangle between them, he sent me a half-lidded, cool regard that said he was quite aware of my reactions and wanted none of it. It was the same look I'd given Paul last night. I swallowed down a curious mixture of sick relief and hurt, trying to focus on my situation, rather than the desire to caress his smooth skin, and the fear of what might happen if I did.

Outside, kookaburras broke into raucous laughter that passed from tree to tree around the house. Butcher birds added their liquid, warbling greetings. The room brightened as the sun rose higher and poured heat and the scent of warming earth into the house.

'So?' Logan prompted.

'So, what?' I asked, bewildered.

'Who were those men and why were they after you?'

'I...don't know who they were or what they wanted,' I said. 'But thanks for helping. I know I wasn't exactly polite in the car.'

He folded his arms. 'You had a pretty good excuse for being scared and angry, so don't stress. But you really don't know what they wanted with you?'

I plucked at a corner of the white, fringed cushion on my lap. Normally I had no problems lying convincingly. For some reason, lying to Logan was more difficult. His eyes seemed to see more than most. The secret wasn't just mine to share. It affected Anna, too, and I wasn't prepared to risk my mother's life to assuage his curiosity.

'This *ocair* thing is what they wanted last time,' I said. 'What do you know about it? If I can give it to them, maybe they'll leave me alone.'

His mouth twisted into cynicism. 'I doubt it. All I know is that it means "key".'

Disappointment fisted in my stomach. If that was true, then I'd wasted my time. And I needed to find another way to stop this madness. So my aim hadn't changed: get Anna to safety and make these bastards leave me alone. I just didn't have any leverage any more.

I rolled my neck and flexed my fingers. It didn't matter. Once I found them, they'd know to leave me be. I wasn't thirteen or even sixteen any more. And I could do a helluva lot of damage without killing everyone. After all, if I killed everyone, who would be alive to tell them to back off.

'OK.' Logan changed the subject casually, yanking me back from my bloodthirsty daydream. 'What exactly happened in the car to trigger that migraine? The dart drugs?'

I rubbed my forehead. 'No. I was getting over that fine. Then you touched my head and it felt like you'd shocked me. I saw...' I changed the words. 'Then the migraine hit like a hammer.'

He didn't reply and, for a long moment, he seemed to stare right through me, blank and abstracted.

With his intensity focussed elsewhere the spell of his charisma broke. What was I doing? I didn't know this man and I'd already said too much. I couldn't trust him just on his say-so? What if this whole thing was a set up? What if he'd "rescued" me from his own hirelings to gain my trust? I stood up, grabbing at the chair as the room wobbled alarmingly.

'I should go. My mother will be worried. If you can't help me then I need to get her out of town.'

Logan rose, catching my shoulders as I swayed uncontrollably. My knees gave way and I sat back down. He knelt once more at my feet, his hands warm on my skin. Wry sincerity momentarily displaced the distance in his eyes.

'You're doing it again, Rowan: running. You don't need to. You're ok with me, I promise. I won't hurt you. And I *can* help you.' His gaze held nothing more than calm honesty as he continued. 'Your mother is fine. As long as she's important to Michael Eisen she's safe. He has rockstar-level security. Maeve and I called her with a secure phone last night. I used your code-words so Anna would know you're ok.'

'How...?' I gaped at him.

His smile twisted. 'You told me the codewords last night. You probably don't remember. You were fretting about Anna.'

'And she believed you?' It seemed absurdly unlikely. My mother was as protective of me as I was of her. I half-expected her to burst through the door any second.

He shrugged. 'Maeve more than me. Maeve's a doctor. She managed to convince Anna you didn't need rescuing at one in the morning. We didn't tell Anna about the attack, just the migraine. Anna said you're usually still weak for a while afterward.' He raked my face with another searching examination. 'And that one seemed pretty bad to me.'

I flinched at the mere remembrance.

'Do you get them often?'

He didn't seem about to lose control in any way, so I relaxed. I didn't feel like driving yet so, as long as he didn't make a big deal, I would stay, at least for breakfast. Well alright, needing breakfast was an excuse. In reality, I had no idea what my next move ought to be. If someone wanted to find me, I couldn't go home. I needed to plan how to get Anna away, and how to turn the tables and find my pursuers before they caught up with me.

'I...' I shook my head to clear it, focussing on his question. 'Migraines. Not too often, thank God. Maybe three or four times a year.' I hesitated. 'But they do seem to be getting more frequent – and worse. This one, and the one the night before, was...extreme.'

Logan sat back on the bed, his spine up against the headboard, legs crossed at the ankles. He picked up a pen and fiddled with it, turning it over.

'So, are there any...triggers you know of?' He sounded too casual.

I tensed. What hid behind that question? I'd been asked the same thing by countless naturopaths and healers of various ilks. I couldn't see any danger in answering.

'Not that I know of,' I admitted, 'apart from you poking me in the head.'

'How about…' He tilted his head. 'Associations.' I must have given him blankness in response because he explained. 'You know: things that happen at the same time – like that dream, for instance?'

The pen blurred, moving so fast I couldn't see it.

'Yes.' I answered without thinking. 'I had that falling dream the last three times.'

'Ah.' His soft, almost-triumphant exclamation brought my eyes back to his face in fear. He flicked the pen aside. It landed neatly back in the cup he'd plucked it from. 'Who *are* you, I wonder?' He eyed me with increased intensity.

That soft question brought all my caution surging back. Why was he so interested in my headaches, but not about the attempts on my life? It made no sense.

'No-one special. I should go.'

'I beg to differ,' he said.

'With which bit?'

'Both.' He smiled. 'You are special and you need to stay here.'

'That sounds like a threat.' I lurched back to my feet.

'Nope. Statement of fact.' Logan sprang up, lithe and silky in his movements; a big cat stalking me. I edged towards my handbag, sitting on a chair nearby. He followed, eyes gleaming in the half-light.

I snatched at my bag. He was faster. I tried to grab it back. He tossed it onto the bed and locked strong fingers around my wrist. I twisted free, turning it into a wrist lock on him. He countered and reversed it with another. I countered. Our hands blurred as I tried again and again to break free, but he eluded me. I had never moved so fast in my life; never been allowed to.

Faster still, he grabbed my arm, twisting it up behind me in a painful lock. I could have freed myself, although maybe not, given how strong and fast he was. Shock held me prisoner more effectively than he did, anyway. No-one, ever, beat me if I didn't let them.

Ever.

He turned me around so my back pressed against his chest; his arm wrapped loosely around my throat. We faced a long mirror, which revealed stark astonishment in my face; thoughtful triumph in his.

'How did you do that?'

'Never met anyone faster than you?' He grinned mirthlessly, eyes mocking.

'No,' I said, made honest by fear. 'You said you wouldn't hurt me. You're hurting me now.'

He released his grip. I turned to face him, massaging the skin where his fingers left white imprints, now turning red.

He nodded at the marks. 'Any normal person's shoulder would have dislocated. You barely winced. And you threw off the effects of that sedative last night in fifteen minutes. It would have put anyone else out for a day.'

I backed away until my shoulders hit a wall, but it still wasn't far enough in this small room. He stood between me and the door.

'Who *are* you?' I whispered around the lump threatening to close my throat.

'Yes, we keep coming back to that, don't we? Thing is: I *know* who I am. And I gave you my real first name, so you should feel privileged.' He quirked a half-smile at me. 'But you…who are *you* and why did they want you alive? If you're serious about getting them off your back, then that's the question you should be asking.'

He studied me, his patience inviting honesty. 'Are you serious? Do you really want to stop running and be free of them?'

Gazing at Logan's darkly handsome face, seeing his inherent self-confidence and utter surety, I decided: he was right. Last night I'd passed the point of just running away again. I had to make a stand; had to find out what was going on and how to stop it. Logan might not know what the *ocair* was, but I'd never met anyone faster and stronger. If I was different, so was he. And he knew *why*. Which meant he might know who was chasing me and how I could find them. That made him useful.

He'd said I had nothing to fear from him and I believed it, although I doubted his reasons for helping were purely altruistic. Still, he knew. I didn't. That was reason enough to stay.

Logan sat down at the small, round coffee table. He snagged my bag and turned it upside down, emptying the contents onto the glass.

I yanked the sheet off the bed, wrapped it around my chest like a sarong, and shuffled closer. I sat opposite, with the – regrettably small – width of the table between us. Logan continued, quite coolly, to go through my bag.

'So,' he said, 'headache and dreams aside, how are you feeling about the last couple of nights?'

The crunch of bone and ligament under my hands; the crack of a skull against pavement. The feral, intent, arrogant sneer on the half-shadowed face staring down at me. I picked up a set of lockpicks that fell out of my bag. My fingers trembled and my stomach knotted. I concentrated on slowing my heart. Turning the tools over, I focussed fiercely on them, unrolling and re-rolling the leather bag, rearranging the picks.

'You know they're illegal to carry outside the house in this state, don't you?' Logan gave a soft laugh.

I shrugged. 'So are quite a few things I own. I have a very low care-factor and I don't plan on being caught.' I certainly wasn't going to mention the additional set of picks sewn into the underwire of my bra.

He plucked my wallet out of the pile of loose change, papers, lipsticks, pens, and hair ties, and flipped through it. 'I'm guessing you didn't plan to get caught last night, either. They were pretty serious, though. You handled it nicely up until the dartgun, but you must've been pretty scared. Want to talk about it?'

'Look.' I set the picks down with a snap and glared at him. 'Just stop, will you? I'm fine. This is not my first rodeo.' I shut my teeth, annoyed with myself for saying that much.

He paused in the act of picking up my passport. 'Oh? Ever had to kill anyone?'

I turned my face away. Dust dancing in sunbeams, soul-deep fear, roaring blackness, falling stone and timber. Pawing hands. The slowing of life's energy beneath my palm.

No. It wouldn't happen this time. I would *not* be taken again. I would put the fear of me into them, but there would be no more deaths. Not if I could help it.

'Not intentionally.'

He continued to regard me calmly, showing no shock or judgement at the admission of manslaughter.

I rose and walked to the window, putting space between myself and the aftermath of my actions. Twisting open the white shutters, I peered into the morning glare. Outside, a wide verandah shaded the window from the rising sun, framing the view into a narrow panorama of rolling grassy hills, green trees and distant, wandering cattle. A small flock of tiny brown birds skittered and jumped around on the broad green lawn surrounding the house. The next visible building was a house at least half a kilometre away.

There was no-one close to hear if I screamed for help.

'Not a very good likeness, is it?' Logan held up my passport, inspecting it then me in turn. 'Were you hung over?'

'Nice. Thanks.' In control again, I sat back down and reached for it but he pulled it away. 'I figure the photographer was trying to make me look like someone just off an eighteen-hour flight.'

A spark of genuine amusement flickered. 'In which case, it's probably a good likeness. Is Greene your real last name?'

'What?' I tugged on a short lock of hair curling in front of my ear. 'Of course it is.'

'Really?' He raised sceptical brows. 'Meghan's not your first name. What's your real last name?'

I weighed up the pros and cons. I knew nothing about him and he knew way too much about me. The moment stretched into awkwardness as he continued to watch me in silent expectation. A small, superior smile twitched at one corner of his mouth. His grey eyes gleamed with cool, derisive humour, daring me.

I had to take the risk.

'Gilmore,' I admitted, suppressing a flutter of fear. 'Rowan Gilmore.'

Outside, the kookaburras laughed again, mocking me.

'Nice to meet you Rowan Gilmore.' He inclined his head. 'I *am* Logan, although my current passport says I'm Fynn, so you'd best call me that if we're in public.'

'Why are you travelling under an assumed name?' I was determined to get some answers of my own. 'Who are you? How did you know my first name?'

He ignored me, riffling through the mostly-blank pages of my passport. I'd used this one for about six months now. It said I was a UK citizen. In truth, I wasn't sure which country I could claim. It didn't matter. It was time to change again, anyway. He paused at the latest, Australia-stamped page then returned to examine my photo again.

'Who was your father? Do you know? Where is he?' He shot the questions at me and I answered, reactively annoyed again.

'Of course I know!' I glared at him for implying my mother didn't know who my father was. 'He left us when I was four and then died a couple years later. His name was Calain Gilmore.'

'Aaahhh.'

Again that expression of understanding; of knowledge deliberately withheld. This time coupled with a hint of distaste. I leaned my forehead into my palms and closed my eyes.

'Do you have any idea how annoying that is?' I asked, weary of all the mystery.

'Of course. My aunt does it to me all the time. Drives me nuts.'

I sputtered a laugh.

Various clinkings and rustlings said Logan packed my things away. Now I'd never find my lipstick in the mess. It would be justice if he was at least embarrassed at the presence of tampons in my bag.

'Did you know there was a Calain Gilmore in the court of Queen Elizabeth the First? He was a Viscount,' he said, apparently not discomposed at all.

He slid my bag across the smoked glass table top. I dropped it onto the floor and leaned back, folding my arms.

'As a matter of fact,' I said, not bothering to disguise the sarcasm, 'I did know. He got made the Earl of Lothien. He's my great-somethingth grandfather. We have five hundred years of family portraits and an ornate family tree with lots of gold leaf on it.' I plucked my phone out of my bag. Reseating the battery, I slid it across to him. 'Since you're so fascinated, there are photos in the album. My father was the last Earl and I'm the last Gilmore. I even have a coat of arms, a motto, a suit of armour and a goddamned money-sucking estate in Ireland if you'd like proof. What the hell has this got to do with anything?'

Logan raised his left eyebrow in arrested surprise. He picked up my phone and thumbed through the photos, both brows lifting as he studied them. By the time he arrived at the last photo, his expression dropped into a deep scowl. The small muscles in his jaw worked and his eyes narrowed.

'You know you're his descendant? Are you serious?'

'Yes.' I brandished the gold and emerald ring. My mother had given it to me for my eighteenth birthday just weeks before. 'Here's his signet. Now tell me why you're asking me a bunch of stupid genealogy questions when you've given me the mother of all migraines, beaten me for speed in a way I didn't believe was possible, saved me from a kidnapping, then kidnapped me yourself. Someone is out to get me and you seem to know something. Tell me what the hell is going on!'

He regarded me for a long, silent moment. Then he went back to inspecting the photos on my phone. All lightness had dropped away. His face was grim, his eyes leaden.

There were only twelve photos, Elizabethan through to First World War era. Not every generation had had a portrait done. Logan examined the final one, a painting of my great-great grandfather as a young man, dressed in full British military uniform, for the longest. He regarded me again, then the painting.

'You've got your mother's hair and face shape, but you also look a lot like him – the light eyes with dark rims and olive skin. Although his is darker than yours.'

'Thanks.' I stroked my upper lip. 'And don't you love my matching handlebar moustache?'

He laughed; a wholehearted sound that made me smile, in spite of my irritation. When the stern distance fell away and the sharpness of his face softened he was…beautiful. An odd description for a man, but true nonetheless. His eyes met mine and the humour vanished. He pokered up and returned his attention to my phone, thumbing through the photos again.

'Only paintings, no photos; not even of your father.' His mouth twisted. 'Well, that's not surprising. The camera never lies but a painting can.' Before I could ask him what he meant, he continued, 'And no wives and or children. Didn't you think that was strange?'

I shrugged, impatient with the whole subject. 'There is one wife – the first Earl's. A redhead named Fionn. My mother always claimed Fionn was the reason my father picked her: because she had red hair, too. After that…maybe they all hated their families – arranged marriages. I repeat: what the hell does this have to do with my current situation?'

Logan leaned forward, his eyes intent. 'Do you know what your father died of?'

'Aaagh! Enough! I'm done. Give me the phone.' I tried to take it from him. He clamped my wrists to the table and raised his brows, daring me to test his speed and strength again. I glared until he let go.

'Yes,' I said, rubbing my wrists as an excuse not to look at him. It was old, old history and not something I liked to discuss, even with my mother. 'He…went insane and killed himself.'

TEN

<Logan, they have men posted at her apartment. Get what you need from her. Fast.>

I am. Be patient. She knows she has to hide, but not why.

<So what's special about her then? Why do they want her so badly?>

Not sure yet. She knows more than she's telling me. I need to see more.

<We know who she is now. What more do you need? Let her lead us to them.>

We still don't know why they want her alive. You told me yourself who Gilmore was; the enemies he made. She could be useful. If they want her badly enough they'll come after her. We need to be ready. If they take her now we may not be able to track her. If we help her now she may help us willingly.

<Excuses. She's dangerous and you know it. She'll never trust you.>

Possibly. Either way, we still need more information. I'll connect her. You'll undo the damage. Then we'll see if she's useful or not.

'I'm sorry.' Logan's tone softened with a sympathy I could hardly bear.

The admission wasn't easy, the stigma still strong, even after all this time.

His hand covered mine. Only briefly, but gently this time. 'That must've been tough on you, Red, and your mother. Do you remember him?'

Were we on a nickname basis now or was he just being sarcastic somehow? I pulled free but there was only grave empathy in his expression; no judgement, no recoil, no discomfort or awkwardness. And, lurking at the back of that, a hint of deeply-hidden pain, swiftly-shielded from my scrutiny. He honestly seemed to understand and that disarmed me.

'Not really. A few half-memories. He used to rub the back of his head when he was annoyed, I remember that. Probably I annoyed him a lot, which it why it stuck with me.' I smiled ruefully. 'And one clear image of him staring at me. Like he was trying to imprint my face on his memory – or his on mine, maybe. And the last thing he said to me.' I hunched a shoulder. 'That was just a few days before he left, I think. I was only a kid. I didn't know about the mental illness or his suicide for ages. When I started getting the migraines at about thirteen, and the medics asked questions about him, my mother told me.'

'You think the mental illness might be related to the migraines? Genetic?' Logan's brow darkened to distaste. He leaned away, his expression shifting to blankness as he stared over my shoulder.

Released again from his subtle spell, I was able to think clearly while his attention was elsewhere. How did he do that? In a few short moments I'd exposed more of my past than I had to anyone, ever.

I folded my arms. 'Look, stop changing the subject. What's going on? Who are you and what did those men want with me last night?'

He frowned. He seemed to do that a lot. I returned the look steadily, not willing to give up this time. He had answers and I wanted them. He was good at getting them out of me. It was time to return the favour. I shut my mouth.

He leaned back on his chair, looped his fingers together behind his neck and turned his eyes to the ceiling. The chiselled line of his jaw and lean torso made my blood rush. I gulped and pulled my gaze away. This was stupid. What was wrong with me? Focus, girl. It was just hormones. Focus.

In the warm, buzzing silence, beams of sunlight crept across the floor. The fan ticked lazily overhead, doing little to stir the now-humid air. Outside the kookaburras chortled to a halt and cows lowed in the distance, mournful.

I just needed to regroup and get Anna out of town. That was my next step. Or maybe she really was safer with Michael? Possibly. I did need to speak to her, though. My car keys were in my handbag. There was nothing stopping me from getting up and leaving, right now. Well, apart from a lack of clothing, but that could be rectified. No, wait. We'd swapped cars last night. I had no idea where mine was.

Logan dropped his chair legs to the floor with a sharp thunk that brought me back to reality. He grinned in that raffish, heart-stopping way that annoyed me all over again for no reason I could think of, except it tugged alarmingly at my self-control. Scraping the chair back, he rose and pulled out some clothing from a chest of drawers. A pair of shorts and a shirt landed on the coffee table and he dragged on a white shirt.

'Those should fit you. We need to take a short walk.'

'What?' I dropped the sheet and dragged the ridiculous blue-patterned board shorts over my hips, tying them tightly to keep them up. The green t-shirt was about three sizes too big. 'A walk? It's seven in the morning. I should get home. Where's my car?'

His hands landed on my shoulders and the certainty in his eyes derailed my decision to leave. 'This is important. I'm pretty sure I know who you are and I can help you find out what's going on. But I need to try something first. It won't hurt and, if I'm right, it should make a lot of things clear for you. Then, if you still want to go, you can leave any time. I promise. But, as you said: someone's out to get you and I do know something. So are you coming with me or not?'

I stared up at him, mesmerised by the profound intelligence in those grey eyes.

'Man, you can be really annoying, you know that?' I shrugged. 'But you make a good point. I guess I'll trust you. For now.'

'One more thing, though.' He picked up my phone and dropped it into a jug of water next to the bed.

I watched the phone sink to the bottom, bubbles forming, electricals shorting out inside, gps... I got a grip on outraged astonishment. Phones could be tracked. I should have thought of it myself.

He jerked his head and I followed, chewing my lip. Was I endangering my own and my mother's life by handing myself over to this man? Or was I taking a step towards solving the mystery of my own existence? There was only one way to find out. Risk had to be taken. Life was risk and I'd had enough of half-life.

I followed Logan through the house.

'Where are we going?' I tiptoed on the cool, polished timber, conscious of the sleeping occupants.

'You'll like it, I promise.' He smiled. My suspicions melted.

I had no idea why, when he irritated the hell out of me, I should feel an almost instinctive trust whenever he pinned me with that steady gaze. It annoyed me to be the follower, like some helpless heroine in a trashy romance. But I followed anyway. In silence, I slid into my waiting shoes and trailed him outside, along the drunken timber fence line of the back yard.

Looking back revealed a stately old house, with wide verandahs and a corrugated iron roof, nestled in a bower of trees, isolated from any visible neighbours. It was a fabulous oasis. I envied his family and their ability to put down roots in such a glorious place.

Logan called to me. He opened a rusted gate, wincing as it gave an ear-tearing squeal. Then he stepped onto a track that meandered into a valley behind the house. I hurried to catch up. Thick, red dirt stuck damply to the soles of my shoes. We left a clear trail of footprints. Mud flicked up my calves.

A white-noise of rushing water became audible. The trees thickened, reaching for the sky, their leaves broad and dark green now: a true, tiny patch of rainforest hidden away here. After about five minutes treading silently on the leaf-strewn path, Logan stood aside and gestured for me to precede him.

'Oh.' I inhaled the sweet, earthy scent of the forest. 'This is just beautiful.'

Dappled shade and pale morning sunlight flickered on the golds and reds of leaves lying on the ground. Troubles sliding aside, I ran towards the sound of gurgling water just out of sight. A bird sounded an alarm call and I watched its movement through the green canopy, entranced by the vivid green wingbeats.

The stream came into view. Clear waters coruscated over round, black rocks. A small pool beckoned, sparkling and clean. Above it a waterfall gurgled and splashed a misty rainbow down the regular columns of a black basalt cliff. Brilliant blue flashed. A kingfisher darted out of the shadows to sweep along the creek and vanish into the overhanging branches.

Impulsively, I kicked off my shoes, put a toe into the water and laughed. It was freezing but I didn't care. A huge tree, possibly a fig of some sort, leaned out over the water on the opposite bank, its massive buttress roots sculptural and beautiful. From deep within me rose an overpowering urge to touch; to feel its rough-smooth bark and embrace its ancient strength.

Picking my way across a shallow part of the creek, I clambered up the bank. A convenient, cradle-shaped root looked comfortable. I sank onto it, leaned my cheek against the coarse-textured, flat surface of a buttress and closed my eyes.

I'd never spent much time in a forest before – my mother's work had always taken us to big cities. The light here seemed fresh and soft, the smells those of damp earth and wood, the space filled with the gentle rustle of leaves and gurgle of water. The air here was cleaner, the underlying throb of life slower. There was a sense of being part of the world rather than separated from it.

Something in me relaxed. This was home. The fears slipped away, and the darkness and constant anxiety stalking my thoughts fled before the encompassing, cool peace of this place.

Nothing could hurt me. Here I was safe.

In my imagination, I opened myself, embracing the interconnection of all the living things around me; my place in it. I almost felt the life force, sensed small animals, even the slow, reaching growth of the fig below my cheek. It was a vivid image and I bathed in it, rested, truly at peace.

'What do you think?' Logan's soft question made me smile languidly.

I sighed, contented as the deep knot of tension coiling through my stomach dissolved and slipped away. 'I feel like I belong here; like I can be myself, not some frightened, half-alive…whatever I am, running from everything and everyone. I used to wish I could disappear into the forest.' I didn't want to open my eyes in case the feeling of being joined to the forest vanished. 'I know it sounds silly.

My mother always said I had an overactive imagination. I just feel...connected somehow.'

He sat next to me and his arm brushed against mine. 'You're not imagining it. I feel it too. If you'll let me, I'll show you something else. Don't open your eyes. I'm just going to touch your forehead.'

'Like you did last night? I'm not sure—'

'No, it's alright. I'll leave that part of your mind alone.'

His words didn't make sense but I felt so damned good I relaxed my usual guard.

The tip of his finger brushed my skin and a curtain slid back. Light, for want of a better word, filled my mind.

Can you hear me? Logan's voice whispered inside my head.

Yes! What the hell...? I scrambled to my feet, stumbling over tree roots and clinging the tree, staring at him in openmouthed horror.

He was still there, in front of me and inside my mind, trying to soothe my spiralling fear. I shoved at the intrusion, pushing his presence out. He slowly rose. I retreated another step, jumbled and disbelieving, each breath jerky and quick, one hand out to stop him coming any closer. As though physical distance would prevent mental intrusion.

'Stay away. What the *hell* did you just do to me?' I glared at him. Could I get past him to the path? Even if I did, he was fast. I wouldn't get far before he caught me.

He raised both hands, palms out. I checked his feet. Yes, that wasn't a placating move, that was a fighting stance. I backed up another step, clutching at the rough tree bark as my head spun a little and my heel caught on a root. Fear flashed and darkness lifted its formless, faceless head, eager. I pressed cold fingertips to my temple. No. There was no threat. I could handle this.

'Stop running, Red,' he said quietly. He seemed calm, assured, unfazed by my mistrust and hostility. 'I'm not going to hurt you.'

'But how did you do that?' I tapped my temple. 'Talk to me here. What's going on? Who are you?'

Do I need to tell you anything? His voice echoed in my mind.

I clutched at my head, squeezing my eyes shut. 'How are you doing that? What did you do to me?'

'I didn't do anything. I undid something.'

I glared at him. 'Not helpful. What does that mean?'

'Someone put a block in your mind, years ago by the feel of it. I just took down part of it so we could communicate. If you'll give it a chance, you'll also be able to sense the forest. Let me connect you properly.' He scanned my face. 'You need it. Before that headache gets worse.'

I eyed him suspiciously. 'But last night you tried the same thing, didn't you and it felt like my brain almost exploded. Why?'

'I tried to take all the blocks down at once but your mind couldn't take it. You're naturally trying to use those parts of your mind. The migraines are the blocks preventing you. Whoever put them there didn't want them removed. Let me help.'

I winced, massaging my temple.

His fingers closed around my wrists, holding tighter when I automatically tried to twist free. He regarded me enigmatically, eyes hypnotic in their intensity. Then he was there, in my head, soothing my shock, his presence somehow comforting and secure, rather than intrusive; as though the connection between us was totally natural. The pain faded.

Trust me a little. His mental voice was a whisper, like the breeze overhead. *I can't lie to you like this. You'd know it. I won't hurt you and it ought to help. You want to know who you are? This is part of you.* He nodded at the trees around us. *Let the forest show you if you don't believe me.*

I stilled, mesmerised by the grave truth in his eyes and mind. I *did* know he spoke the truth. Reluctant, curious, afraid, ready to pull free at the slightest hint of deception, I sank down at the base of the tree again.

He sat beside me, fingers loosely entwined with mine and somehow a part of that same missing section of my life the forest filled. He swept me back into connection with the tree. Its steady, deep strength gave me courage and I relaxed. Now Logan was part of the forest with me, even deepening my bond with it. Together we were entwined in the life and beauty of the natural world.

With his firm guidance, I touched small lives all around me, lived the slow, deep pulse of the forest; the quick brush of birds flitting past; the warmth of sun on leaves and the taste of water and soil through roots. Through my bare feet and skin, I joined the world, blending with it; tasting its energy; in complete harmony with every living thing; contented; whole. Fear and darkness, blood and pain were distant, vague memories.

This was the truth. I laughed at the green-lit leaves overhead. Every leaf, stem and insect shimmered with a silvery-green not-quite-light that mesmerised and entranced me.

It's beautiful.

...you can see it?

Oh, yes. Can't you?

No, only feel the pulse of the energy flow.

It's kind of silvery-green and feels like a thousand tiny pinpricks inside my skin; like if I tried too hard to grab it might hurt, but if I don't it's just...energising. And it tastes like ozone.

It feels different for everyone. To me it's cold water and the taste of snow.

Logan's presence withdrew and physical discomfort intruded as my body clamoured for attention. My backside hurt. I reluctantly disconnected myself from the lure of the forest. I said goodbye to the fig and opened my eyes. Logan looked back at me, his eyes almost dreamy. It was the most relaxed I'd seen him.

Impulsively, I pulled his face closer, kissing him without reservation, with a joy and completion I'd never felt before with anyone. He kissed me back, his mouth warm and tender, his thoughts twined with mine, his arms around me gentle as he cradled me close. I deepened the kiss, hungry, wanting more, sliding my arms around his shoulders, revelling in the strength in him.

He broke free and shoved me away, wiping his mouth.

Don't do that. His mental voice was hard, his eyes snapping. *It's not me you want. You're just feeling the earth-connection for the first time. It's all new. If we took this where you want it to go now, you'd hate yourself and me for it later. We both would.*

I looked at my hands. He'd held them. They'd cupped his face as we kissed.

I'd touched him again, palm to skin.

But this time nothing had happened. No visions, no draw of power. No fear. No darkness.

What the hell?

'We need to cool off. Let's take a swim,' Logan said aloud. Standing and brushing his pants off, he avoided my eye.

Rejection stung. My cheeks flushed. I said nothing; still reeling from his mood-switch and my discovery. Paul Eisen must have felt like this last night.

Logan's face clouded to black irritation. 'Paul? I thought you'd decided not to keep dating him.'

I gave him a cold look. 'Aren't there some sort of ethics of telepathy that say you're not supposed to intrude on private thoughts? Wow. That's a sentence I never thought I'd say.'

He pressed his lips together, eyes glittering with some emotion I couldn't identify. 'There are but it's difficult when you're broadcasting. The point is: how well are you planning to get to know Eisen?'

'You're not my keeper, Logan. He asked me out again, yes, but…my life's complicated – even before all this.' I indicated him and the surrounding forest. 'And I have a feeling things are going to be even weirder. Am I right?' I eyed him narrowly. He hid important things and I wasn't going to let them go now.

He stayed silent a moment, then turned away, his face once more expressionless. 'You have good instincts. You're safer away from someone as visible as Paul Eisen.'

'Like I said,' I said mildly, returning his cool with hauteur of my own, 'you're not my keeper and I barely know you. You have no say in who I see. I still don't know what you want from me, either. Or why you're helping.' I cocked my head at him, knowing my next words were truth. 'Especially since I get the impression you don't even like me all that much.'

Logan stilled and hardened. 'I don't want to be your keeper, but I can help you stay safe. If you'll let me. Liking you or not has nothing to do with it.'

He flung his t-shirt aside and dove smoothly into the deepest part of the pool. I stood. My backside was numb and my back ached. After a brief hesitation, I tugged off the shirt and shorts and dipped a toe in. Grateful for the freezing temperature, I slid into the pool, catching my breath as the icy water caressed the sun-warmed skin of my stomach. It brought me fully to my senses and the intimate connection with the forest receded further, dreamlike.

A small part of me was still aware of Logan's thoughts, though. In his mind was an image of me: sparkling water on my bare, olive skin. He dwelt on the curve of my waist, the swell of breast above my bra. I turned to see him rising from beneath the water. He was beautiful. Stripped to his shorts, his lean, muscular body caught in the dappled sunlight, he was meant to be here, meant to be part of this place; as I was.

He saw me watching and grimaced. Diving into the clear depths, he swam across the pool and surfaced not far away. A shake of his dark head sent glittering drops of water flying through the sunbeams.

I slipped beneath the surface, and the chill enveloped me entirely. I stayed under as long as I could, watching the sunlight flicker across the rocky bottom, trying to regain equilibrium. Eventually my scalp ached with the cold and I had to breathe. I broke the surface with a gasp, sweeping hair and water from my eyes.

Logan stood over me, his eyes as cool as the water. The light-reflections slipping across his face disguised any emotion. His mind was blank, our connection severed.

'We should go soon,' he said.

ELEVEN

<Did you hear her? She saw the sianfath. I've never heard of anyone who could.>

What does it mean?

<I have no idea. Do you know what she was expecting when she held your face?>

Maybe another precog. She's repressing that knowledge thoroughly. She's afraid.

<Of what?>

...Herself. Who she might be. What's buried in her mind. Schizophrenia?

<No, I don't think so. Something else, entirely, I think. Something much worse – and much more powerful.>

'But we only just got here,' I protested, unwilling to return to the wound-tight, frightening world I inhabited. It seemed unreal and distant right now and I wanted to keep it that way.

Logan checked his watch. 'We were in thrall with the forest for almost four hours. Time passes quickly in the *sianfath*.'

'Four hours!' I stood up in the shallow water, only now noticing the length of shadows and quality of light. 'Is that what it's called, that glow; that feeling of...connection: the *sianfath*?'

He nodded shortly. 'Yes, it means something like...one-and-all. Bit hard to translate.'

Overhead, the sun edged out from behind the trees, pouring heat and light that sparkled and glittered as it caught the drops of water floating in the air. I trailed my fingers across the water's surface, still feeling the tantalising dregs of the connection to the great fig tree, clinging to a tiny bit of peace. I swished the water, watching the purple-white, glittering ripples, thinking and struggling to put those thoughts into words.

'So...who am I? Why can I feel the forest? Why can I hear your thoughts? Who put these blocks in my mind and why?'

'All good questions but it's a long story and you're getting cold,' Logan replied. 'Let's get out. We'll get lunch, a hot drink and talk.'

A shiver sleeted across my skin and I waded out of the pool. As I grabbed my clothes, Logan reached towards my face, then hesitated and dropped both hands away, merely staring deep into my eyes.

You'll never lose this ability to hear me now. Does that bother you?

Yes. No. I'm...not sure. Somehow it seems normal.

That's because it is normal, to our people.

Who are "our people"?

He turned his back. 'Get your clothes on and I'll get food then tell you what I can.'

'Wait.' I folded my arms.

He turned back, brows lifted.

'I'd like answers more than food or hot drinks. Start talking, Logan.'

His eyes turned past me for a moment and he compressed his lips. With abrupt movements, he spun back and sat on one of the many large, black rocks lining the watercourse.

Taking that as assent, I dressed and made myself comfortable with my back against the sun-warmed basalt.

'So tell me who you are; what's going on. Who these people are chasing me and why are they?'

He stared off into the distance for a long, silent moment, then nodded.

He talked and I listened.

After a minute or so, I held up a palm, not sure if I was halting him or the disbelief welling up inside me. This was just ridiculous. What he described couldn't possibly be true.

'Hang on, hang on. This is madness. *Homo sapiens silvis? Silvis* must be Latin for what, forests? Intelligent Man of the Forests? Are you saying I belong to an entirely different *species* of human? That's... ridiculous!'

'Yes, I know it sounds impossible,' he said, 'but it's true. You've heard or read the stories of the Faery folk; the Beautiful ones; the Shining ones; the Forest Folk. That's us. We are the *aes sidhe*; the Elvenkind; the sidhe – whatever you want to call us.'

'Elves?' I laughed. 'That's just plain stupid. There is no such thing.'

He shrugged, his ice-grey gaze slightly scornful. 'I don't much care if you believe it. It's the truth. You're a half-caste, and I'm three-quarter. Your father was a full-blood, as was my father. My mother, my Aunt Maeve's half-sister, was half-caste. So technically, I believe, we're a sub-species, since we can interbreed. We call ourselves *Daoine sidhe*.' He smiled wryly. 'Which just means "people", so it's nothing mystic.'

'You're serious?' I stared at him in disbelief. 'Frigging Elves?'

He nodded. 'We typically mature mentally much faster than humans, but physically slower. You probably remember most of your childhood very clearly and you would have been small until you hit about sixteen.'

I nodded, mouth agape.

He continued. 'We live a lot longer, but our reproduction rate is much slower, so we're dying out as a race. We're an endangered species.' His smile was bleak. 'Unflattering though it is, the mating instinct is why you're attracted to me so strongly. Your body knows who I am.'

I started, my cheeks flushing, shaken by his casual reference to my reaction. On a purely academic level, it made a lot of sense, if what he said was true. It was just so damned hard to believe.

'Both sexes,' he continued calmly, 'are faster and stronger than humans, although males more so than females. Both are gifted in learning languages and information of any sort. Both have telepathic abilities, but women often also have other abilities: precognition, telekinesis, that sort of thing.'

I said nothing, unable to believe it, but unable to disbelieve it either. There was too much that rang true in too many ways for me to dismiss it as pure bullshit.

'What you felt today,' he added, indicating the lush vegetation around the pool, 'our connection with the forests of this world is ancient and integral to who we are. That's the other reason we're dying. The forests are part of us and we of them: the *sianfath*. You've lived in cities all your life, but you don't belong there.' He fell silent, watching me as I stared at the rippling water at my feet.

'OK. Let's just suspend disbelief,' I said, 'and assume for a moment it's all true. Why?' I swatted a mosquito on my arm and considered the broken little body. I had extinguished a life, small though it was.

I shuddered. 'Why are people chasing me?

'That,' Logan replied, 'is a more complicated story.' He checked his watch. 'If I promise to tell it will you let me get lunch first? I'm starving.'

'Fine!' I glared at him. 'But you'd bloody well better come back or I will hunt you down.'

His reply was just an ironic half-smile.

'Wait,' I repeated.

He paused.

'Will you tell me what the *ocair* is as well?'

He stilled and his eyes slid from mine as he looked back at the house. I couldn't see his face as he replied,

'Like I said. I don't know what else it is, so I can't tell you. Sorry.' He stalked away.

That was a lie. Something in me knew it. But even a lie was a good thing, because it meant I was on the right track. I'd found someone with the information I needed, even if he didn't trust me enough yet to share it.

My irritation with him slid away as he vanished up the path. I didn't need him to like me, just to tell me what the hell was going on. As soon as I had the information he kept dangling, and whatever he hid, I would go.

Elves? My thoughts kept returning to that idea. Could it really be possible? In the midst of the powerful swell of life and peace in this little valley, it was easy to believe. But was that because I *wanted* to believe? After all, everyone wanted to think they were special. I didn't. My differences had always been something terrifying; to be hidden. But if I wasn't some freakishly-weird human…if I was really *meant* to be different, and to live with others like me. That made the world a far more interesting place.

And more complicated. Which I didn't need, right now.

Could I believe him? Could I trust him when I'd vowed never to trust anyone other than Anna? Logan already knew far more about me than was safe.

The best I could achieve, at the moment, was to suspend disbelief.

Wanting to regain peace, I leaned back against the rock and soaked up the feeling of being free and relaxed for what felt like the first time ever. I closed my eyes and raised my face to the brilliant warmth. Red and orange lights danced on the inside of my eyelids. My lips curled in a languid, satisfied smile.

After a few minutes, a cloud seemed to pass before the sun, even though it still shone brightly. The back of my skull ached with tension. Something dimmed my sense of freedom and I opened my eyes, searching for the cause. The creek hadn't changed. The water still glittered, the trees still sighed gently in a light breeze, birds still flitted in and out of the sunlight; living jewels.

So, what was wrong?

Uneasiness seeped in, pinpricks under my skin, displacing calm. I sat up, brushing my hands together and pulling my feet out of the cold water. Instinctively, I gazed north, towards the path and the house, towards the source of my unease. What was it?

I waited, still tense and uncertain what to do. Logan appeared on the path, sans food and drinks. Instead he carried two laden backpacks, one large and one smaller. He'd changed into different clothing and wore his leather jacket. I squinted up at him, shading my eyes from the afternoon sun, trying to pretend everything was normal.

'Pretty crap service. Where's....' I stopped, recognising my own tension in him. I wasn't imagining it. 'What's wrong?' I flicked grit off my feet and shoved my sandals on.

Logan checked the path. 'They've found you. They're almost here.' He passed me the smaller backpack. 'Your handbag's in there, and a couple of changes of clothes. Maeve has everything from your car with her.'

'What?' My heart stuttered. 'Who's here? The men from last night? They couldn't. I broke two of them at least.' Sliding the pack over my shoulders, I scrambled to my feet.

'More of the same. Hired to find you.' He grabbed my wrist, pulling me not to the path but into the shallow water. We crossed to the other side, splashing awkwardly over the uneven bottom. 'I should have drowned your phone last night. They must have tracked it when we turned it on this morning.'

'But it was a burn phone. I've only had it three days. Who the hell can do that? Who hired them? Why do they want me?' I tugged free and stopped. 'I can't keep running, Logan. If you don't know what the *ocair* is then I need to confront these men and find out from them. I want them out of my life. If it's all they want, then I'll just give it to them.'

He made a noise of exasperation. 'You can't be so naïve. They don't just want that, whatever it is. They also want you – alive. Look.' He glanced back up the path. 'I promise I'll explain but there are at least fifteen of them this time. We *have* to run. Pick your battles. This isn't one you can win. Not against that many with guns.'

Without waiting for my agreement, he spun on his heel and sprinted away.

I swore. A loud, metallic squeal said the intruders had found the garden gate and trail to the valley. I wavered then followed Logan, struggling to keep up with his long-legged stride as he ran down a barely-visible path.

'What about your aunt and cousin?'

Glancing back, he put a finger to his lips and tapped his temple. *Voices and sounds echo down here. Tread carefully. Maeve and Jen are well away. We'll meet up with them later. Right now we need to get to the shed at the bottom of this hill.*

I couldn't easily reply. Telepathy took concentration and I had to watch where I put my feet. I refused to be some damned ankle-twisting heroine. Sweat trickled down my back. I wasn't as fit as I thought, apparently.

Logan picked up the pace. He barely breathed hard as he leapt from boulder to boulder and wound silently through the trees. He seemed at home, never snapping a twig, never stumbling. There were times he almost vanished in the dappled green gloom.

I was an elephant: all big feet and flapping appendages as I tried to balance on the slippery rocks. A branch broke under my flailing hand. A shout sounded from above, somewhere on the hillside. A face appeared between trees, on the path from the house.

Logan swore aloud. Angry at myself for betraying our location, I snatched up a fist-sized rock. I stopped behind a tree, steadying myself. I drew my arm back and stepped out. Something struck the trunk next to my head, spraying slivers of timber.

Shit. They were *shooting* at me? What happened to wanting me alive?

Seething, I sighted and threw the stone with all my strength. A pained cry; followed by satisfactory thrashing as a body rolled, through the underbrush and crashed against a tree trunk.

Logan chuckled. *Nice throw. Now run. Look forward, not down. Trust your feet. They'll find the right way for you.*

I lifted my face and ran. He was right. Running without looking worked better. I stopped thinking about twisted ankles and focussed on him. Christ, he was fast. For the first time in my life, I had to push to keep up. He flew over the leaf-strewn, rocky ground like it was a straight, flat running track.

Another shot exploded near my leg, sending chips of stone in all directions. A sharp sting to my calf said I'd been hit by the shrapnel. Logan sped up. Another explosion of bark showered splinters over me. The leg could wait until later. These guys were serious.

The creek bed levelled out, the water pooling in a small, idyllic dam. Grassy slopes and eucalypts surrounded it on either side. The scene was pretty, but distressingly short on cover for fugitives. Incurious black and white cows eyed us from beyond a dilapidated wire fence.

Logan paused at the edge of the forest. An arm out stopped me passing him. The noonday sun baked the verdant hills, water almost-visibly evaporating from the dam. The scent of warm cow-dung mingled with the earthy aroma of leaves and dirt from the forest floor as I bent over, hands on knees, panting as quietly as possible.

'There,' he said.

I squinted up, following his line of sight.

A small shed squatted not far away, its grey timber walls far from vertical, its single window grimed with years of dust. I couldn't see a door on this side. We had to cross at least twenty metres of exposed ground to get to the building. If there was someone inside, or further up the road, we'd be seen.

I caught the sound of distant crashing and swearing. 'They're coming.'

Logan nodded. 'I can't tell if there's anyone waiting. We'll have to chance it. My bike's inside.'

'You went back for your bike last night?'

'Sleep's overrated. If something happens to me, do you know how to ride?'

'Yes, but—'

'No arguments.' He scowled at me. 'Just get on it and go. The key's tucked under the seat. Here's the safehouse.' He flashed an address to me, mind to mind, so it seared fluorescent red across the inside of my eyeballs. 'Maeve knows what to do.'

'Well, shit,' I said feelingly, 'I'm glad someone does. Stop being so damned melodramatic. Let's go.' I dashed from cover, crouching low.

He swore but his light steps followed.

No shots. No alarmed voices.

We edged along the eastern end of the shed, furthest from the road, until we could see around the corner. The door stood partly open. Logan withdrew and closed his eyes for a moment.

I didn't leave it like that. There's someone in there. Just one I think. Ideas?

I concentrated. *A frontal attack would be mad. He'd just pick us off. Here. What's behind this?* I pointed to a broken board, low by my leg. The gap was big enough for someone my size to squeeze through.

He inspected it. *I think there's an old wrought iron fence leaning up against that wall. There should be enough space to get in, but what the hell do you do then?*

I smirked at him. *I'm just the distraction. You're the main event.*

Without waiting, I shed my pack, dropped to the ground and squirmed in through the gap. A nail tore the skin over my hip. I stopped and unpicked the spike with deliberate care, releasing the pain on a slow breath.

At last I was inside. I crouched behind the jail-bars of three or four fence panels. Too many to move at once. My eyes adjusted to the gloom and I peered over a stack of timber. A burly, bearded man sat astride Logan's bike, playing with the controls, a stupid grin on his face.

I flashed the image to Logan, who responded with a curt acknowledgement.

Spotting a way out from behind the bars, I eased into open space. My next options were limited. I could take off my shirt and play the sex-kitten distraction card, but any henchman with half a brain would be ready. That was a slippery path to damnation again, anyway.

So I picked up a solid piece of timber, tiptoed closer and whacked him upside the head. He toppled like a felled tree and lay still. The bike landed on his leg. Leaning over the bike I checked. He was still breathing. Good.

'I thought you were the distraction,' Logan whispered. He slid in through the door. 'Did you have to drop the bike?'

'I lied. I do that. Besides, I'm not a distraction kinda girl.'

He sent me a look full of ironic disbelief.

I shrugged. 'If you don't like how I do things, next time you can be the distraction.'

'Get on.' He heaved the bike upright. 'We'll have to go out full steam so keep your head down.'

Flipping the kickstand he turned the bike awkwardly in the small space and aimed it at the door. Next he strapped the backpacks to a rack, swung a leg over and gestured to me. He tried to give me his helmet, but I refused. There was no point protecting my head when he was the one driving. Besides, I'd need full vision for the next few minutes.

I climbed on behind, tucked two small plastic bags under one thigh and wrapped an arm around his waist. Three short, iron timber-spikes went under my butt. A forth lay in my hand. A fifth I shoved into my bra, where the iron grated against my skin and smelled unpleasantly of rust. Uncomfortable but they wouldn't be there long.

'Go then,' I said. 'I know how to ride pillion.'

'Of course you do.' He growled and the engine echoed him.

There was a shout from outside, somewhere behind the shed.

With roar and a jerk, the bike leapt forward. The front wheel slammed open the wooden door. A short scream and a flying pair of feet showed someone no longer stood behind it.

I hefted the spike, trying to get a feel for how it would spin. My shoulders twitched in anticipation of a shot in the back. I felt exposed and out of control. I hated feeling that way. Another shout. The zip of a silenced bullet. Too bloody close.

The wind lashed my eyes. I caught a glimpse of three men, running at an angle, aiming at the road. They would get there before the bike. Logan swore.

'Keep going!' I shouted.

The bike wavered, probably reflecting his indecision. I poked the spike into his ribs and waggled it at him.

'Keep. Going!'

He gunned it. I took a bead on the leader, a large man who waved a nine millimetre pistol as he jogged heavily in our direction. He was never going to hit anything. I switched focus to the second gunman. He stopped and lined us up rather more professionally. I swore aloud. It was my dart-gun wielding attacker from last night; his angular features perfectly calm and focussed.

This time he held a more lethal weapon.

I threw the spike. I knew it would hit as soon as it left my fingers. Whether it would hit with the point or the solid end was hard to tell. The gunman threw himself to one side, yelling as the spike smashed into his shoulder. I snatched out the second and flung it. That one missed and so did the third. The fourth and fifth followed in swift, accurate succession. Three men down. All with what looked like non-fatal wounds.

From the ground, my would-be captor got off a couple of shots. I ducked instinctively as the first zipped past my shoulder. Too close. Another shot buzzed. The bike jerked to the left. Logan swore again. His jeans showed a long, ragged tear. Blood oozed from a thigh wound. It looked shallow, but I couldn't tell if the bullet had exited.

I concentrated on my new mental connection with him. *Bad?*

His reply came back with overtones of gritted teeth. *Hurts like you wouldn't believe but superficial. Shit.*

What?

There.

We swept around the bend leading away from the house and shed. Three black four-by fours roared down the hill. Behind them, black smoke smudged the hot blue sky.

Another bullet whistled past our heads. Several smacked into the dirt on either side of the bike.

I pulled out the two plastic bags. The plastic tore under my teeth. Metal pieces dropped onto my legs. They bit into my skin through the thin board shorts and pinged off the exhaust pipe. Logan scowled at me. His brow cleared to approval when he saw what I had.

Risking a slide-out, he floored the bike into the corner of the dirt road. We screamed towards the highway, using every bit of power in the twelvehundred engine. The cars roared, close, but falling behind.

I sprayed one bag of flatheaded nails onto the road behind us.

The first fourby blew a tyre and slewed to a halt, one wheel in a ditch. I scattered the second bag of nails. Another tyre blew on a second car. The vehicle careened across the road, dust billowing from its tracks. The front jerked sideways and the car flipped, rolled and slid to a halt on its side, blocking the road. The third car slammed to a stop nearby. Three people leapt out, weapons pointed at us.

I hunched my shoulders and closed my eyes.

TWELVE

<We're clear and heading for the Edge Hill house. You?>

Yes.

<The girl?>

She's with me. She's...been helpful.

<Be careful with her, Logan. She may yet prove—>

I know exactly what she is. She trusts me enough now and she's still our best shot. I just need your help with the blocks in her mind.

<They'll know she's not alone now.>

You cleared the house of trace?

<Didn't you see the fire?>

'Anna?' I spoke quietly, cupping my hand around the phone and turning my back to the staff in the shop.

'Meg!' She sounded surprised and pleased, not frightened. 'Are you home? Are you alright? Paul said he dropped you off last night. How did you end up with that Fynn boy and his aunt? I've been so worried.'

'It's a long story.' My heart slowed and I let out a shuddering breath. She was alright. 'You're at work? How's the weather where you are?' Our code question. One she knew meant I was serious.

There was a pause and the background noise quietened, as though she'd found somewhere private to speak.

'Yes. Special staff meeting. It's lovely and sunny here. You?'

I hesitated. If I said it was stormy our protocol meant we had to leave straight away. Was I ready to do that? Logan hadn't yet told me everything I needed to get to whoever was chasing me.

'It's a little overcast. I think maybe Spain would be nice this time of year.' That meant I wanted her to leave town. There was a long silence. I chewed my lip and glanced over my shoulder. The plump lady making our sandwiches waved cheerfully at me and held up two paper-wrapped parcels. I gave her a thumbs-up.

'Sweetheart,' Anna said, reluctance in her tone, 'if it's just a little overcast, maybe I can make do with an umbrella. I have a good one, right here.'

Which meant she thought she was safe and didn't want to leave me. Dammit. I expected she'd be stubborn. We'd never been separated before.

I sighed. 'Just keep it close, then. Don't go home. You'll get wet. I'll call you at six.'

'We're having drinks with a specialist IT guy after this. I can't leave because he's here to see me. I will make sure I'm free at six. Then we can talk. But call me if something urgent comes up.' Which meant she couldn't say more because there were people close by.

'Love you.'

'You too, sweetheart. Please be safe. And if you need to get out of the weather, just go. Please?'

I hung up before her and stared at the phone. Call time less than a minute. Good. I pulled the battery and threw it and the phone into separate bins.

'Black coffee and a ham sandwich.' I passed them to Logan and eased myself onto the splinter-ridden grey-timber bench next to him. I didn't even question how I knew his preferences.

After a long time winding along narrow country lanes that sliced through the red dirt, rainforest patches, and grassy hills, we'd reached more populated areas and stopped at a little suburban set of shops. Logan waited by the bike while I bought food and first aid supplies with cash he gave me. The park next door offered a resting spot.

I used my pocket knife to cut away a chunk of his jeans to expose the wound, cleaned and bound it as best I could, then did the same for the various small nicks and scratches I'd sustained. The nail-scrape into my hip stung. At least I'd had a tetanus shot a few years before. Pulling the sliver of stone out of my calf tried my fortitude, though. It was deeper than I thought and bled freely.

Logan watched me dress the wound, mild amusement in his grey eyes.

'What?' I raised eyebrows at him as I tucked the medical scraps and supplies away in my backpack.

He waved the question aside. 'Just something I'll have to show you later, when we get to the safe house. Now's not the time.'

I opened my mouth to object then decided not to. If he wanted to play stupid games I just wouldn't participate. Quite frankly, I'd had a trying last eighteen hours and wanted answers, not more mysteries. Right now, I was hungry enough even answers could wait a few minutes.

We ate and drank in silence, watching traffic stream past and children play on the distant playground. A black, turkey-like bird strutted by, pausing to eye us warily and scratch at the leaves and red dirt. The bird's life was the faint flicker of yellow; a single glimmer amongst the fireworks of unseen light emanating from the surrounding trees.

I blinked and the silvery-green non-light faded.

I turned to inspect Logan. 'Right, if I'm going to be seeing weird shit, shot at, and throwing pointy things at people, I need to know why. Who are those people and what's going on? If they don't just want the *ocair*, what do they want? Give. Now.'

Logan rose, seeming unimpressed by my demands. 'Now's not the time. We need to get moving and get to the safe house. I know you're afraid, but you'll have to trust me a little.'

'I'm not afraid. I'm frigging-well *angry*.' I stayed where I was, arms folded. 'We need to talk. You haven't answered my question, Logan. In fact, there are several you haven't answered. Who's after me? And why? What's so all-fired important about me that you risked your neck to save me?'

He pinched the bridge of his nose and closed his eyes. 'Look, as far as I know, there's nothing particularly unique about you.'

'Huh, thanks.'

The look he gave me was distilled sarcasm. 'There are people who hunt the sidhe just because of who we are. Over time, stories sprang up about sidhe abilities – you've heard them. Some people believe. Enough to be a threat. The most organised aren't dreamy new age types that dance around Stonehenge on Midsummers Day. They're serious. They call themselves the Mors Ferrum. Run by a cold-blooded bastard named Alexander Dyson.'

'Seriously?' I eyed him with scorn. 'Are you really expecting me to believe in some mysterious, ancient organisation of badguys out to get me?'

'Whether you believe or not is irrelevant,' he said. 'They exist. They're the ones after you. Do you want to hear the rest, or not?'

'How do you know they're the ones after me?'

'Remember this guy?'

An image appeared in my mind: my angular-faced attacker from Christchurch, last night and this morning. I flinched and threw up a hand in automatic self-defence.

Logan took that as assent. 'His name is Connor Blake. We *know* he's with the Mors Ferrum. It's them, alright.'

'Mors Ferrum.' I scowled at the brightly-painted steel bars of the play gym equipment nearby. 'Iron Death, in the Latin. Do they call themselves that because iron is supposed to be fatal to elves?'

Logan's smile turned wry. 'Ironically those legends grew because of their name, not the other way around. Real iron has no more effect on us than it does on anyone. Its threat to us is more symbolic of civilisation and the destruction of our forests. The Ferrum is far more dangerous, though.' He ran restless fingers through his hair.

I sat up straight, regarding the cerulean sky. Thunderheads gathered on the eastern horizon, piles of grey and white. A flock of brilliant, green-and-red lorikeets scrawked as they flew overhead and settled, squabbling, in a nearby flowering tree.

'So they're hunting all the sidhe, not just me?'

Logan stilled, gripping the bench so hard the timber creaked. His jaw worked and the muscles in his forearms twisted beneath the thin skin.

'Yes. My father died at their hands.'

He brushed aside my uncomfortable "sorry" and straightened, rolling his shoulders back and lifting his chin. 'It was a long time ago. The point is, we're now hunting *them*. That's why we're here. At least three of our kind have disappeared in Cairns. One was my cousin, Jonathan, a half-brother of Jen's. We need find out who's targeting us here, and how much they know.'

I raised an eyebrow at him, sceptical. 'Who would be after the sidhe, though? And why?'

'Think about it. The commercial applications of understanding our genome: telepathy, telekinesis, greater speed and strength. The potential for exploitation is staggering.' He turned his level gaze on me. 'If they want you alive, it's mostly likely for medical research purposes. That scares the bejeezus out of me.'

I swallowed and lifted my chin. 'But what if it's not that? What if it's something to do with this block in my head? Maybe if I get rid of that, I'll know who put it there and what it's hiding. Maybe it's hiding information I know about the *ocair!* How do I get it removed?' I leaned forward, inspecting his face, searching for truth in his reactions.

'I don't have the skill to remove it. My aunt does.' He took a drink and put the coffee cup down slowly.

'Who put it there?' Even as I said it, I knew. 'Oh! My father did it. Oh my God. The paintings. You said long-lived. How long are we talking?' The pieces fell into place before he opened his mouth. 'The original Calain Gilmore was in the sixteenth century! Apart from Fionn, there are no pictures of wives or children. Only adult males all the same age. That's what you saw, isn't it? They're all him. How stupidly Phantom.'

He nodded and sipped at his coffee, not looking at me.

'So I guess you saw me and realised what I was, then saw the pictures and realised whose daughter I am.' I sucked in slow breaths of moist, warm air. 'I still don't get it all. You asked if Greene was my real name. Is Litson yours? How old are you? Even if I accept what you're saying as true, how does my father fit into this? Why did he put the block in my mind?'

Logan grimaced. 'I'm twenty. My aunt's name and mine is Freyson. She's two hundred and eighty, but don't tell her I told you. We move a lot too, but not just because of our age. There's more to it.'

'Wait, wait, wait,' I interrupted. 'If I remember my History – and admittedly I did fall asleep in class – the Norse legends of the Vikings. Your name "Freyson", does literally it mean the son of Freyr, lord of the Light Elves of Norse Mythology?'

He nodded, rubbing his thumb over the back of his hand. 'Children in our culture take the name of the higher ranking parent. But I don't know what family my father belonged to. He…died without ever telling me or Maeve. My aunt and mother however… their great-great-great grandfather was the son of Freyr, three thousand or so years ago.'

I dug thumbnail marks into my foam cup, waiting. Children giggled and screamed in the park. I squinted against the sunlight, watching them play, trying to absorb everything and failing. This had to be bullshit. Elves? Then I caught the pulse and flare of the *sianfath* from the trees nearby and had to accept his words as truth. Or at least some of it.

Logan said nothing so I filled the silence he seemed content to let lie between us.

'So are the Light Elves you...us?'

'The humans have called some of our people Light and some Dark Elves but both are us.' He skirted the edges of answering my question, his eyes flat and hard.

'Well that makes no sense.' I slanted him a look under my lashes. 'What's the difference?'

'In every society there are those who work for peace through non-violent methods. Then there are those who believe force, ironically, is the only path to peace,' Logan said. There was a tension in his voice and shoulders that belied his calm words. 'When human farming threatened the wild forest places, some of our people advocated working with them. Others wanted to fight the inevitable, put off the dilution of the gene pool; even destroy the humans altogether. Or, at the least, rule them.'

'And?' I prompted, shivering again at the images his words conjured. A spark lit the inside of my mind: swords raised, flashing in the sun; men in armour; arrows darkening a blue sky. Pain displaced the images and I grimaced, pressing my temples.

'And the issue divided us.' He seemed unwilling to elaborate.

'C'mon, you're holding something back.' I folded my arms, glaring at him.

A sliver of something, cold or apprehension maybe, slipped down my spine.

Logan brushed imaginary crumbs off his shirt, avoiding my eye. 'Some of the worst tyrants in history were Dark Elves or advised by them: Genghis Khan, Hitler, Attila the Hun, Pol Pot. But some of the best were Light Elves: Gandhi, the Buddha, Confucius, Mother Theresa, Jesus Christ.'

'Seriously?' I gaped. 'Well that puts a different slant on things, anyway.'

He smiled thinly but still didn't meet my gaze. 'Yes. And because of the worst of the Dark, people like the Mors Ferrum hunt us all. Typical human intolerance and ignorance. And greed.'

'So how can I get them to leave me alone?'

Logan made a sound of frustration, crushed his coffee cup and threw it into the bin with unnecessary force. 'You don't, Red! Don't you get it? They won't leave you alone until they get what they want.'

'Well, I know what they want: this *ocair* thing.' I lifted my chin and met his eyes unflinchingly. 'If I give it to them, they *might* leave me alone. Did that ever occur to you?'

His lip curled. 'You're a fool if you think that. It's not going to be that easy.'

I opened my mouth. His head snapped up and he scanned the road, ignoring me. I followed his gaze, but there were only rows of quiet suburban houses marching into the distance. Then a half-familiar discomfort roiled in my stomach and pressed against the base of my skull. A thousand pinpricks under my skin.

'Shit.' He snatched up our rubbish and jammed it the bin, before limping back to the bike.

'What?' I hurried after him. 'What is it?'

He rounded on me. *Who did you call?* He gripped my shoulders, grey eyes drilling into mine. *When you were in the shop. Who did you call? Your mother?*

'I had to let her know I was ok, and warn her we have to leave. I didn't tell her where I was.'

Logan jammed his fingers through his hair. 'Goddammit, Red. You've been on the run your whole life and you do something that basic? They tracked your call.'

'They couldn't have.' I glared at him. 'I'm not an idiot. I bought a burn phone, used our codewords. Kept it under a minute and pulled the battery straight away after the call.'

'Damn!' He shoved the helmet on and, with a grunt, swung a leg over the bike. 'That's worse. It means they're watching Anna closely and they have resources. Seriously high tech resources that tracked your call straight away and at least gave them a cell area to search. They're coming. Get on.'

I slid on behind him. 'But that means they may have her already!'

'I doubt it.' He flipped down the visor. 'She's pretty safe with Eisen's security. More likely they have her phone tapped.'

He revved the engine and took off from the carpark in a spray of gravel, looking over his shoulder as he did. I followed his gaze. Two black four-by fours rounded the corner at the end of the street. They sped up.

I clung to the bike, overriding instincts to lean. I willed myself to act like a gearsack so as not to hinder Logan's control of the machine. He threw the bike around corners in a way that spoke volumes about his anger. I couldn't blame him, only myself. I'd underestimated whoever was after me and that could prove fatal.

The bike screeled around a corner and tarmac filled my vision, leaving me white-knuckled. The bike was faster and more manoeuvrable. But the SUV's were close and the streets in this country town were broad and open. There were no convenient alleys too small for cars. No backstreets to hide in. Logan gunned it down a straight section of road. I risked a quick check behind. Our pursuers trailed but were still in sight.

Our speed dropped so fast my cheek smacked into Logan's back. My grip tightened reflexively. He slammed on the front brakes and slid the back wheel out sideways. At the end of the road, a third black SUV slewed around the corner and closed that exit. Dropping the clutch Logan took off again, straight at what looked like a driveway. A quick peek under his arm showed a narrow concrete easement between two timber fences. Steel bollards at the entrance should make it impassable to cars.

How far did it go and how did we get back onto the streets?

Behind, tyres squealed as the three cars ploughed to a halt. Plastic and metal exploded as a bullet destroyed the bike's rear taillight. I flinched, my heart pounding. Another showered us with timber shrapnel as we rounded a backyard fence. Then we were hidden from view. A temporary reprieve.

The easement forked. Logan drew the bike to a halt, glancing both directions. One seemed as good as another, to me. He chose the more northerly route and I had no reason to object. As long as it got us out of the area I was perfectly happy. This was turning out to be one helluva day.

The easement segued into a walking track. We followed a little creek, shaded by weeping eucalypts and flittering with bird life. Of course that meant a predictable exit and therefore a high probability our trackers would find us. Anyone with a smartphone could pull up a map and see where we had to emerge.

Timing was everything.

Logan pushed the bike dangerously fast on the narrow path. I bit my lip to stop a scream as he slipped between another pair of bollards in the track. My heart beat so hard it stole my breath. All I could do was catch it back and hope.

We burst onto a larger cross-road, narrowly missing a woman with a pram. Logan opened the throttle. We flew along the tarmac, dodging cars and earning angry gestures and beeping horns from everyone we passed. I twisted to check behind. The black SUVs were nowhere in sight.

I silently passed the good news on to Logan. He acknowledged it curtly and took several turns at random, gradually slowing down to the speed limit and heading away from the main road. Open farmland and patches of rainforest lay ahead. Not an ideal place to hide unless you knew the routes intimately.

After half an hour through winding back roads, Logan manoeuvred his way to a highway and opened the throttle. He headed east. Signs appeared, pointing to Cairns. Without slowing, Logan hit the first curves of the Kuranda Range. The tightly-winding road clung to the steep escarpment that dropped from the Tablelands to the coast. I closed my eyes as he skimmed between two thundering trucks. The acrid scent of exhaust fumes hit my face.

Is the bike registered to you? I threw the thought at him tentatively, unsure of my reception.

No. His mental voice was terse. *We'll stop at the bottom of the range and I'll flip the plates, just in case.* He cut the connection.

It felt like a slap.

We passed the major shopping centre at the base of the range but he didn't stop. He swung the bike off the main highway and headed for Cairns by a back route, through cane fields, past farmhouses and across the Barron River.

I gave up trying to reach him. His mind was a blank wall. He was obviously still mad at me. I had bigger things to worry about: my mother was possibly being held captive in lieu of myself. I couldn't be sure about Logan's blithe assurance of her safety. What the hell did I do next? I needed to get in touch with her, or the kidnappers, and find out what they wanted. I'd trade myself if I had to.

But I had no right to endanger Logan or his family, and no real reason to involve them either. Sure, Logan had helped, but I'd paid him back by saving his ass at the shed. Anna's safety wasn't his priority and he clearly distrusted me. I wasn't interested in playing any more mind games. I had the information I needed – the name of the organisation and idea of what they wanted. Anna was more important than any other morsels of information he felt like doling out. Once she was safe, I could focus on taking these Mors Ferrum bastards down. I didn't need anyone's help.

THIRTEEN

<Are you safely away?>

Yes, now. They are closer than we thought, though. Whatever they want her for, it must be important. They're throwing everything at finding her.

<Cut her loose then. Don't risk yourself.>

She's not prepared for this sort of encounter. Up until now she's skirted around the edges of their awareness. She's had a few close calls when she got careless, but nothing on this magnitude. If she's caught she will break.

<And?>

...

<Logan. We're not here to rescue damsels in distress. There are bigger things at stake than one insignificant girl.>

That's where I think you're wrong, Maeve. I don't think she's insignificant. As much as I'd like it to be otherwise, I think she may be the most important player in this. I just don't know why, yet.

<Logan! Don't—>

Logan, I have to go to the bathroom. Can we stop at that gas station up ahead? You can switch the plates.

He didn't reply, but veered into a suburb the faded green signs labelled 'Redlynch'. If he chose it as some sort of black dig at me, I wasn't amused. He stopped at a small petrol station which had a good collection of food, touristy crap and mechanical bits and pieces cluttering up the display area inside.

Two rather ancient security cameras covered the bowsers and the store interior. Anna's work had taught me the majority of security cameras were low-resolution and not as easily accessed or enhanced as the TV crime-shows would have their audiences believe. Logan must have seen them, for he parked the bike in a camera blind spot. We dismounted out of view of the passing parade of cars filling up and families with children traipsing to the bathroom and shop.

I grabbed my backpack and headed for the shop, keeping my face averted. It suited me for Logan to be annoyed enough not to watch me. He busied himself switching the plates on the bike.

Inside the shop I acted swiftly. A baseball cap and cheap sunglasses hid my face from the ATM camera as I drew the maximum daily cash limit from both my cards. Even if my cards were flagged it would take the fourbys a little while to get here. By then we'd both be long gone. I grabbed the rest of what I needed and dumped it on the counter. Chirpy conversation kept the serving girl's mind busy while she scanned and totalled.

Behind, I half-heard whispered conversations – not loud enough to understand the words, though. Hopefully nothing about me. How could it be?

On the way out I passed Logan and wordlessly handed him a cap. He took it. I raised one shoulder and jerked a thumb at the bathroom sign.

'I'll be in there. Give me five minutes. I had to draw cash out so we can't stay long.'

Once outside, I checked to make sure he was occupied, in line for the counter. In the surrounding streets, I spotted what I was after. There. A nineties model Ford. Easy. Perhaps one of the employee's cars. Hopefully they wouldn't notice it missing for a few hours.

Even with my slightly rusty skills, it was the work of seconds to gain entry. A screwdriver into the ignition, a few other tweaks courtesy of my strength, and it was ready. My foresight in seeking out the seediest elements at school in LA had paid off. Logan hadn't emerged by the time I turned over the starter. Grand theft auto. I grimaced. That was a new one. Although this wasn't a particularly grand auto.

I had no idea if my mother was still at the MJE offices, or if she'd been abducted. The office seemed the best place to start, though. Pity I had no contacts here in Australia who were capable of tracking my mother's phone. With a twinge of guilt at abandoning Logan, who may have those resources, I pulled out into traffic, obeying all the road rules and watching for police cars.

A few kilometres down the road, I spotted signs for a large shopping centre. Perfect. Driving a stolen car into the middle of a city, for which I had no mental or physical map, was plain nuts. I parked the car and left it unlocked with the screwdriver in the ignition. With any luck some enterprising thief would re-steal it. Before leaving I wiped every surface with wetwipes I'd bought for exactly that reason.

Inside the cool of the shopping centre I bought a phone, changed clothes, and donned a new blonde wig. Then I stopped in the food court for food, coffee and a few minutes to think about my next move. The backpack Logan had given me held no more than what he'd described. Which meant my second set of throwing knives, karambit blade and boot knife were still in my gym bag – in the boot of my car. But Logan said Maeve took everything from my car with her.

Damn. I would have to either get them or replace them quickly. Unfortunately, that posed a whole new set of problems, since all were illegal to carry in Australia.

I took a long sip of coffee, trying to plan my next steps. How did I find Anna?

It was difficult to think in all the noise. People chattered all around: talking, whispering. Weirdly, though, none of the conversations made sense. They almost sounded like running commentaries; a series of unconnected observations about other people and events. The din seemed to slide sideways through my ears and into my brain, derailing my train of thought.

Irritated, I focussed fiercely on the steam rising from my coffee. After a minute I managed to block out the noise and think clearly again.

I replayed my lunchtime phone conversation with Anna. My mother hadn't sounded at all odd. Nothing even vaguely sinister. She'd used none of our emergency words. So what was the story? Was my mother's phone tapped? Was she in danger from these Mors Ferrum?

Or was Logan behind this? After all, I only had his word he wasn't. If I operated under the assumption *he* had something to gain, what was it? Was this all some elaborate ruse to gain my trust? But again: why? Nothing sprang to mind.

There were too many 'what ifs' to make sense of it. The only thing I could do was confirm my mother was safe. If she wouldn't leave, maybe I could get her to stick close to Michael and his security. But if I could get her out, that would free me up to force these Mors Ferrum people, if that's who they really were, to back off.

I finished my coffee and marched towards the exit. Outside the automatic doors, heat slapped me in the face, reflecting off the tarmac, turning the air into steam. My new clothes stuck uncomfortably to my skin, and my scalp itched under the cheap wig.

Two in the afternoon and the sun burned like a blast-furnace. What a ridiculous climate.

At the taxi rank I let two go to other people then stepped into the third. It might be paranoid, but what the hell. Absently, I gave the driver the address for the MJE building and leaned back against the seat, staring out the window at nothing.

The driver tried to catch my eye in the mirror. He seemed to be one of those chatty taxi drivers who felt the need to make cheerful conversation. He soon gave up when I replied in single syllables or simply didn't bother to reply at all. He couldn't help himself, though, and kept up a low-key muttering; a long monologue about how much he disliked his job, how annoying the passengers were and how little he got paid.

I ignored him and took care to keep the brim of my cap low, obscuring my face from the camera pointed at the back seat. Overhead, a plane climbed into the sky. Would that Anna was on it, safe. Sky and plane vanished as we travelled through the lush greenery of older suburbs.

Ten minutes later, the taxi slowed and pulled to the side of the road, opposite the MJE Building's sun-glinting glass front. I counted out cash, but held it back and glanced over at the building.

Being Sunday afternoon, the middle of town was pretty much deserted. Even the few occupants visible in pub opposite were practically motionless in the enervating heat. Shimmers rose off the asphalt, distorting the sharp lines of the buildings.

The front doors of MJE slid open. My mother strolled out, radiant and laughing, arm in arm with Michael. Her red hair glinted in the golden afternoon light. Michael strode directly to a waiting limousine. The couple were surrounded by six watchful security staff and joined by three other women and two men. Presumably other office staff.

My fingers were on the door-handle before sense caught up with eagerness and put a collar on it.

'Hang on,' I said to the driver, 'I might need you to take me somewhere else.'

He gave an easy shrug.

Anna threw a smiling comment at one of the workers and waved to them. Michael handed her into the black-windowed limo. Two of the security staff climbed in with them. The other four slid into a matched pair of grey Mercedes – one in front of the limo and one behind. All three vehicles pulled away from the curb.

I tucked the cash away, debating.

Anna was perfectly fine, and far better-protected with Michael than anything I could do. The chances of anyone kidnapping her at the moment were pretty much zero. So were my chances of getting close to her, unseen. There was no point spending money driving around, following them to drinks. I'd have to find another way to reach her.

I was about to give the taxi driver the address for a motel I'd pulled off Laterates.com, when movement across the street caught my eye.

A tall man, in cargo shorts and a blue polo shirt, stepped out of the shadows of the pub. He touched one finger to his ear and watched Michael's cavalcade vanish around the corner. His lips moved. He turned in a slow circle, surveying the empty street around the building. A cap shadowed his angular, lean face. Sunglasses hid his eyes. But it was him: Connor Blake. Just waiting for me to show up.

'Shit!' I slid down in the seat. My heart raced and my head began to pound. Darkness broke free, erupting, rage-filled to protect me. I cried out and pressed my palms against my head. My whole body shook with the effort of holding it back. Kicking the back of the driver's seat I yelled at him.

'Drive. Go!'

'Where?' The driver sent me a bewildered glance in the mirror.

'Just go!'

He shrugged and pulled away from the curb, leaving the threat behind. My head thumped. The ink clouding my thoughts retreated.

He was right. Where? I couldn't go to any friends' houses, partly because I had none and partly because anyone I knew from school might be watched. I couldn't go home. I couldn't leave town and abandon Anna. What was I supposed to do? I couldn't get to Anna, or even call her to make plans, without being tracked.

As much as I hated to admit it, I had no idea what to do next. I wanted this over with. I wanted these people to back the hell off, but how to achieve that was beyond me. Anger and determination would only get me so far. And it was a fine line between anger and stupidity. I couldn't take these people down on my own if I couldn't control what was inside of me.

I needed help. I had to trust someone; to put my safety and my mother's in someone else's hands. The thought galled but I couldn't see any other options. And, if Logan was telling the truth about being able to help me, what he knew might also set me free.

I had to take the chance. When I went after these men, I couldn't risk releasing what lurked in my head.

I gave the driver the address of Logan's safe house.

He accelerated me away from danger, but towards the unknown.

A short while later, I stood somewhere in the middle of suburbia, still hesitating, still unsure. The street waited, quiet and calm: a haven after the last twenty-four hours. It was pretty, for a suburb; full of established trees and a hodgepodge of house styles covering at least a century. One side was a set of modern townhouses, all clean rendered walls and square outlines. Next to that stood a timber and fibreboard construction perched on breeze blocks and badly in need of razing. Beside it a small timber cottage, its porches adorned with more lacework than a wedding dress, hid behind a hedge of glossy green bushes bearing white flowers that smelled like orangeblossom.

All along the street, poinciana trees bloomed. Their fire-orange flowers clashed with the blue sky and scattered like blood-offerings over the road. A car swished past, fluttering petals into little flame-storms. To the northeast, a small thunderhead piled grey and luminous-white pillows high into the stratosphere. The air thickened with the foreknowledge of rain to come.

I stood outside a graceful old timber house and stared through the security gates. Behind the house, sunset's lurid pinks and oranges flared. A distant rumble of thunder thrummed through my body as I hesitated. Grey clouds roiled higher and the sky darkened.

Inside that house, I assumed, were Maeve and Jennifer; Logan's family. They held the answers to my questions and, possibly, help to get Anna. On the other hand, I'd never met them and I barely knew Logan. What if I was walking into some sort of trap? This peaceful street was hardly the place, but....

Oh, good grief. Paranoia was taking over. What had I told myself before about the need to stop living a half-life? So far Logan had done nothing unforgivable or given me any big reason not to trust him. I'd just spent too many years mistrusting everyone. If he could help me get Anna away and had answers to some of the most fundamental questions of my life, I needed to walk through the gate in order to ask them.

Squaring my shoulders, I pushed the buzzer on the gate-post. The gates swung inward with expensive efficiency. I marched inside, crunched up the long driveway and climbed the stairs onto a broad verandah. Huge windows, designed to be open to catch every breeze, were closed and shuttered, the muted hum of an airconditioner audible. I knocked and the door swung open to reveal...Logan.

He gazed calmly at me and folded his arms. 'Finished stealing cars?'

I stayed where I was, mirroring his pose and raising my chin at him. Unable to think of a witty, snappy return, I pressed my lips together. I wasn't going to beg for help.

'You don't *have* to beg,' he said. 'We were going to help you anyway. You just have to stick around long enough to let us.'

I glared at him, unnerved. 'Stop that. Stay out of my head!'

A faint smile flickered and he indicated the house again. 'If we're going to argue you may as well come in. It's hot out and it's going to rain soon.'

'Only if you tell me what the *hell* is going on!' I strode past into the cool interior.

He didn't rise to that, only suggesting mildly that I lay my hat, glasses and blonde wig on a hall table. I followed him deeper into the house. The outer door clicked shut. Logan touched several buttons on a sophisticated computer screen on the wall and a series of red lights blinked.

'Security system.' He answered my unspoken question. 'As far as we know this house is off their radar, but it pays to be cautious now you've arrived in a taxi. That does leave a trail.'

I pursed my lips, biting back a sarcastic rejoinder. The twist of his mouth said he'd probably heard it anyway.

He led me through a central hallway, bypassing spacious, open plan lounge, kitchen, study and dining areas to either side, until we reached the back verandah. Two wings of the house carried the verandah around a freeform pool that was nestled in amongst a veritable rainforest of tropical and subtropical plants. With a sigh of pleasure, I sank into an outdoor chair. Surrounded by a transplanted forest, I was almost able to relax.

Logan vanished into the kitchen and returned with an iced drink. I drank it appreciatively. Homemade lemonade, it's tart chill a perfect counter to the humidity. He refilled my glass without comment, this time adding a dash of vodka after I nodded to his silent question. He settled into a chair opposite, watching me silently, with that leashed stillness so peculiar to his character.

As my shoulder muscles relaxed under the warm influence of the alcohol, I slid a look under my lashes at him. I'd effectively ditched him and he had every right to be angry with me. Then again, he still hadn't told me everything, so I should be pissed off at him. Maybe that made us even.

His lips curved, softening into humour. Dappled afternoon sunlight flickered across his face, showing hints of auburn in his dark hair.

'You're broadcasting again.'

'What?'

He tapped his temple. 'I wasn't in your head before. You were broadcasting. You need to learn to shield your thoughts.' His eyes narrowed. 'You have fairly good natural shields. It probably comes from growing up living in cities, around so many people. Otherwise their thoughts would have driven you insane by now. It's probably because I took down the first block that I can hear you so easily now.'

I sat back, rubbing my hands over my face. 'OK, it's been an...unusual twenty-four hours. I've about had enough of being kept in the dark. Not being a mushroom, I've always hated it, real and metaphoric.'

'A mushroom?' He groaned. 'Ah. In the dark and fed crap. Got it. I haven't fed you any crap, by the way. All of it's true.'

'Well,' I said, trying to maintain the angry momentum I'd had on the way over. 'I'm pretty damned pissed off and I'm not in the mood for more put-offs. Answer a few more questions, will you? Then I need to work out what to do next.'

'By all means.' He leaned back in his chair and spread his palms. 'Ask away.'

FOURTEEN

<We are almost there. Do you need more time?>

A little. She's handling it well, but she still doesn't trust me.

<Remember that this is a war, Logan. She's just a weapon in it. Do whatever you need to, to convince her to help us. She has no mental defences. If she won't co-operate then take what you need from her, wipe her memory of the last day and let her go. We can watch what they do.>

...

<Logan. Don't allow your emotions to cloud your judgment. She has the potential to be very dangerous, you know that?>

Oh yes. I'm not likely to forget, am I?

'What you said before,' I began, 'about special abilities other than speed and strength. What else do the *Daoine*...the sidhe...we...have?'

Logan traced patterns in the condensation on his glass. 'There are a few other skills. Mostly in women. Telekinesis, precognition, psychometry, animal affinity are the main ones. And a few no-one's seen in several generations: teleportation, the shadow-thought, pyrokinesis. Both sexes can channel the forest's life-force into healing. Which explains some of the miracles in the Bible, if you think about it.'

'Oh!' I sat up straight. 'Is that what you were going to show me? Is that why you were laughing when I bought bandages?'

He half-stood, unwound the gauze I'd wrapped around his thigh and revealed his injured leg. Through the torn jeans, his skin was clean and healed, just the faintest white scar showing where, only a few hours before, blood dripped from a gouge in the flesh.

I gazed in open-mouthed astonished belief and disbelief. That, more than his words, convinced me.

'But if we're so frigging brilliant,' I objected, 'why are you scared of humans?'

Logan gave a sardonic crack of laughter. 'You have to be kidding. There's a limit to what we can heal and we need substantial connection to the *sianfath* to do it. We're a minority and we do die. Do you remember what modern Easter celebrates? Remember what happened to Gandhi? Our very existence is a challenge to so many philosophies and beliefs it's staggering. Humans are terrified of things they don't understand.'

I leaned back again, taking a sip of my drink to steady myself. 'So that's why you rescued me last night? Because you thought I was one of you? That's very altruistic.' I pointed at myself. 'How did you recognise me?'

I had little faith in altruism. He clearly had an agenda of sorts but I doubted he would reveal it yet.

He looked up at the ceiling, as if considering his answer. 'Partly it's just a sense of…connection, I guess you could call it. A feeling that you've met someone before when you know you haven't.' When I nodded my understanding, he continued. 'Partly it was your eyes.'

I touched my face. 'What about them?'

'The blue or grey eyes with very dark rims is a gene from our people. It's pretty uncommon and recessive, so it won't be your *only* clue. And it doesn't tell you what percentage caste the person is. Or whether they're Light or Dark. Just that they have sidhe ancestry.'

He shifted in his seat. 'We don't think anyone's yet worked out that connection, but it's only a matter of time and then people will start disappearing.'

'Damn! I knew I should have worn contacts.' Unable to contain my restlessness any longer, I rose and paced a few steps before turning back. 'So, you really think these Mors Ferrum people want to dissect me?'

Logan shrugged, hooking his elbows over the back of the chair and stretching his legs out under the table. 'It's a possibility. I don't know exactly what their motives are.'

I leaned on the railing and stared out over the lush garden and pool, not seeing it at all. 'It's scary they spotted me so quickly. I've only been here a couple of weeks.' I turned back to study him. 'Five years ago they said they wanted to ask me about the *ocair*. What is it? Why is it so important?'

'I told you.' He switched his gaze back to his drink and shrugged. 'I don't know.'

I glared at him. 'You're lying. Again.'

'No.' He caught my eye, sincerity in his. 'It's true that it means "key" but that's all I know. I promise, Red.'

No amount of staring caused him to flinch so I looked out over the peaceful garden and up at the rustling leaves overhead.

'Fine. But you said there was more; some reason why my father put this block in my mind. I can't see how being afraid of humans would cause that. He'd survived. Surely he could've taught me the same skills. Just my speed and the—' I caught myself and changed the sentence, '—strength has set me apart my whole life.'

Logan stood beside me. 'It probably has more to do with his own history. You can make a lot of enemies in five hundred years.'

'They'd mostly be dead, though,' I returned sarcastically. 'I'm sorry, but I'm struggling to see where I fit into all of this.' I put my hands on my hips. 'I still don't see how helping me, benefits you. Nobody risks their own life for nothing.'

'You don't trust me,' he said. 'I don't blame you. I've known this my whole life. I've had my aunt around for guidance.' He leaned on the railing and turned to face me. 'Perhaps your father put the blocks in to keep you from accidentally betraying yourself to a dark-aligned fellow sidhe, or an enemy of his.'

'But why did he leave?' I sounded like a stupid, hurt kid. Annoyed with myself for revealing too much, I picked up my drink and threw it back, grimacing at the alcoholic bite.

He still hadn't answered my questions about his motives and that bugged me.

Logan shrugged again. 'I only know a little of your father's public history. He appeared rather suddenly in the court of Queen Elizabeth and earned her favour in some unspecified way when she was young. She granted him the title & lands to his family in perpetuity. From then on, he and his "descendants" spent a lot of time meddling in politics; making enemies. I suspect that's why he never wanted children. Families make you vulnerable.'

There was a hint of bitterness in his tone that surprised me, but probably shouldn't have.

'You said you'd lost your father,' I said gently. 'What about your mother?'

'My mother was murdered by a Dark sidhe.'

'Oh.' I touched his arm. 'I'm sor—'

He jerked out from beneath my touch, eyes blazing. He backed away, his body tense. Then the look was gone and his face was calm and distant once again.

'It was a long time ago.' He poured another drink and swallowed it in three gulps. 'We were talking about your father and the Mors.'

I shivered and wrapped my arms around myself. What was that all about?

In the gathering darkness, a rumble as thunder rolled around the city yet failed to deliver the promised rain. Frogs in the thick undergrowth around the pool began to sing their welcome.

'So,' I said, trying to find a way under his guard, 'what are you saying? You came to, what, kill whoever is responsible for Jonathan's disappearance?'

He nodded again, face grim. 'We've been doing it for the last five years, since Jen's been old enough. Travelling the world, trying to keep the sidhe off the industrial research radar; keeping tabs on genetic research.

'How many sidhe are left?' Had I found my place, only to lose it to people like that? It didn't bear thinking about.

'My aunt thinks maybe fifty thousand or so full blooded,' Logan said, 'and maybe double that in half castes aware of who they are. Many more whose genes are so diluted that they're just better sports people, or gifted linguists.'

I eyed him. 'So, if you're so focussed on whoever killed your cousin, why did you risk exposure by rescuing me? Were you hoping to recruit me?'

He looked at me with steady expectation then shrugged one shoulder. 'We could use your help, yes.'

'No way.' I backed up a step. 'I don't want to be part of your private war. I just need to get these people off my back and my mother out of town safely to where she can start over.'

Logan's head lifted and he looked in the direction of the front door. He shoved off from the railing.

'Maeve and Jen are here. Come meet them.'

I grabbed his arm, intending to make sure he understood my position. But at the first brush of my palm on his skin, a montage of images flashed into my head, so sharp, so perfect, but so narrow, it was like peering through the wrong end of a telescope and seeing only part of a close scene, without context or sound.

Darkness. A lamp. A flash of electricity. The thud of something heavy falling. Darkness...The glint of light on metal; a gun held in my outstretched hand. A bracelet on my wrist: emeralds and gold. A muzzle flash. A spray of blood. Logan, lying on artificial turf, eyes closed; lifeless. Darkness...A pillar of light within me, reaching out, destroying everything it touched, draining every life it encountered, growing stronger with each moment. Destruction. Death. Power.

I snatched my hand back, staring in bewildered horror at Logan. The words tried to spill free. I held them in my throat, behind clenched teeth.

He frowned at me. 'What is it?'

The image faded into dreamlike surreality. I scrubbed a palm over my face. 'I'm... no...it's nothing. Let's meet them.' I managed a smile and gestured for him to lead on.

I'd never had so sharp an image before. No, three images. Separate visions. Two about Logan. But the third image was different – more like I was watching through the eyes of someone else. It frightened me more than the other two combined, for it felt solid with the weight of inevitability.

I followed him to the front door in silence. He checked the camera image, disengaged the security and opened the door.

On the verandah, her arms full of grocery bags, stood a girl of about ten or so, willow-slender with raven black hair, honey skin and dove-grey, black-rimmed eyes. She wasn't beautiful in the classic sense, for her face was thin and angular, but she was certainly arresting.

'Mum, she's here!' she called, smiling cheerfully at me as she offloaded half the bags to Logan.

An exclamation from further along the verandah hailed the appearance of a tall woman elegantly dressed in flowing white linen pants and a gossamer green silk blouse. As she emerged into the porch light, I took an involuntary step back. Like her daughter, she had grey eyes, but her hair was auburn coffee, her skin nut brown and her face so narrow and sharp, I could only stare at her, speechless. There was a familiarity about her, too. I knew her, but also didn't know her. Exactly as Logan had described.

'Rowan.' Her smile was serene. 'I'm so pleased you arrived safely. Let's not stand in the doorway, though. Do, please, return inside.'

'You're Logan's aunt?' I asked the obvious as I backed away to let them enter.

Even if I hadn't heard the whole "elves" idea, I'd still have thought there was something odd about Maeve. I couldn't decide if it was the sharply angular cheekbones or the wide-set, large eyes, but Maeve was both beautiful and strange. I tried to discreetly check for points on her ears, but her long hair covered them. How on earth did she walk abroad without causing a sensation?

'I cast what, in the old stories, is called a "glamour". An illusion in other people's minds in which I appear very ordinarily human,' Maeve replied, answering my unspoken question. 'So much easier than wigs and contact lenses. My dear, I know you're mistrustful of Logan but the truth is that you need to be here.'

'Oh really?' Unnerved, I couldn't help the sarcasm lacing my reply. 'Why? So you can drag me into your fight? No thanks.'

The older woman eyed me with a gentle half-smile as Logan returned from the kitchen and relieved her of the bags.

<Because the taxi driver wasn't speaking out loud.> Maeve's voice whispered in my mind.

'What…what do you mean? Of course he was.'

She seemed amused. 'Perhaps we could discuss this inside? Our eyes are more adapted to lower lighting, so I find the brilliance of the sun a little distressing.' Her pupils were the tiniest pinpoints.

I followed her into the cool, dark interior.

Maeve waved a graceful hand at the surroundings. 'Relax for a moment while I confer with Logan. I'll send Jennifer out, with refreshments, to keep you company. Oh, and Logan, would you kindly fetch Rowan's things from boot of the car? I've put her in the front bedroom.'

I was not in the mood for company and light refreshments. It was irritating to have my conversation with Logan interrupted.

Jennifer seated herself opposite with unconscious grace and teenage self-consciousness. She appeared to be around ten, but given her heritage, she could be older. After a minute of slightly stiff conversation about inconsequential things, in which she revealed she was thirteen, Jennifer looked at me ingenuously.

'Wanna see something cool I learned a couple of years ago?'

'Uh.' I paused, collecting my thoughts. 'Sure.'

'I'm not very good at it yet, but Mum says I'll get better with practice.' She screwed up her nose. 'I don't practice enough. Boring as. Anyway. Watch that.' The girl pointed at a broken branch, about as thick as her arm, lying partially in the pool.

The branch shook, then lifted from the ground and drifted off the pool before settling gently onto the leaf-strewn garden bed. Jennifer beamed with pride.

'It's harder than it looks. The first time I tried I almost broke a window trying to move a little pebble. The trick is in how much force to use. It's different depending on the weight of the object.' She sounded too serious for such an outrageous demonstration. 'Plus you kinda have to push backward at the same time to stop yourself falling over. Something to do with Newton, I think.

'Of course,' I replied absently, still eyeing the branch in wonder. 'Newton's Third Law: every action has an equal and opposite reaction.'

'Probably.'

Still stunned, I grinned. 'The Force is strong with this one, Obi-Wan.'

'Huh?' Jennifer eyed me like I was insane, which wasn't unreasonable.

'Star Wars.' I chuckled at her blank expression. 'You haven't seen it? Your education is sadly lacking. What you can do – it's practically the Force. Awesome!'

She gave a puzzled, pleased little smile. 'Wanna try?'

'I can't do that.' My reply was automatic. I reconsidered. The image of me as a Jedi was deeply appealing. 'Can I?'

'Sure.' Jennifer tilted her head. 'Well, maybe. Dunno. It's the most common skill girls have, after telepathy. About one in fifty or something have the gene. Runs in families, though, so I guess it depends on who you are.'

'How do I find out if I have the gene?' I interrupted the chatter.

'What? Oh, like this.' Jennifer touched my temple.

The knowledge flared in my mind, tearing into my thoughts with precise, exquisite agony. I clawed at my head. Stripped-bare, brain-wrenching pain obliterated lucidity. Shadows strained against their bonds, deep in my mind. No. No!

'Jennifer!' Logan's angry cry, speared through me. 'What were you thinking?'

'I just taught her telekinesis.' The girl sounded frightened.

'Dammit, Jen, you can't interfere with this. Maeve specifically told you not to. You could have killed her!'

'I didn't know! Why are you always so mean to me? I can't do *anything* right!' Sobbing, Jennifer retreated.

Logan gathered me close. 'Hang on. Maeve's coming.'

I struggled against his hold. The darkness emerged and stretched through me, reaching for him. I fought for control. My hand brushed his arm. Power flowed into me, brilliant, green-white, stronger than anything I'd felt before.

He gasped and thrust me away. Our connection broke. Pain arced behind my eyes again and I collapsed to the floor.

'Ah, Red, I'm sorry,' he said. 'I'm sorry. Hold on just a little longer. She's coming.'

There was a scuff and the light fall of feet. Then cool fingers stoked my temples and¹ the pain drained away like water under Maeve's touch. Within seconds it vanished. The darkness withdrew. Shakily, I climbed to my feet; embarrassed, weak. How could it be over so quickly; so easily? The others gathered around: Maeve thoughtful, Logan angry and Jennifer, peering around the corner, resentful and afraid.

'How did you do that?' I turned an amazed gaze on Maeve.

The older woman exchanged a look with Logan and nodded.

'We have a few things to discuss but I'll leave you in Logan's care for a moment. Jennifer, you will come with me, please.' Her tone brooked no argument and the girl followed her mother back into the kitchen. Jen's voice rose in protest as she argued with Maeve.

'Come outside and sit down,' Logan said. 'You'll need to recharge.'

I watched Jennifer through the glass as she raged against the rock of her mother's calm. The girl burst into tears and stormed off into the house. A door slammed.

'Don't mind Jen,' Logan said. 'She's just a kid. She'll get over it.'

I turned away, uneasy over her outburst for no reason I could determine.

Logan hesitated, then took my wrist and led me out to a bench tucked away in the garden, past the end of the pool. From there we were hidden in the greenery and close to a small waterfall that gurgled pleasantly into the pool. I sank onto the bench, still reeling from the onset and release of the headache. I patted my head in disbelief.

'How did Maeve do that?'

Logan shrugged one shoulder. 'Years of practice. She's the most skilled technician I've ever met.' His mouth twisted. 'Not that I've met all that many, to be honest. She also has several degrees in psychology, neurology and cell biology. She's determined to understand our psychic abilities from a purely scientific point of view.'

'Psychic...' I sat up straight, staring blankly into the waterfall. 'So....the taxi driver...all the people in the shopping centre...I was really hearing their *thoughts* not their conversations? That's what Maeve meant? I can hear anyone's thoughts now, not just yours?'

He nodded, leaning back casually on the bench, elbows hitched over the back, legs outstretched. He'd changed into clean, loose linen pants. He allowed the silence to extend as I pondered. What did I do next? I'd have to learn this shielding thing or I'd go mad listening to people like that driver and those idiots at the mall. If Jennifer's demonstration was any indication, I had a hell of a lot to learn.

FIFTEEN

<Ah. She believes now. Be careful what else you say, though. She's still hiding something.>

We all are, aren't we?

<I have a feeling her secrets could get us all killed. What did she do to you?>

Just an uncontrolled power transfer. She didn't do it on purpose. Instinctive attempt to heal herself, I'd say. I broke the connection before she hurt me.

<Hmmm.>

I sent Logan a quick, apologetic smile and picked up a dead leaf, folding it over and over. 'Sorry I ditched you.'

He snorted. 'Fat chance. I was never far away. There's too much at stake here.'

I considered him. 'So what, you're going to keep me prisoner? What do you need me for? What's at stake? I already said I'm not fighting your war for you.'

'Hardly keeping you prisoner. Leave if you want.' He leaned back and folded his arms, putting distance between us again. 'I heard what you said. But the truth is: we could use your help. You'd already decided it was time to stop running. This is what you were running *from*. Not just some random people, the Mors Ferrum. It *is* your war, too, whether you like it or not. And we can help you in return. Assuming you want to know more about your heritage, that is. And how to get rid of those headaches and control your gifts.'

'Do you really think Maeve can help me?' I touched my head.

'She already has, hasn't she?' Indifference coloured his tone. 'After dinner she wants to have a closer look into that block in your mind. Ok with you?'

I turned away from the coolness in his eyes. It had been a crazy day. I still wasn't sure what to think. The prospect was tempting, but not if it hurt as much as Jennifer's experiment, and not if it meant being sucked into a world that sounded like the product of a half-crazed film writer. I wanted to trust them, but it had to go both ways. Why did Logan seem to dislike me so much?

'I...don't know.' I flicked the much-abused leaf away and wiped damp fingertips on my shorts. I tucked my fingers under my legs and hunched forward, staring at the pattern of paving stones and pebbles at my feet. 'Letting someone I barely know mess around in my mind is a little daunting. Especially after what just happened. Let me think about it.'

'I'm glad you're here, Red.' Logan leaned forward, hands relaxed between his knees. His expression was calm, with nothing in it to support his statement. 'I didn't like letting you go today, but you're smart and talented and stubborn when you want to be.' He sent me a wry smile.

I ignored that jibe, since it was inarguable anyway.

'But you don't have to be so alone anymore,' he finished. 'Let us help you.'

My heart stuttered. I drew and released a long, slow breath, trying to calm my mind. He'd hit me where it hurt but, if he heard my thoughts, he'd know that. I shut down my emotional reaction. I needed to think about this, about him, logically.

Silence fell between us as I contemplated the day; what he'd said; what had happened; trying to make sense of it all; trying to decide what was best. It was just too ridiculous to be believable. Had

I felt the forest before? Maybe it'd just been my imagination after all. It wasn't possible to talk to a tree. Was it? I was tempted to try but the potential onslaught of agony, and the darker possibility that might be set free, deterred me.

In the long silence between us a now-familiar prickling of uneasiness intruded. Restless, I shifted on the bench. Tension twisted tighter, winding and prickling through my whole body until I couldn't sit still. I shot to my feet and took two hasty steps away, only to turn back to Logan when movement didn't resolve the feeling.

'What's wrong?' He rose, frowning.

I grimaced, turning to pace again. I moved towards the house and the feeling increased. 'I don't know. There's…there's something not right. Can't you feel it? I had the same feeling, at the other house. Before you came back to the creek.' I touched my lips. 'And I taste the connection.'

Logan's eyes took on an abstraction I now associated with telepathy.

'Maeve can't …No, wait.' He snapped his mouth shut. When he turned on me again his eyes were hard. 'Get your things, we're leaving.'

When I didn't move, out of confusion, he growled. 'Go! No! Hang on.' He snatched at my arm. 'What do you have that could contain a tracker – either on you or in your bag?'

'Someone's still tracking me? How? You drowned my phone and I haven't even used the new one. Everything I have on is brand new today!'

He shook my arm. 'What *else* do you have? Something you've been given by someone in the last few days or weeks?'

'Stop a second! Let me think.' I pressed two fingers into the centre of my forehead in an attempt think straight through the tension that built like the thunderstorm on the horizon.

I groaned. 'A hairclip. But my mother gave it to me Friday morning. Oh man! It's in my gym bag. *That's* how they knew I was at the gym Friday night.'

Even as I finished the sentence I ran, Logan close behind. He pointed out the room I'd been given. I dumped out my gym bag on the bed. I scrabbled amongst the jumble of towels, deodorant and socks, grabbing the ornate, silver-metal hairclip.

'This.' I passed it to Logan, who inspected it closely. 'But who gave it to my mother? And why should they only track it now? I've had it…No, I guess Maeve had it today with her. Why didn't they find her?'

'Right, yep, that's it.' He levered it open with a thumbnail to reveal a small chip glued inside. 'They couldn't track it because all our cars and houses have EM-proof areas – to prevent wireless hacking of any of our gear. The boot of Maeve's car; the safe room here and in the other house. The signal must have started when I put your bag in here. They're still a fair way off, though. I'll take this and lead them away from the house. You go with Maeve and Jen to the next safe house.' He pulled keys out of his pocket.

'No way!' I grabbed the smaller backpack and stuffed the curved karambit blade and a few other items from the gym bag into it. On impulse, I threw in the scrap of paper on which Paul Eisen had written his number. The last couple of items went into my pockets. The rest I could abandon without regret. 'This is my mistake, not yours. Give the clip to me. Lend me your bike. I can lead them away. They're looking for me, not you.' I held out my hand.

He pursed his lips and stared into the distance for a brief second. A frown flickered across his face. He tucked the hairclip into a pocket.

'This is bigger than just you, Red, and more than just the people chasing this clip. Whether you like it or not, we're in this too. They know you're not operating alone. You can either go with Maeve to the safehouse, or you can come with me, but I can't let you run this time. There's too much at stake.'

I snatched the keys from him and glared. 'I had no goddamned intention of running. I need your help to fix whatever screwed up crap is in my brain, and to get Anna to safety. I do this, you help me with that. Pretty sure if you hang around me long enough, the Mors you're after will fall right into your hands. So then we're even.'

After that, I was done. When Anna was safe and I'd taught the Mors to leave me alone, I would get on the next plane. They could kill each other all they liked and leave me out of it.

I caught a glimpse of Logan's compressed mouth and scornful expression.

I slung the pack over my shoulder. 'Once this is done, the first thing I'm learning is how to shield my thoughts from people like you.' If he was right, then any damned "Dark" sidhe I came near would know everything I thought. It was already hard enough to hide my differences.

His eyes glittered. 'I am *not* of the Dark. The only—' He snapped his teeth together on the word. 'Fine. Let's go. If we can get away fast enough we may be able to keep this place instead of burning it to the ground!' He flashed me a quick, humourless smile. 'We lose a lot of houses that way. Hides DNA trace.'

He led the way to the garage, passed me a helmet and thrust out his hand.

'Keys.'

I jammed the helmet on and swung a leg over the driver's seat. 'Your turn to pillion. I know where to take this hairclip.'

He didn't reply, but his hands fisted at his sides. He slid on behind me and flicked down his visor, anger fairly seething off him.

Out on the street, the bike roared between my knees as we sped through the soft warmth of the night. Fear sleeted through my body. I wasn't usually afraid of much, but today I honestly felt like I wasn't coping, and that was new.

Where are we going? His voice sounded harsh.

Somewhere we can ditch this hairpin and maybe lead them on a bit of a goose chase for a while. Keep them busy while you and Maeve get me up to speed.

Where?

There. I flashed an image and he grunted. His anger eased.

They're getting closer but they've turned away from the house to follow us. His tone held satisfaction.

I gunned the engine, flying along the quiet suburban streets, only slowing to the speed limit when we arrived in more populated areas. Even then, I risked police notice over and over as I dodged between cars and slipped through the tiniest of gaps. Logan's fingers dug into my hips. I grinned in fierce enjoyment.

We reached our destination and I yanked off the helmet. A mournful horn tooted and we ran towards the dock. All around, laughing, jostling crowds of people waved and shouted. Music blared from a nearby restaurant and coloured lights danced off the harbour's smooth, inky water. The smell of diesel mingled with mangrove and saltwater scents in the still air.

High above, towering far into the dark sky, the bulk of a cruise liner blotted out the stars with regular lights and shadows of its own. The entry ramp had already been taken away and the boat's great motors thrummed a low-key, disconcerting rumble that stirred unease in my stomach. We stopped at the edge of the dock as the boat slid, ever so slowly, through the still water.

I groaned. 'We're too late!'

Instead of replying, Logan peered through the dark at the passengers lining the railing. Several waved to friends and family seeing them off, or admired the night time cityscape.

'Give me the clip.'

I slapped it into Logan's outstretched palm.

He released a soft exclamation of satisfaction and drew back his arm. I caught the edges of a thought, not directed at me. Far above, her face just a white-and-shadow blob in the darkness, a girl named Michelle peered down at Logan. He threw the hairpin with all his impossible strength and accuracy. The girl snatched the glittering gift. A 'thank you' drifted down and Logan turned away with a satisfied smile.

I raised my brows at him. 'What the…?'

He pulled me away from the thinning crowd, heading back towards the large darkness of the nearby parking lot.

'I suggested she heard me shout her name and that I was her boyfriend, come to give her one last gift before she left.' He watched as the ship eased its way to the open ocean. 'That should keep our guys busy for a while.'

Clutching at his arm, I pointed. 'We're not out of the woods yet, lover.'

A black fourby screeled to a halt in a spray of gravel. Doors opened and spewed forth men in black and grey camouflage. Armed with tasers and dart guns, they cut us off from the bike. My hard-faced friend from previous encounters was not among them. Which was almost disappointing. It would be satisfying to hear bits of him go "crunch".

The parking lot was empty, poorly lit, and distant from the restaurants and shops. That left us without either witnesses or assistance. I turned back to the enemy. Rain drifted down from a heavy, orange-grey sky; light and cool. Thunder rumbled.

Logan smiled grimly. 'Two for me, two for you. And they haven't yet called in that they've found us. We still have a chance to make them think you're on that boat. But we need to take these guys out now.'

My heart pounded. I tried to calm my nerves. 'What's the plan?'

'Jen Gifted you the knowledge of telekinesis,' he murmured. 'Think you can use it?'

I edged backward as the men approached. 'Not a chance. Instant brain-fry. Not going there.'

'Right.' His mouth stretched into a humourless grin. *Then try and stay out of the way of the darts.*

Helpful.

Rain plummeted in fat, cool drops that turned the oily tarmac slippery. Steam rose from the still-warm ground.

A man with a taser rushed at me. I bared my teeth in a snarling grin. People were idiots sometimes…ok, a lot of the time. Too keen for glory. All he had to do was stay back and let the darts guy shoot, but this moron chose not to. Good.

He came within range to use the Taser and paused. He was still too far away for someone to get to him. Someone normal anyway.

Lightning flashed.

No need to hide my skills here. I launched myself at him. Not quite fast enough. He pulled the trigger reflexively. His eyes widened as I twisted aside. Only one barb connected, making the weapon useless. I ripped it out of my thigh, grabbed his gun hand and squeezed. The weapon, and his bones, crunched.

The man's strangled scream drowned in thunder. His cry became a squeak as I spun him around and held him before me as a shield. Two darts slapped into his body – one into a thigh and one into his bulletproof vest. He glanced down and gave his companion an angry glare. His body sagged in my arms as the drug took effect.

I swore and dragged him forward until he became too much a dead weight and I had to stop.

Off to my right, movement and grunts said Logan dealt effectively with his assailants. My second man stood out of reach, dart gun wavering between myself and Logan. Fool. He shot at me. The dart hit my cover, just millimetres from where my arm wrapped around his chest.

I drew out my favourite throwing knife. Lightning flashed and thunder rolled almost simultaneously. My opponent flinched and glanced up. One quick flick and the dart gun flew from his hand. My blade protruded from his forearm. I dropped my shield-body and covered the remaining distance in the time it took the man to blink at me in shock.

He screamed as I yanked the blade from his wrist. I slid an arm around his neck, choking off the sound with a sleeper hold. I lowered him to the ground. His left hand scrabbled against my shoulder. His movements weakened and he slipped into unconsciousness. I released the sleeper hold, picked up the dart gun and shot him in the thigh.

The scuff of feet on gravel brought my gun-hand up, ready. Logan staggered towards me. Two dark, crumpled bodies lay motionless behind him, glistening in the rain.

'Hurt?' I slid under an arm as he listed to one side.

'No. Caught a couple of darts. Must be getting old.' He grimaced, his words and movements deliberate. 'Assuming it's the same drug they used on you, I'll be out for a while. Before that happens, I need to cover our tracks and add to the … misdirection. Drag whichever are still… alive together.'

His two attackers were dead. Their bodies were already cooling, necks broken, eyes staring into darkness. Mine lived. Shaken, I did as he instructed. He knelt in a puddle and placed his fingers on both of their heads at once. His handsome face twisted with the effort of whatever he did. At last, with a satisfied nod and a faint sigh, he slumped into oblivion.

I groaned. Left alone with two bodies and three unconscious men in a dark port facility, in the torrential rain. What the hell did I do now?

Logan had killed two men. Yes, he was protecting me, but I'd sworn never to kill again. How could I trust and work with someone who did that so easily?

His bike wasn't far away. I could take it, his phone, find Anna and get her out before any of them woke up. Then I could work on these Mors Ferrum on my own terms. At the thought of them, the caged darkness in my head rattled against its prison.

I looked at the black-clad, gun-carrying men lying on the sodden ground beneath Logan's still, helpless form.

Dammit! I couldn't leave him. Not when he and Maeve might know how to help me govern whatever was so desperate to control me.

I dug through pockets until I found the car keys, opened the vehicle and stuffed bodies and men into it. Next I pulled out a coil of rope I found in the back and, as an afterthought, both of the dart guns, tasers and all the darts I could find. I'd never known a drug to put me under so fast, so it might be useful to have a sample.

The rain eased to a light drizzle, making the next task slightly easier, but not much. Using all the rope, cut into pieces, I tied Logan to the bike. I climbed on, balancing it awkwardly as I strapped him to my waist. Then I threw the car keys as far as I could into the darkness and gunned the bike into life.

I rode at a painfully slow speed. The extra, uncontrolled weight made the bike hideously unstable. The wind turned my wet clothes ice-cold, even in the warmth of the tropical night. Luckily, being a rainy Sunday night, traffic was minimal and I avoided most of it. I had no idea which way to go to the new safehouse. The best I could achieve was to put distance between us and the last place my pursuers had seen us.

Shelter had to be my next priority. Unfortunately, most shelter also included people. Logan's condition would only invite unwelcome questions and medical attention. There had to be a motel somewhere nearby. But in my efforts to avoid main roads and traffic, I'd picked an area of town remarkably devoid of motels. Houses, closed shops and the occasional kids' parkland were all that seemed to be around.

Desperation made me consider the possibility of breaking into one of the darkened houses in a quiet street. There was just no way of knowing which ones were long-term empty and which ones had occupants that would turn up any minute. It was, frankly, a relief when, after about half an hour of aimless riding, Logan stirred and groaned behind me.

Ahead lay a small, triangular garden in the middle of the road. An afterthought of poor road planning, or maybe saved by environmental activists. One giant fig tree, surrounded by smaller bushes around the edges of the drip line, sprouted from the centre. Shadows plunged the area beneath into gloom.

It would have to do.

Mounting the gutter with difficulty, I scraped through the bushes, eased the bike into the shadows and killed the engine.

My fingers were cold and clumsy. I fumbled with the knots and cursed my own rope-tying efficiency. Logan grunted as I struggled with the bindings that held him safe. Finally they loosened. I dragged him off the bike. Hauling him to the tree, I kicked away the litter of crushed beer cans and broken glass then propped him up between the buttress roots of the ancient fig.

A car approached, its lights cutting through the night and turning the rain into silvery mist. I flicked up the kickstand and lowered the bike onto its side to hide it behind the shrubs. The last thing I needed was some do-gooder stopping to help. The car swept past with a swoosh, spraying water from a puddle. I shielded Logan from the worst of it and swore as it trickled down the back of my neck.

Beneath the giant tree was relatively dry and sheltered. Logan groaned again and raised heavy eyelids, his eyes clouded by vague non-recognition. It seemed to be taking him longer to recover. Perhaps because he'd taken two darts instead of one.

If he felt anything like I did, he'd want water when he woke. I rummaged through my bag and pulled out a half-empty bottle salvaged from my gym bag. I held his head and trickled water onto his lips. It dribbled down his chin and his eyes closed again.

Not good.

We couldn't stay here long. Rain poured from the heavy sky with a seriousness that spoke of monsoons. Thunder rolled again. Fat drops of water found their way through the leaves. I shivered as adrenalin drained away and the chill seeped into muscles, leaving me clumsy and vague. There must be a way to wake him up.

He slid sideways and I hauled him upright again. When I withdrew my hands, one glistened dark-red in the streetlamps' orange-sick light. I yanked at his shirt, tearing it open, searching for injuries.

I stopped, blinking rain away. Beneath his shirt Logan wore some sort of metallic-threaded, flesh-toned vest. Thin and flexible, it could only be a bullet-proof vest of some sort, though not anything I'd ever seen or heard of. There were no tears or holes in the material. The blood on his shirt wasn't his. He sighed slightly, head lolling to one side. Relief flushed me with temporary warmth.

Another search of my bag, and the guns and darts scavenged from their attackers, revealed no convenient antidote. Frustrated, I stood up and leaned my back on the gritty tree trunk. Looking up at the rustling darkness of the leaves above I shivered and wiped a drop of water off my face. The leaves sounded like voices.

Voices! That was it. I needed to connect him to the *sianfath* thing. But how?

SIXTEEN

<Logan? Logan?>

   ...

I touched Logan's throat. His pulse was thready, his face pale and damp. His mind was a messy blur of nausea and confusion that made me want to retch. Right, so he wasn't going to be able to guide me. What then? How had I done it before, at the creek?

On impulse, I leaned his cheek against the tree trunk. Then I placed his hands onto the rough surfaces of the roots to either side of him, pressing his palms firmly onto the bark.

He twitched and grasped the buttresses weakly. His face, slack with the drug, firmed into something close to awareness and though his eyes remained closed. A furrow appeared between his brows.

I opened my mind just enough to follow his skill, to see how the Healing process worked. Given the earth-connection had not caused me pain last time, it shouldn't this time, either. The ability to heal myself would be invaluable.

There followed a subtle shift closer to full consciousness as he pulled from the tree what he needed to eliminate the drug from his system.

He opened himself to the *sianfath*.

Easing in with him, I took a moment to orientate. The giant tree became my anchor point from which to explore this surreal connection to the world. I tasted ozone and earth in the life-pulse of the tree and the bushes around me; even the ragged grass clinging to the verge along the concrete gutters. The edges of Logan's thoughts brushed mine. I withdrew, far enough that I wouldn't interfere, but close enough to sense what he did.

Describing the experience wasn't easy. Words didn't do it justice. The right ones didn't exist. Every living thing seemed to have a sort of muted silver-green glow, even Logan himself, although it wasn't a light and also not a colour. The prickling under my skin energised and woke me.

Logan drew only from the little parkland around. I watched him draw strength from the plants and channel it back into his own body. He used the energy on a cellular level to break down the drug into more basic molecules. His skill was extraordinary; delicate; precise. Was it instinctive or learned? Would a knowledge of biochemistry help?

Drawing the energy wasn't difficult. It just took a degree of control to make sure none of the plants was overly-stressed; to make sure life went on after the small amount of energy was drawn. Individual strands of force were visible as greenish non-light, twisting and intertwining into one thicker strand that wound its way back into the centre of Logan's chest.

Why, didn't he take from animals or the hot, orange pulse of humans? Surely they were equally valid sources? Some sort of ethical choice? As far as I could tell, there was little difference and the proximity of so many humans gave the *sianfath* a brilliant luminosity; one that exerted a powerful attraction. The urge to stretch out and encompass all within my reach, to pull strength from them to augment my own, was almost overwhelming.

I gave up trying to analyse it and extended further, into this other world, tasting not only the trees, and humans, but the darting small lives of insects and the swift squeaking flight of insect bats overhead. I explored my newfound freedom and connection, excluding Logan's focussed thoughts. This experience needed to be mine, alone.

In the surrounding houses and a nearby cafe, diners ate and chattered, their auras of orange non-light varied; some clear, some muddy swirling messes, some vibrant, some dull with physical or emotional pain. I heard their skittish inner thoughts running at odds with their mouths: a mother worried about her sick child; a father angry at his teenage son's defiance. Lying to each other and themselves, hiding secrets, laughing, crying, pain and joy intertwined.

Following life-threads, I reached further, drifting on the gossamer connections like spiderlings on the wind, touching a thousand diverse lives, drawing a thousand diverse breaths. I revelled in the sense of both union and utter freedom. Union with life itself. Freedom from the limitations of physical form and the power imposed by chemistry and hormones, flesh and bone.

With this much energy within my grasp anything was possible. If I opened myself a little more to the world, stretched a little further, I'd have enough power to cure Logan and more. I could absorb enough to destroy his enemies, and mine.

The darkness, ever vigilant, flew with me, eager. It stretched through me, with me, until I was one with it and the *sianfath*. It whispered in my thoughts, promising me safety and strength. Tempting. Together we could do anything. Control anyone. Burn everything.

Logan sucked in a shuddering breath and raised his face, opening those extraordinary grey eyes. They widened. His brows snapped together.

Still stretched and basking in the euphoric power of the *sianfath*, I saw his mental presence as both warm and bright. He dropped his smooth mental shields and wrapped me in an embrace more intimate than a physical one. Within him lay incredible mental and physical strength, extraordinary intelligence, and great depths of hidden pain and anger.

Then, before I could make him aware of the power at my disposal, he pulled on all the delicate threads of my consciousness and flung me back into the doughy heaviness of my body.

I gasped, forcing air into stagnant lungs, lifting eyelids weighed by something more than sleep and less than death. Bereft of a thousand amputated ghost limbs and bodies, I was reduced and had lost something vital. Even the knowledge of what I'd had, the power I'd had access to, slipped away. Ephemeral panic became solid, threatening to choke me as I fought for control over my body and emotions.

'Stop!' The command tone in Logan's voice stopped cold my rising fear but I trembled with reaction as a weakness sapped my body of warmth.

My head thumped in warning. Logan hauled me onto his lap, cradling me like a child. Soaked, small and cold, I shivered uncontrollably. Rain pummelled my skull, drumming pain into every follicle and inch of skin.

'It's ok,' he murmured, stroking my hair. 'It'll be ok.'

'Wha...' My recalcitrant tongue refused to obey and form words. 'What happened?'

Logan pushed wet hair back from my face. 'You just stretched yourself a little thin in the *sianfath*. I'll take you to Maeve and I can help you learn to control it.'

'Control!' I clambered to my feet, fighting the sag in my knees and the fear in my heart. Struggling to stay upright, I steadied my body and voice.

'Logan, I...' My throat tightened. 'This is all too much. That was more than just being stretched a bit thin. That was...I could've…there was something…' I pressed a hand to my stomach, unable to put into words the feeling of foreboding that tore at me - and at the chains binding the shadows deep in my head.

Fear shifted to anger, tightening my stomach and throat, curling my fingers into fists.

'I don't think I can do this. There's something wrong with me. There's something…*inside* that wants…I don't want to be like this. I just want to be *normal!*'

He got to his feet, eyeing me levelly, with a hint of scorn. 'There's nothing wrong, but you aren't a normal human, Red. You never were. You know that. But it's like any ability – you just need to learn to use it properly. You can't pretend this isn't happening, because it is. I know it's frightening and overwhelming but we're here to help.'

'Fine.' I covered my face for a moment, then raised my chin. 'Get Maeve to put all the blocks back in place. Then I'll be ok and I can forget I ever met you.'

'It doesn't work like that. Your headaches will just keep getting worse until the block breaks down. Or until you take some drastic action to stop them, like suicide,' he said harshly. 'Maeve can help you make the transition less painful. I promise.'

I thrust him away as he approached. 'Get away! I need time to think. Stop pushing me. Ever since we met you've given me no time to process things. It's all happening so fast that I can't control the dar…I don't *want* this!' The scream tore at my throat and mind.

The anger I'd held so tightly locked away for so many years surged to the fore. Years of pretending, of isolation, and fear, and yearning, congealed into awful understanding.

I was destined to be alone, hiding who I was, fearing discovery, for my whole, very long life.

Rage curled my hands and curdled my stomach. Tears blurred the world. I clutched at my head as darkness blossomed forth and fought for domination. But now it was worse, for it knew how to reach through me to the power in the *sianfath*. Desperate, I fought it, only aware that I mustn't let it dip into that well or I would lose the battle forever.

Logan touched my shoulder. His consciousness impinged on mine as he tried to work out what was wrong; tried to soothe what he thought were my fears.

Let us help.

I lifted my face and glared at him, baring my teeth as I battled the shadow spreading its cloak over my thoughts. His eyes widened and he took a step back.

You can't help me. None of you can. I don't need your help. Was that voice mine?

Logan jerked as though I'd slapped him. His face firmed into determination. His eyes narrowed. He touched my forehead.

Sleep, Red.

The darkness roared in denial.

I fought. I fought Logan and the shadows, rejecting both, afraid of both. But the fight against the darkness was one I couldn't win. Not this time. It was stronger. So I went willingly into the arms of unconsciousness to escape.

It followed, haunting my dreams with scenes of fear, and death, and falling.

I surfaced slowly. Lethargy pinned me to a comfortable bed. The energy of awakening slid into my limbs in a leisurely fashion, like honey, until muscles responded to my requests for motion. I opened my eyes to stare blankly into darkness. My mind skittered away from the incident that had put me here. I was afraid to even think about it.

The memory of my time in the *sianfath* was already faint and dreamlike, but the recollection of the darkness was ever-present.

Anger, pain and fear fed it. I needed to control myself better, in order to manage it. I couldn't afford to let it take over. It just waited for me to make another mistake. To set it free again. It was only a matter of time.

I thrust the thought aside.

A few minutes of meditation settled the flutter of uncertainty. I could do this. I'd just scared myself and given in to fear. I wouldn't again. Fear was only stories. I didn't have to believe them. I could control them.

The room was cool and dark with only a faint glow of orange seeping in around the edges of thick curtains in a bay window. I turned my head, glad to feel well, and spotted a green, luminous clock face beside the bed. Nine. It must be evening, since nine in the morning would be brighter. So I'd slept for only around two hours. Readjusting my thinking to fit that in, I flipped the duvet aside and sat up.

At least I was still dressed this time. Where was I, though?

The door opened and light sliced into the gloom.

'We heard you wake up.' Jennifer skipped into the room and sat on the edge of the bed, her smiling face half-lit. 'We're in another house now. Good thing you felt them coming. We got away fast enough. Looks like they didn't know exactly which house, so we might be able to use that place again sometime. I like this place better, though. The dojo is awesome. It's so nice to have another girl in the house, too. Mum and Logan are always like, sooo serious about everything and I'm always getting in trouble.' She glowered. 'I hate having no friends. Did you feel the same way? Logan said you moved around a lot, too. Oh, Mum sent me to fetch you to our now very late dinner, if you're hungry.'

'Are you kidding?' My stomach growled audibly and we both laughed.

A quick side-trip to the ensuite gave me the chance to see myself for the first time in many hours. I squinted into the mirror and grumbled. There wasn't much I could do about the unruly auburn hair except run a brush through it and hope. I patted the thick waves into some semblance of order, washed mud off my face and applied a little eyeliner - just as a token to make myself feel better.

As I put the pencil away, I spotted my new phone. Dammit! At lunch I'd told my mother I'd call at six. Now I'd missed that deadline. Leaning on the sink, I closed my eyes, chewing on my lower lip. If my mother was free to follow our agreed protocols, she should be on the next flight out. Anna knew the drill. Heroics were out. She had neither the physical ability nor training to undertake a rescue mission. But would she stick to the plan or would her fear for me and attachment to Michael Eisen hold her here?

I straightened and tucked the phone into a pocket. I couldn't risk calling from it. That would lead the phone-tapper straight to this safehouse. I wouldn't make the same mistake twice.

I stepped out into the main house and followed the sounds of dishes and cutlery to the kitchen. It was a relatively small place, another renovated house, with smooth timber floors and high, white ceilings. Cool and elegant, like Maeve herself. Logan and Jennifer sat already at a large, timber table. Maeve sent me a quick smile and waved at a place setting next to Jennifer, across from Logan.

I looked over at him and encountered a calm gaze accompanied by a raised, questioning brow. I shook my head and sent him a quick apologetic smile. His expression softened, his mouth twitching.

Maeve placed a large bowl of chicken and salad in front of me. I applied myself to the salad in silence. The other three were quiet, but I had the distinct feeling a rapid-fire dialogue swirled around me. It had to be about me but there was no way of knowing the details. I got the impression that Logan sat firmly on one side, Maeve on the other and Jennifer wavering. I dismissed the idea I could join in. It wasn't worth the headache.

Maeve said aloud, 'Yes, it's perfectly understandable you want to try but it might be safer if we wait until I've had an opportunity to assess what's going on. I'd prefer to proceed with care so you don't hurt yourself.'

My thought must've been unshielded. I flushed and thought hard about food instead, but my appetite vanished. I rested my aching forehead on my hands, heels pressed into my eyes. The silence carried whispers of voices I couldn't quite hear and couldn't quite block out.

Maeve touched my wrist and I jerked it away out of habit. Her gaze carried understanding and empathy as she leaned across, deliberately grasped my hand and held it. I tensed, waiting.

She smiled. 'There's nothing to be frightened of. You won't get any visions from touching me. I can shield you from it. So can Logan, now I've shown him how.'

I stared at her in silence, not certain how to respond. I'd lived in fear of touching anyone with my bare hands for so long I doubted I could do it naturally any more.

'You're what's known as a precognitive,' Maeve continued, sounding much like my last English teacher. 'But most I've met only have vague feelings of impending trouble, like you did before. But you see glimpses of a future when you touch people with your hands. That's right isn't it?'

I nodded slowly. 'I've only had the feelings a couple of times, though. Normally it's visions. And only very narrow, like watching a movie through a telescope. It's always hard to tell the context.'

'And is it always about unpleasant occurrences, like the motorcycle accident from which you saved Logan?'

I hunched a shoulder and pushed salad around on my plate with a fork.

Maeve sighed. 'I'm not surprised you dislike contact, then. I'm dreadfully sorry it's been so onerous for you, Rowan, but you must see what a blessing this could be?'

'No! It's not. And I won't be a lookout in your stupid war.' I glared at her. 'Just try, for one second, to imagine what it's like to *never* be able to touch someone you love. And when you do, to see nothing but destruction and…' I swore.

Tears blurred my vision and the room swam with the pent up grief of so much life and time lost. I stood and ran out the back door, into the garden.

No! I could do this. Tears spilled and I dashed them away angrily. Staring up, through dark, whispering leaves, towards the dimly star-speckled sky, I tasted the rainwashed air and let it soothe my fears.

I felt, rather than saw, Logan come up behind me.

He gripped my shoulders. 'Red—'

'Look, Logan.' I turned away, brushing him aside. 'I know you're not telling me everything. I know you don't even like me. And I know you want something from me, so just stop pretending you care, ok? This is tough enough as it is, without you screwing with my head, too.'

He regarded me, unspeaking, his brows knitted, grey eyes showing hints of uncertainty.

'Forget it.' I headed back into the house.

Jennifer gave me a quick, scared look and picked at her food. I addressed Maeve where she still sat, calmly finishing her meal.

'Maeve, I need to let my mother know I'm safe. If she stuck with our plan she should be on a plane out of the country by now.' I glanced out the window at the glowing lights at the centre of the city. 'But I'm pretty sure she hasn't. She'll be worried and I need to contact her. Is there a safe way I can call her?'

'I'll show you.' Logan brushed past me. 'We've got a scrambler and a voip connection that's routed through so many servers there's no way of tracking it.'

He led the way to an office in the back of the house and flicked the light switch. The room stayed dark. With a muttered curse, he flicked it again. Then, by the light of the open door, he strode across the room and reached under the curved green shade of a brass lamp on the desk.

Compulsive apprehension seized me. A shout forced its way out of my tight throat. 'Don't!'

SEVENTEEN

<What's happening?>

Another precog. I'll deal with it.

<Watch her. I want to know if the headaches are connected to the precognitive events. And make sure she doesn't say anything to her mother that would betray us.>

You underrate her, Maeve.

<Perhaps. Or you overrate her.>

Logan's finger hovered over the switch.

'Don't turn it on,' I blurted, trying to make sense of the images I'd seen. It was often hard to find the context of what I saw until too late but I was sure this time. 'I saw…it's…there's a short. It'll electrocute you.'

Logan dropped his arm. He left the room with nothing more than a curt instruction for me to wait. I stood in the dark room, unsure and shaking, my head aching again, but faintly.

Footsteps approached and I felt silly standing in the same place, halfway into a room lit only by the oblong of light from the open door. I moved to one side as Logan entered carrying a lightbulb and a stepladder. Quickly and efficiently he changed the overhead bulb and flooded the room with soft yellow light.

Next he showed me how to use the voip computer system and waited while I spoke to my mother.

'Anna?'

'Oh, thank God, R..Meghan. You didn't call! Are you ok?' Anna's voice cracked. 'I've been going out of my mind with worry. I almost called the police but Mick talked me out of it.'

'I'm sorry. Another migraine. Just woke up.' Relief at hearing her voice almost overwhelmed me. I wanted to feel her arms around me; have her tell me it would be alright. 'You alone?'

'Yes,' she said, sounding surprised. 'I'm at Mick's. It's lovely here, I assure you. *I'm* fine. I've left a message for your school that you're off sick. What's going on? Are you still with that Fynn boy?'

I hesitated. I had intended to tell her everything, but something prevented me. Perhaps my own uncertainty; perhaps because Logan was still in the room. I asked Anna to use Michael's computer to return my call over the net. The scrambler would prevent electronic eavesdropping or tracking once Anna was on a computer voice internet connection.

A minute later, we reconnected and Anna's face appeared, her brilliant blue eyes dimmed by worry. She seemed to be in a library, complete with gilt-leather books and a brass ladder to the ceiling-high shelves.

'Yes, I'm still with Fynn and his family,' I said when she asked again. 'There've been a couple of…problems.'

'What kind? Are you hurt?' Anna touched the screen, her lips pursed.

'No. Just had a few run-ins with our friend from Christchurch.'

She gasped, her eyes wide.

I gave a sanitised version of the last day or so, leaving out everything Logan had told me about the sidhe. It was best she knew nothing that could be used against me. Lying to my mother wasn't easy and I needed all my years of practice to keep my expression bland. If she suspected there was more going on she didn't say so. Without question she agreed to get a new phone in the morning so we could communicate without being traced. But after she three times guaranteed Michael had adequate security, I gave up trying to convince her to leave.

She frowned at me. 'This is getting too dangerous. I want you to leave, Rowan. Now. Get back to Ireland.'

'Are you going?' I shot back.

'No, but—'

'I'm not leaving you, either.'

With a sigh, she nodded. 'You're as stubborn as your father was.'

'I think I get it from both parents,' I said drily. 'At least promise me you'll stick close to Michael. Don't go back to our apartment without his security people. Promise?'

'I promise,' she said, grimacing. 'But we're not ready for this level of intimacy. How am I supposed to explain it to him?'

'Pest problem at the apartment? Leaking roof? I don't know.' I sighed. 'Exactly how close are you guys, anyway?'

Her eyes twinkled and a dimple appeared in her cheek.

I groaned. 'Spare me the sordid details. I meant how serious?' I'd never expected us to separate so soon. I thought we'd have a couple more years. Until my trust fund was released and she didn't have to work. The prospect of not seeing her every day closed my throat and blurred my vision.

'I don't really know,' Anna replied. 'It's been a long time since your father...' She gazed through me, into memories and sadness.

'Actually, I wanted to ask you about Dad.' I cleared my throat, uncertain how to proceed. I believed Logan, but I wanted to hear from Anna who Calain Gilmore was.

Logan's presence somewhere behind, itched on the back of my neck.

'What's happened to make you ask?' Anna countered.

I hesitated, not sure what to reveal. The muted thrum of the airconditioner filled the silence I left.

'I'm just trying to make sense of why these people are after me. It has to have something to do with who he was. What he passed on to me. Or maybe he had this *ocair* thing and hid it somewhere. Did he say anything when he left us?' I'd never heard all the details. Perhaps this was the time.

'No.' Old pain darkened Anna's brilliance. 'He just said he had to go to keep us safe.'

'And after? Did you hear from him?'

'Not until his lawyer came, when you were about six, and told me...' Memory of loss pulled at her mouth. 'Told me Calain had drowned. A dozen witnesses saw him jump off the cross-Channel ferry. Wait.' She rummaged in her wallet. 'I have a letter the lawyer brought. You're old enough to read it now and it might help.'

I sat in dumbfounded silence as Anna teased open a much-folded letter and held it up to the camera. Somehow, I doubted my father would write anything in plain speech, but the hope flickered in my belly anyway.

My dearest Anna

I am sorry I've hurt you. But this is the only way I can keep you both safe – from me and my past. Sometimes I wish I'd never let you talk me into having a child, but it had to be. I've done what I can to ensure Ruadhán can lead a normal life, but my past will catch up to her, one day.

You know our daughter is different. I wish I could tell you exactly how, but it's best you and she never know. I've put her money and the estate in trust for the day she turns twenty-five. Until then, keep her safe. Blend in, move often and keep a low profile. One day, people will come looking for her. Be ready. Make sure she learns the things we talked about. Her skills will save her life, and yours.

I love you both and hope you'll forgive me. Trust me, just this once more.

All my love,
Calain.

I read it twice, slowly. What did he mean by "my past will catch up to her"? Why didn't he want to have me and why did it "have to be"? What was he keeping me safe from? Connor Blake and the Mors, or other enemies I didn't yet know about? Did my father even know about the Mors? He must if he'd been around as long as Logan said.

And Japan, two years ago, had that been arranged by the Mors Ferrum, or someone else? How many enemies did Calain have?

I shuddered, dragging my thoughts by force away from the hot, fleshy, dark memories; from the pain, from the gasping, distressed cries, the blackness, the lost hopes, the final, iron nails in the coffin of innocence. Darkness stirred at the memory. I clamped down on it, afraid. If it escaped and took over, as it had tried to do under the tree…

Behind me, a rustle of cloth recalled me to my location and unwanted company. I refocussed. That was past and I needed to concentrate on the now if Anna and I were to survive.

'I don't understand.' I touched the letter on the screen. 'What does this mean?'

Anna shrugged, folded the paper away and tucked a strand of shining hair behind her ear. 'I wish I knew. When you were born, he loved you, but he was afraid of something about you. Maybe something to do with his own parents. He once said he'd never known them but I think he did, and was deeply angry with them.' Her eyes were full of sympathy and worry.

I closed mine, trying to put it all in perspective. 'I'm no closer than I was yesterday.' I rubbed my temples. 'All I have is more mysteries.'

'Did that Fynn boy know anything about the *ocair* thing? You were going to ask him.' She didn't try to disguise the sharp suspicion in her tone.

I resisted glaring over my shoulder at Logan. 'Nothing useful except that it meant "key", which we already knew.'

Anna frowned. 'So you're in exactly the kind of trouble we've been trying to avoid. All because you chased after him in the hopes of finding out more, and nothing came of it? I think it's time to let that go.'

'It's not his fault, Anna,' I said. 'It's mine. I'd already decided to do whatever it takes to get these people off our case. I can't stand running away any more. I can't live like this.'

'Rowan, you're not ready!' She paled, her hands twisting together on the desk. 'It's too dangerous. You said you're having trouble controlling the—'

'Stop! It's ok. Fynn and Maeve are helping.'

'Helping!' Anna's eyes widened. 'You're trusting them? Are you insane? You don't trust anyone and you barely know them. I can't believe this. Get out, now, Rowan. I'll be fine. I think—'

'Ah! There you are.' The door behind Anna opened and Michael strode into the library.

Behind me, there was a click and the office plunged into darkness. I started and looked around. Logan stood by the door, out of camera sight.

'Megan? Is that you?' Michael peered over Anna's shoulder at me. 'Why are you in a dark room? Where are you?'

'Hi, Mr Eisen,' I said. 'Um... bulb just blew, I guess. At a friend's place.'

'Good to see you again.' He smiled and laid a hand on Anna's shoulder. 'Have you asked her yet?'

A doubtful frown flickered over Anna's face. 'No.'

Michael squeezed her shoulder and shook his head. He smiled at me again. 'Your mother's too humble. She keeps trying to convince me not to celebrate her birthday on Wednesday but she's just going to have to put up with a small party. You'll come, won't you?'

'Ummm…' I shifted uncomfortably in my seat.

His smile became slightly forced. 'Not you, too. C'mon. Humour me. It won't be anything too big. Just us, Paul, and a couple of people from work. Say yes and help me convince her. She needs spoiling.'

Wednesday was only a few days away. Probably not enough time to settle things. And I'd never cared much for parties.

'I'm going to be away for a few days, Mr Eisen,' I temporised.

His brows snapped together. 'Really? Where? Don't you have school?'

'Mick, it's fine, really.' Anna touched his arm. 'We'll have the party. If Meg can make it, she will.' She smiled up at him. 'Just give me one more minute and I'll be done. Mix me one of your cocktails?'

He hesitated then lifted her fingers to his lips in old-fashioned courtesy. With a short nod to me he disappeared out the door.

'Sorry,' I said. 'You got backed into a corner there. Now you have to have a party.'

'I'll survive.' Anna smiled wryly and glanced back at the door. 'It would be nice if you could come, though. I do miss you. But I'd rather you went to Ireland. Please?'

'No. I have to finish this.' I grimaced. 'I miss you, too but it's not really safe to put me in the middle of a mixer with a lot of handshaking. And…' I wasn't sure how much to say; or if she was even in danger at all.

It certainly didn't seem like it. Yes, the appearance of those black fourbys was a pretty clear indication her phone was tapped, but that didn't mean Anna herself was in danger. Whoever wanted me just hadn't yet reached the point of using her as leverage. The appearance of Connor in front of the MJE building said the possibility was on their to do list, though.

'No, I can't come. I'm safe at the moment, but if I come to something as public as that I'm just asking for trouble if they're watching you to find me. Just be careful, ok? I have a lead on who might be after me. I'm hoping I can get them off our backs in the next day or so. Then we can both go, or both stay. I'm not leaving you.'

Anna sighed and tugged at a curl of hair that slipped over her shoulder. 'I get the feeling you're not telling me everything.'

'I can't. For your safety as much as anything.'

'That bad?' Her gaze sharpened.

I nodded. 'That bad.'

Anna closed her eyes briefly. 'Alright. I'll get that phone first thing. Just be safe? I'll be ok with Mick.'

I blew her a kiss. 'Take care. Love you.' I closed the connection and my aching eyes.

'You ok?' Logan's voice was gentle with understanding. The light flickered back on and I flinched.

I slid out of the chair, uneasy and unsettled by my mother's words and my own memories. There was so much I'd never know about my father and I had a feeling it was important. I glanced again at the dark screen.

'I'm just worried about her. Do you think she's in danger?'

Logan was silent for so long I looked sharply at him. His expression was pensive, abstracted. If he spoke with Maeve, I couldn't hear his thoughts; just feel the smooth warmth of his shielded mind as a reassuring presence in the room.

He raised his brows at me and shrugged, shoving his hands into his pockets. 'I think, if you're concerned, maybe you *should* go to that party and convince her to leave. You'd both be safe in such a public gathering. And, as she said, Michael Eisen has security coming out his ears.'

I gestured around the room. 'After today? You think I should be out in public? That seems...insane.'

'If you run,' he said, grimacing, 'they'll just take her and use her as a hostage to bring you back. If you ask me, you're best off getting her away. Clearly she won't leave of her own accord.'

'So what, I should kidnap my own mother?' I laughed.

A smile flickered, not even approaching his eyes. 'Just see if you can talk her into leaving. You can't risk seeing her alone if someone is just waiting for that opportunity. The party seems like the best place to talk to her safely. Think about it, anyway. In the mean time...' He took my hand, holding tight when I tried reflexively to tug free. 'Use the next couple of days to let Maeve help you. Right now, though, you need to get some sleep.'

'You're right,' I said. 'I should. Will you thank Maeve and wish them both goodnight for me?'

Logan nodded then, just as I left the room, he spoke my name. I turned back.

'The lamp.' He indicated the green lamp I'd prevented him from switching on.

'What about it?'

He leaned down and picked up a cord, the end was frayed, wires exposed. 'You were right. It might not have killed me, being who I am, but it certainly would have incapacitated me for a while. Thank you.'

When I didn't reply, but just regarded him in silence, Logan dropped the cord and moved closer.

'Why did you warn me?' There was a tension about him that spoke of strong emotions, tightly held. 'You'd just finished pointing out that I don't like you and I don't care, but you still warned me.'

I backed away, folding my arms. 'I...I can't help it. It's like my tongue is hardwired to the visions. It takes a huge effort *not* to say something.'

'But you could have. You had the precog the first time earlier today. I caught the edges of it when it happened. You stopped yourself from talking then. Now, you warned me.' He stepped closer still. 'And you could have left me at the port tonight and run. You must have been tempted, but you stayed.'

I nodded, backing away again. My shoulders pressed against the cool timber wall. He gazed down at me, his expression slowly changing from wariness to something unreadable. His jaw clenched and he made a noise of frustration. He moved away, restlessly touching things around the room.

I wasn't sure whether to be relieved or upset he hadn't kissed me. Had he even wanted to? He was so hard to read, I wasn't sure. At times he seemed to dislike me intensely, but occasionally I caught a glimpse of something else through the wall he kept up. If he wanted me, it was against his better judgement.

While my attraction to him was certainly real and distractingly strong, it was also atrocious timing and possibly just an artefact of our genes. Now was *not* the time to be romantically involved with someone. Especially someone I didn't entirely trust. My thinking and emotions were screwed up enough. I needed more control, not less.

In addition, somewhere in all this mess lurked a hidden agenda. I wasn't sure whose or what it was, but it was there, none the less.

Logan picked up the frayed wire again, staring at it thoughtfully. 'Anything else you want to tell me about? Other visions?'

I swallowed. Cold realisation sleeted across my skin and I had to steady myself on the wall as flashes of the rest of the image came back to me. Would it come true too? The gun, Logan lifeless on the floor? What could I do to stop it?

'Yes.' I frowned. 'That is...I don't know. I can't remember it clearly.' I pressed at my temples. 'Somewhere high. Fake grass. Nighttime. A gun in my hand. A shot. A body...yours...on the ground. I'm wearing a bracelet I don't recognise. Emeralds and gold.' I left out the final vision of power and death, unwilling to even try and put it into words; as if speaking would bring it into fruition. 'Is it truth? You tell me? I have no frigging idea what to expect next, quite frankly.'

He gave me a slightly amused, slightly troubled smile.

At the door I looked back at him. 'Is that why you want me around? For my visions?'

His grey eyes were steady and calm, with no hint of deception I could see.

'No.'

He walked away.

He hadn't said what they *did* want me for.

EIGHTEEN

Her mother's not in immediate danger.

<No. And if we do this right we can use that to our advantage>

...

<Logan? Remember why we're here. Remember what we need her for and who she is.>

I'm the least likely person to forget, Maeve.

It was a relief to close the door behind me, even though the family could probably still hear my thoughts. I prowled the room and focussed on putting up some semblance of those "natural shields" Logan had mentioned. There was no way of knowing if my attempt succeeded. My thoughts kept wandering away to contemplation of what had been a surreal day.

A hot shower helped and the temptation of the cool, soft bed was too much to resist. Squirming under the covers, I closed my eyes and tried to relax, slowing my thoughts. Outside, a thousand frogs, awoken by the rain, shouted their availability to potential mates. The noise was deafening, even through closed windows and with an airconditioner running. A pillow over my ears reduced the ruckus to a bearable background chorus. I drifted towards sleep.

Whispers of voices tore at the ragged edges of my mind, fading when I tried to understand them, surging back when I tried to ignore them. More voices joined in, one raised in anger, one in song;

conversations, arguments, laughter, tears. The noise became the roar of a football stadium, of a waterfall; drowning me.

I threw off the covers and flicked on a light. Yanking open my bag and dumping the contents on the floor, I scrabbled through until I found a pack of herbal sedatives. I took one, then another, as the voices swelled again to mingle with the frogs and the whole world was just noise, inside and out. I cried myself to sleep, curled into a ball with my hands over my ears.

What little sleep I got was haunted by dreams of Logan's death and my own terrifying fall. This time a new dream surfaced, one in which I floated above the world and a million strands of silvery-green and orange energy poured into me, engorging me, empowering me until I was all that existed and the Earth was laid to waste below my feet. Anna, Logan, Maeve, Jennifer – and everyone I'd ever met and cared for lay strewn as shrivelled husks, twisted in agonised death poses.

I woke before dawn the next day with tears still damp on my cheeks. My brain was cottonwool on fire. Every waking second I spent struggling to block out the unwanted connection to the world around me. There were no forests here to give solace. Backyard gardens weren't far away, but they offered no real peace. Their fight to survive in an urban environment too closely mirrored my own. I bowed under the weight of the small lives of mice, roaches and possums living in the city, along with the frenetic, petty thoughts of neighbours.

Even worse was the temptation to simply drain the energy out of every living thing around me just to shut them up. Could I do that? Oh my God, the dream: I could! The darkness within could. That's what the dream meant.

No! What sort of monster even considered that option?

I paced the room, trying not to scream, palms pressed over my ears, repeating the mantra *I am alone, I am alone* over and over. Half a dozen times I hovered on the verge of calling Logan to ask for help. Only the early hour stopped me from yelling the house down.

The door flew open. Logan spun me roughly to face him. He scrutinised my face closely and grimaced.

'I'm sorry, Red. I didn't realise you were so open. I should have taught you to shield last night. Maeve's waiting. Let her help.'

'Can she?' I groaned. 'I can't take too many more migraines and I can't stand the voices, either. There's too many. Tell me she can help before I go insane.'

Logan caught my face and forced me to look into his intense grey eyes. *I promise she can help. You have to trust her, though. Trust me. Focus on me when it's all getting too much and I'll do what I can to help until you can control it.'* He kissed me, hard and swiftly then let go and grabbed my wrist before I could react to the warmth of his mouth. *Focus on that until she can help.*

He led me to a Japanese-style cottage built in the middle of a large garden behind the house. Inside it was decorated like a dojo, complete with tatami mats and weapons on the wall. It was familiar, calming and, somehow, quieter inside my head and out.

Gesturing for me to sit on the mat, Logan moved away. 'She's on her way. Take a few minutes to settle. You'll find the garden buffers you from the neighbours. Later we can spar, if you like. Focuses the mind like nothing else.' With that, he retreated to a shadowed window seat, leaving me to try to calm a besieged mind.

Maeve appeared in the doorway and glided in, serene and beautiful as usual. She knelt on the mat.

'I'm sorry your introduction to our world has been so difficult. Will you let me help?'

A neighbour's spat broke into my thoughts and I groaned. 'I don't think I have much choice, do I?'

Maeve smiled. 'There are always choices. Sometimes we just don't like them.' She settled, crosslegged, tucking a silken skirt around her knees like a schoolgirl. 'Let me begin with how to shield yourself from intrusive thoughts. Imagine your entire mind is inside a house or a building – somewhere you can feel safe. Then you can open windows 'tuned' to different people in order to speak telepathically with them, or you can let groups of people into the entrance hall, or you can close everything to keep people out.' She chuckled. 'Polite etiquette requires you "knock" on someone's shield if you need to speak with them. Let's try it, shall we?'

I closed my eyes and tried to create a vivid mental picture. But I'd moved house more than twenty times in the last fourteen years, so a house was just a place to sleep. Instead, I pictured the last place I'd felt safe: my estate in Ireland.

I'd only ever spent a short time there, once as a child when the vast medieval stone fortress inspired a fixation with all things knightly, and once last year, as a tourist. My trustees managed the place as a bed-and-breakfast and wedding venue that did a roaring trade and earned enough to cover its upkeep. I'd spent two weeks there during school holidays, unrecognised and under a false name, learning my own family history from the lectures and tours, savouring a deep connection with my father and enjoying a sense of belonging I'd never experienced.

So I recreated the thick stone walls of the medieval section around my deepest self, adding later Elizabethan and Georgian extensions, with their leaded-glass or sash windows, to protect my surface thoughts. The thick door to the lower levels protected what I saw as my innermost self. And I relegated the chained, bound *thing* that lurked in the depths of my mind to the dungeon. Perhaps now it would stay entombed and never emerge again. I reviewed the castle, pleased with the result. I opened my eyes.

Maeve watched me, her expression one of curiosity and surprise. 'You do make very clear pictures, Rowan. Did it block out the voices? I can see it perfectly and it looks like it should be an excellent sanctum. Somewhere you're familiar with?'

I nodded, but kept the name of it locked away, not wanting to share the key to my security with anyone. Had it worked? I listened. Nothing. Not a single intrusive thought or voice; not even a connection with the plants close by the dojo. After a moment of relief, that troubled me. Even in the short time since Logan had connected me, I'd become used to being aware of the natural world. It was an extension of self that felt perfectly normal. Now it was gone, leaving me bereft and lonelier than ever.

How did I get it back without losing the safety of the walls? Closing my eyes, I pictured the buildings again and saw the answer. Of course. How stupid. I ripped up some of the flagstone floor in the great hall, connecting myself, symbolically, to the Earth. It worked. Silver-green energy from the *sianfath* glowed through the floor. It seeped in through my feet; warm and cool at the same time; comforting.

'Goodness,' Maeve murmured, 'how original.'

Logan, who watched from a window seat in the dojo, arms folded, silent, shifted in his seat.

I raised my eyebrows. 'Did I do something wrong?'

'Nothing at all, my dear. You simply have a somewhat unique approach to these things.' She smiled. 'I foresee you'll be teaching me as much as the reverse. Shall we begin?'

More capable of thought now the onslaught of half-heard voices had stopped, I sat up straight and agreed.

'We have a great deal to do in quite a short time if you are to learn what's required to protect yourself,' Maeve said briskly. 'However, to release your gifts, we must first remove the blocks your father constructed. It is, unfortunately, the only way to stop the headaches. I also want to teach you how to modify memories, so if you do err in your dealings with humans, you can cover your tracks.'

'Is that what Logan did last night at the docks?' I leaned away from her. 'I don't know, it seems…wrong somehow to mess with people's heads.'

'I know what you mean. But if you recall who I am you'll understand.' Maeve swept back her long hair. 'I've lived this life for almost three hundred years and I know how to protect my family. I'll "mess with people's heads", as you put it, to protect you and them and us, nothing more. We're such an impossible secret to keep I'd rather not let anyone be tempted.'

She cast me a quick, narrow glance. 'Your mother, for example. She's being courted by her boss, who seems to be one of the most influential men in this town. If you told her, she might unburden herself to him. The information could then find its way to the wrong person. That would be a death sentence to all of us, including Anna. Please believe I know what I'm doing. The Mors Ferrum have a long reach and huge resources.'

Her sincerity was real although the drama seemed a little over the top. Isolated as we were in this little regional Australian town, it was hard to imagine my mother's love life could be the cause of a catastrophe. On the other hand, Anna was in love. Love had a tendency to loosen anyone's tongue, even one schooled in secret-keeping. Maeve was right. I sighed.

'You are young and this has all come as a shock.' Maeve patted my leg. 'Don't reproach yourself, you're handling it all beautifully. Let's begin, shall we? I want to understand what your father did. I believe he was attempting to protect you but, knowing Calain as I did, I'm not entirely certain he knew what he was doing. His own origins and upbringing were...unusual.'

'You knew him? You know about his past?' I gaped at her, not sure whether she spoke truth or simply dangled information as bait to keep me around.

'A little. Suffice to say I knew him well, for a short time.' She sent me a mischievous smile. 'Well enough that you have a half-brother, Dante, who's ohh...I think a hundred and fifty and lives in Italy. He's quite a gifted Hunter, with a skill for collaborative telepathy – what we call the *lorntinn* – and finding sidhe abducted by the Mors Ferrum. Calain didn't know of him, of course.' Her smile turned pensive. 'It's a story for another time, my dear. Right now, we need to see what he did to *your* past.'

Stunned, I could only nod weakly.

I found it difficult to relax as Maeve slowly, painfully unpicked the psychic blocks placed there by my father so many years ago. Having someone play inside my mind was a disturbing, unnerving feeling. The lack of control, and a niggling concern about what else Maeve might feel inclined to tweak or might find, troubled me. I kept the door holding my deepest self – and the dungeon – firmly closed against her.

At one point, she straightened and frowned at me. 'This would go much faster if you'd allow me to connect on a deeper level. That door you've created to hide your inner self also protects the strongest of Calain's blocks. I can't force you to open it, but trusting me a little would make this less painful for both of us.'

I said nothing, merely staring levelly at her. She sighed and resumed work.

The process left me drained and shaking, in pain and nauseated. After an hour, having removed two blocks, Maeve siphoned the pain away.

She eyed me, frowning, one hand still hovering near my head. 'You really do have a remarkable physiology, my dear.'

'What does that mean?' I rubbed at my temples, weary beyond belief.

Maeve touched her own throat. 'You're missing a small organ we call the *reollid*. It wraps around the thyroid and acts as a control and regulator for the flow of energy to and from the *sianfath.*'

'Is that bad?' I stroked the base of my throat.

She tilted her head. 'I'm not really sure. Theoretically it means you could draw, store and release much more power than normal. But it also means you could easily drain your own body completely and exhaust yourself. Possibly beyond recovery if you're not careful. Normally our bodies automatically retain enough energy to function. You'll have to regulate it consciously; always hold a little in reserve to keep your body alive.'

'But how?' Panic lodged in my throat. 'I have no idea how to do that.'

Maeve patted my leg again. 'It's alright, dear. We'll work it out, I promise. We aren't talking about huge amounts of energy, so you'll be fine.'

She sent me to eat and rest awhile. I did little of either, worry distracting me.

After breakfast, Jennifer taught me the rudiments of control of my shields and abilities. I felt like a fool, fumbling through exercises Jennifer had learned as a five year old. I gathered the basics of telepathy quickly, but the key to telekinesis eluded me. After an hour's frustration, we were forced to conclude I didn't have the gene for it. It was a bitter disappointment as, of all the skills, it seemed the most useful. Not to have it was a blow to the ego.

Working with Logan came as a relief. His cool distance and calm good sense exercised a soothing influence on my overstretched nerves and temper. We sat in the garden, learning how to merge with the plants and understanding how they connected intimately within the greater matrix of the *sianfath*. In that moment, I felt most relaxed and peaceful, the most able to control myself. With the trees and with Logan I dared to open up and let the green tendrils of the *sianfath* do their work on my tension. Once I'd learned now to keep hold of myself, regulate the energy flow, and not stretch too thin again, it all seemed so simple and clean.

After that, we ate lunch and Maeve went to work again on the remaining blocks in my mind. At the end of that session, German, Italian, Spanish and Mandarin tripped off my tongue as though I were a native-born speaker of each. It was bizarre and my brain felt both full and lighter.

Early in the evening, as the sun blazed its way behind a glory of pink clouds to hide behind the western mountains, I sat holding my head, waiting for the pain and nausea to subside after removal of one more block. Maeve asked me a question.

'Do you recollect anything more about your father in the days before he left?'

I stared at the floor, determined not to succumb to illness. 'Not really. Just that he stared at me for ages and he looked sad.' I smiled bleakly. 'He said he hoped my stories would never be challenged, as his were. And then he told me that if they were, survival was more important than proving the stories right. I remember that.'

Maeve gasped. 'What language did you just speak?'

'I...I don't know. Wasn't it English?' I squinted up at her.

'No,' she whispered. Tears glistened in her eyes. 'It was the language of the *Daoine*. It hasn't been spoken as a living language for over a thousand years. I barely understood you. It's called *Henath.*'

NINETEEN

This is invaluable.

<We have little time for such things, Logan.>

There is so much we can learn from her!

<Later, if she survives. This work is delicate and I'm having to rush. It's exhausting and dangerous for both of us. There's a real possibility I'll injure her.>

Then don't. Take down only what is necessary to stop the pain.

<It's a little more complicated than that. She's still fighting me, unconsciously. We have little time and we need her to lead us to them. If I can't get the remaining blocks down or gain her trust soon, I'll have to wipe her memory.>

...

<We should probably rest. Why don't you work with her? She trusts you more than me. See if you can get her to...relax. I'll take Jennifer out for a while.>

Outside the dojo, crickets began their evensong, competing with a chorus of hoarse-throated frogs singing an invitation to the inevitable evening rains. The warm, humid air barely stirred as a breeze shuffled leaves high overhead. A high-pitched squeak and the leathery flutter of wings spoke of the passage of enormous fruitbats in their nightly search for food. A car swooshed past outside, muffled in the silence of the sheltered dojo.

Sitting up, I stared at Maeve in bewilderment. 'If the *Henath* hasn't been spoken in that long, how do I know it? How do you know it? Why do telepaths need a language anyway?'

Maeve laughed, tucking long hairs behind her ears. 'Even telepaths want to keep secrets. Language is still a part of the culture, although admittedly *Henath* is quite a simple verbal syntax, as it's always nuanced by telepathy.' She sank back onto the heels of her hands, staring up at the dark timbered ceiling. 'As to where I acquired it? Some from my parents and some from Calain in the short time we were together. I assume he taught you. He never told me where he learned it and he would never Gift me the whole language, mind to mind. My parents both lacked the ability to do so.'

She studied me thoughtfully. 'It is possible you and I are some of the last few who speak it at all. Will you teach Logan and Jennifer?'

I measured the suggestion against an increasing sense of indebtedness. I disliked owing anyone and if I could repay Maeve's work in this small way, I wanted to.

'Sure.' I shrugged. 'But it'll take some time and my life isn't exactly settled or easy at the moment.'

Maeve's seemed both amused and little sad. 'It will only take a moment. The whole language is there in your mind, I saw it. You can pass it on as a Gift, the same way Jennifer taught you telekinesis. It is a pity you don't seem to have telekinesis, isn't it? Don't take it too hard. It does run in families. We may find you have other skills.' She patted me lightly on the knee. 'Gifting will be your next lesson. Go now, you're tired and so am I. This is proving more challenging than I thought. Your father was heavy-handed. We are down to the last two, one of which is the strongest. You'll have to let me into your innermost shield to work on that one, though.' She stretched her elegant neck. 'You do have other, weaker ones, but I suspect they are ones Calain taught you to put in place as a child.'

'What for?'

She shrugged. 'Why do any of us block things from our conscious mind? Things we don't wish to remember, perhaps? You'll learn, in time, to access and release them if you wish.'

'What if they're hiding something important?' I asked.

'Unlikely,' Maeve said, her smile condescending. 'What could a four year old know that was so important, really?' She waved dismissively. 'We'll work on Calain's last two blocks next. The second-last is masking your precognitive abilities. Once it is removed you'll be able to control when you receive the visions, and touch people without fear. Behind the other one – the one you've hidden behind your inner shield and the dungeon door – lies…well, I'm not certain what it is. Another ability, as well as what appears to be all Calain's memories of his life.'

I sat back, overwhelmed by the enormity of Maeve's words. 'What does that mean? What happens when it comes down?'

In the car, when Logan had found me: those flickering images of someone else's life, they must have belonged to Calain. If his life held as much trauma as Maeve implied, would I be able to live with his memories active? Would they overwhelm me and subsume my life beneath his until I couldn't distinguish my history from his?

And what else lay behind that block? Would taking it down release everything caged in the depths of my head?

With a shrug, Maeve arched her back and stretched. 'Calain's memories I can teach you to keep locked away until you're ready to deal with them. As to your abilities, I'm not certain exactly what you'll be able to do.'

She touched my wrist lightly. 'But perhaps we should take a short respite before we attempt the last two. You look fatigued and even Logan is getting restive after being compelled to remain inside all day. Why don't I go out, buy some dinner and leave you two to make use of the dojo?

She smiled benignly and rose to her feet, moving more like a thirty-eight year old than someone of two hundred and eighty. A significant look passed between Maeve and Logan as she left. What was that about?

The last golden afternoon shaft of sunlight faded away, leaving the dojo in deepening darkness and soft humidity. Logan rose from his place on the window seat and flicked a switch. Around the edge of the ceiling, a line of dim, yellow bulbs illuminated the space with an easy, indirect light. He moved around the edges of the mat, silent on bare feet.

I rose and stretched the kinks out of my back and neck, eyeing him curiously. He wore a tight-fitting black t-shirt and loose kneelength shorts. I couldn't help but admire his lithe physique as he circled slowly around the dojo, watching me. His expression was enigmatic, his mental shields so solid it was as though he didn't exist, belied by the fact he stood right in front of me.

Truth be told, I was relieved to be done with the mentally exhausting work with Maeve for a while. I welcomed the prospect of a good workout.

I shifted into an open, relaxed fighting stance, hands up, feet apart for balance, waiting. Logan altered his stance to mirror mine, his face still impassive. He jerked his chin and lifted an eyebrow.

'Let's see what you've got, Red. No holding back, no hiding. Just you and me and no-one breakable to worry about.' His teeth showed white against the olive of his skin.

I hesitated, watching him move. I'd never had a full-on session. Never met anyone who wouldn't break when I let fly. I'd been restrained my whole life. I wasn't sure what my true limits were.

Logan, though, grew up knowing who he was and what he could do. He'd also probably had a few years more training than I had. Perhaps my only advantage lay in him not knowing what styles I'd learned. Then again, I didn't know what he'd done either.

'We could just stand here and watch each other, but someone has to make a move.' He flashed out with a punch so fast it almost took me by surprise.

Some instinct made me slap it aside just in time. I continued the motion with a backfisted flick to his nose – meant to sting and cause his eyes to water, rather than injuring.

He jerked his head aside and caught my hand. Twisting it into a lock he pulled me close. Before I could retaliate or break free he pushed me away, out of reach.

'Too slow.' He wagged a finger. 'Too soft, and too predictable. I can take your best. You've held back you whole life; trained for self-discipline and to learn human limits. You've trained to *not* hurt anyone.' He flexed his neck, circling me smoothly. 'And not hurting anyone will be your result if you don't let go of the social niceties. You can be sure the Mors Ferrum will *not* restrain themselves. Let go now. Show me what you've got.'

I glared at him. 'Really?'

His answer was to lunge for my arm. Too obvious. I relaxed my peripheral vision. His foot lashed out at my knee. I shin-blocked, stepped inside his guard and grabbed his arm. He countered the armlock, moving faster than I'd ever seen.

He hauled me up against his body, slid a hand behind my neck and planted a kiss on my mouth. Then he let go and thrust me away again. I staggered back, stunned into immobility.

'You need more training in dealing with the unanticipated.' His tone was sardonic. 'We'll have to work on that.'

'I hardly expect an enemy would ki—' I shut my teeth with a snap, biting off the word and the memories that went with it. Old, helpless anger rose hot in my belly. Darkness rattled its cage. I contained it ruthlessly, circling him, hunting for an opening. Twice already he'd made me feel like an idiot. I was better than this.

'That's the point: it's the unexpected that will negate all your natural advantages and your skillset. You'll freeze into a reaction-loop as your brain tries to process new information and work out how to respond.' He tapped his temple. 'That takes too long. You'll get hit before you work out what's happening. You're dealing with people who know our kind. They've tested you three times now. They *will* know what to expect and they'll be prepared. If they have to break your arms to control you, they will.'

He lunged at me again. I waited until the last second and side-stepped. One arm slid under his elbow and over his collarbone. I turned and flipped him over my hip. He twisted to land safely. I followed him to the ground and sat astride his hips, hands on the mat on either side of his head.

'My sensei said things almost always end up on the ground. How's your ground fighting?' I grinned fiercely down at him.

He raised an eyebrow, apparently not at all fazed. He bridged beneath me, shifted his weight and reversed our positions. Now I lay on my back in the guard position, legs locked around his waist. Bending forward, he pinned my arms to the mat.

'Not bad. Yours?' He leaned closer, his mouth just inches from mine. 'How would you get out of this?'

The energy between us changed in an instant. I knew exactly what to do to get out of it. Did I want to, though? I smiled slowly at him. His eyes flicked to my mouth and his own lips pressed together. He raised both brows.

'Well?'

On my mettle and annoyed he was so easily able to control his reactions, I raised my hips. Tightening my grip on his body, I twisted left and unbalanced him. I pulled his right arm across my chest and wrenched my other arm free as he fell. Using all my flexibility and speed, I slipped out from beneath him. One leg went over his neck and the other across his chest as he fell onto his back.

Arching my back, I straightened his arm into a bar. He clenched his fist, trying to break the lock by sheer strength. It almost worked. He was extraordinarily strong. I gritted my teeth, tucked my hips closer to his body and held on. At last he tapped out and I released his arm.

Logan sat up, flexing his elbow, showing a hint of admiration. 'Nice.'

'Gracie jujitsu. Five years.' I sat up, stretching out my legs and straightening my shirt. 'Do I pass?' I leaned back on my hands.

He shrugged. 'You should have gone for the blood-choke rather than the armbar. A broken arm will cripple but not incapacitate. You can't afford to leave one angry and conscious. Guns can be fired left-handed, too.'

'I'm not going to kill anyone. Ever again.'

Logan's face blanked. He shifted onto his knees, crawling across the mats towards me, grey eyes intense. Did he intend to attack me or kiss me?

He knelt beside me, his eyes drifting from my bare feet, up the length of my shorts-clad legs, over my body and to my face. I resisted the urge to move; to arch my back and send him a sultry look beneath my lashes. It took a great deal of effort, though. There was no denying I wanted him and, unless I was mistaken, the attraction was mutual.

But he'd already made it perfectly clear than he wanted none of me, so what was with the sudden change? Besides, all the reasons for not getting involved with him still stood. If I slept with him, he would seduce more than just my body and I wasn't ready for that. Sex clouded issues already murky and uncertain.

'Maeve actually suggested…' He trailed his fingertips down the line of my jaw. '…that I should seduce you to help you relax. Would it?'

I froze. Definitely unexpected. Or… had I been broadcasting my thoughts again? I checked my mental image. No, the castle was intact. He shouldn't be able to read me.

He lay down beside me, cheek resting on one fist, elbow on the mat. He chuckled, low in his throat, when I moved and put space between us.

'I keep forgetting you're not used to our ways. In a telepathic family it's difficult to keep these things private. One tends to become quite open about all aspects of life, including sex. Sorry if it bothers you.'

I cleared my throat, trying to reorientate my thinking. It made sense there would be less privacy in a houseful of telepaths, but it was still embarrassing to think that way.

'Not exactly upset,' I managed, 'just a little stunned. It will take a little getting used to; this whole "telepathic family" thing.'

'Understandable. Intimacy to telepaths is more about deep-sharing of your inner self, rather than sex. You have a strong shield up around your inner self, so Maeve figured you weren't yet ready for that level of trust. But, you didn't answer my question.' He moved closer and tilted my chin up so I was forced to meet his eyes. 'Would making love help you relax?' His grey eyes darkened and his grin turned wicked. His hand dropped to my shoulder, slipped down the curve of my breast and trailed along the line of my bra under the thin t-shirt material.

Blood rushed to my cheeks and my breath quickened as my body reacted to his touch. It was difficult to keep in mind the several, good reasons for abstaining when his hand slid under my shirt and caressed my stomach.

But I needed to. Besides, there was something too studied, too trite about his actions. He was going through the motions but holding tightly onto himself, keeping his feelings for me, whatever they were, controlled.

I rolled away, onto my knees, smiling a little to soften the blow. 'To be honest, Logan, right now what I need is a decent sparring session. Anything else would…complicate things.'

'So that's a No, then?' He sat up, eyeing me with wary amusement.

I cocked my head. 'You're taking it rather well.'

He folded his legs, kneeling on the dojo mat. 'To be honest back at you, I was mostly interested in seeing how you'd react to the proposition.'

'So it was what, some sort of test? For what?' I turned away, gritting my teeth against a flash of memory.

A quick frown, tinged with sympathetic horror, flickered across his brow. He smoothed it back to faint speculation before I had a chance to speak. What right had he to judge me? Or manipulate me like that? Did everyone just want to use me?

In the dungeon, deep in my mind, the door rattled. The prisoner seeped past blocks and filtered into my thoughts, tinging them black with self-hatred and recollection. I glared at Logan, anger and disgust welling up. Yes, even he saw me as a tool, something to be used in his war. I opened myself to the *sianfath*. Logan's presence was a tempting beacon of silver-green non-light. It would take no effort at all to take what he was and use it; to take from everyone who hurt me and turn it against them. So little effort and all the pain would be eliminated forever.

TWENTY

<We have an opportunity. I've just seen them. They're in this area, but not looking for us or her. Security is minimal. It's a chance to get close without too much risk. But we'll need Rowan to do it.>

You're using her as bait? She's not ready for this.

<This may be our only chance. She won't suspect. She'll believe it's her idea. Give me a few minutes to take down the second last block, then I'll send her out.>

Are we doing the right thing, Maeve?

<Don't, Logan. I know you care for her, but remember why we need her. This is about more than your lovelife. Remember why we're here.>

Dammit Maeve, I know, but there has to be another way. She doesn't deserve this.

<Do you have a better suggestion? We may never have a chance to get this close to them again. What if Jennifer is next? Are you prepared to sacrifice her for Rowan's safety? Remember who she is!>

Why the hell do we have to sacrifice anyone?

<War entails sacrifice, Logan. You know that better than most. Now stop letting your emotions govern your thinking. Make this happen. Now. I'm sending her out in a few minutes.>

You're leaving the last block in place?

<I'm...not sure what's behind it. I think, given who she is, it's safer that way.>

'Oh, God,' I choked, covering my face.

'Red?' He leaned toward me.

I scrambled backward across the mat. 'Don't touch me!' Backed against the dojo wall I fought the seductive pull of the thing inside me. How was I supposed to resist it? Maeve's work had made its release easier, in spite of the dungeon door. I was under barely any stress at all, but holding it in check took all of my concentration.

'What is it?' Logan moved closer. 'I'm not going to hurt you.'

I closed my eyes and focussed all my efforts on caging the beast. Slowly, it retreated behind its door, leaving my heart racing and palms sweating with fear. Fear for Logan; fear for me.

When I opened my eyes Logan was watching me narrowly, intent.

'I didn't mean to scare you,' he said gently. 'My very lame seduction attempt was a test, yes. To see how good you are at controlling your emotions.' He rose lithely to his feet. 'In combat the person who controls and overcomes their reactions best often wins. I'd say you just did pretty well.'

He didn't get it; didn't understand how close to death he'd been. Controlling my sex drive was easy.

He must have misinterpreted the fear flickering through me, for his expression slid into wry regret. 'Don't get me wrong, I'm not blind to what's between us, but there are…issues we need to deal with first. I heard your thoughts about me last night, after you called Anna. I agree with you. The timing is wrong and...' He shook his head. 'Well, I wasn't expecting you to say "yes".'

I focussed on my irritation with him as a distraction from a worse possibility I'd just barely controlled. I couldn't tell him how close I'd just been to killing him.

'You haven't exactly been open about being interested before this. I had the impression you don't particularly like me. Why should I believe you?'

Logan held out his hand. After a moment's hesitation, I took it and let him haul me to my feet. Wrapping an arm around my waist he tucked me close under his arm.

Hs eyes fell to my mouth then returned to mine. 'When this is all over, and you're a little less off-balance, and things here are sorted, we'll talk. I just…' He stopped, grimacing. 'Look, I can't…' He left the sentence unfinished and just gazed down at me with an expression of hesitant regret in his eyes.

Acutely conscious of the lean, muscular strength of him, the warmth of his thigh against mine, the spice of his skin and the bitter twist to his lips, I dealt with the rapid emotional shifts in myself as best I could. I wanted him, there was no denying it. I resented him taking sex off the table, even while I was grateful for it at the same time. It irritated me that he'd somehow taken control of the situation, yet I also appreciated his admission that he found me attractive.

There was still something, though. Something in him that spoke of a deeply-shielded thought or emotion. He liked me, but he was torn for some reason. His words and body carried just the slightest hint of tension as he awaited my response.

With regret, I nodded and stepped back. 'Just don't be surprised if, when that time finally gets here, I say No again. You're still hiding things from me.' And I was more dangerous than he knew.

The little flicker of wry, self-deprecating surprise was gratifying, but he simply inclined his head in acceptance. 'So are you.'

Before I could reply he nodded at the mat. 'Shall we spar?'

I shifted into a fighting stance, eager for the mindless focus training provided. Anything to take my thoughts off the fact that

Logan had, moments before, been seconds from death, even if he didn't know it.

Logan's head snapped up, turning towards the front entrance of the house. 'We'll have to do this after dinner. Maeve's back.'

He paused, obviously communicating with his aunt. Whatever she said seemed to bother him. His eyes narrowed and his brows knitted in a black frown. He looked sidelong at me, then swiftly away again. With a faint sigh, he grimaced.

Then he closed the gap between us. Hesitantly, he slid a hand behind my neck. His lips brushed mine, briefly and sweetly. He pressed our foreheads together and closed his eyes.

'I'm sorry.' Turning away, he cleared his throat. When he faced me again, his usual calm imperturbability back.

'I'm sorry,' he repeated, but any grief he felt didn't reach his eyes this time. There was nothing but coolness and distance in him. 'I'm afraid we'll have to put our sparring off 'til tomorrow. Maeve has an errand for me and she wants to work on those last blocks of yours now. I'll be back later.'

Without any further explanation, he gave me a quick, troubled glance and vanished into the house.

I stared into the darkness, trembling uncontrollably.

A few seconds later, his bike roared away into the purple evening's silence.

'Shall we continue?' Maeve took a sip from the glass of lemonade on the floor by her leg and put it aside, wiping her fingers fastidiously on her loose, grey cotton blouse. 'With that second-last block gone, your precog should be under your control, now. When you touch people, you'll only receive visions if you want to – or if you forget to block them. So we only have that one left – the dungeon door. Then you'll be free of the headaches. And free to use your gifts and to understand your father better.'

I massaged my neck, feeling muscles made stiff with tension. I was resisting Maeve's work and it made things harder for both of us. Partly anticipating pain and partly difficulty in letting go my mistrust. And this work required a great deal of trust. I would have to open the shield protecting my innermost core and that scared me. Releasing the fear of what Maeve might put into my mind, not what she would take out, was the hardest.

I also feared what lay behind that last block. Not only Calain's memories, but this last ability Maeve mentioned. The darkness that lurked in my mind, that broke free when I was in danger. Was that the ability? It must be. If so, I didn't want it to be free. The latent power it carried terrified me. The things I'd done; that I could do; that I'd almost done…Who would I be when it was released?

'Actually, I could use a break.' I eyed the dojo door, breathing in the sweet, flower-scented, humid evening air. 'Would it be safe enough to walk down to the shop? I just need...'

Maeve squeezed my arm. 'I understand. We tend to be an introverted people and you've been in close proximity with us for two days now. You must be desperate for a few solitary moments. It is a lengthy walk though. Logan's still out retrieving some belongings of mine that we were obliged to leave behind at the old place. So if you're content to walk, go ahead. Take your telephone and please don't be long.'

I looked over at the older woman with a mix of irritation and amusement. 'You sound like my mother.'

Maeve raised one perfect eyebrow, but didn't comment.

The truth was, it wasn't solitude I needed so much as a chance to talk with Anna. I missed her calm good sense and advice. I'd never been out of communication with her for so long and fear for her safety lurked in the back of my mind, distracting and worrying. I needed to speak with her in a way that wouldn't be overheard by the Freysons, or lead these Mors Ferrum people, if that's who they were, straight to them.

I rummaged in my backpack, where it lay on the windowsill of the dojo. As I plucked my wallet and phone out, my fingers brushed a piece of paper. An idea blossomed, full-blown, in my head. The paper held Paul Eisen's phone number. He was distant enough from Anna that he was probably not under direct observation. I could contact him. It wouldn't do to say anything important over the phone, but perhaps I could pass on a message.

With a nod to Maeve, I strode out of the dojo. At the end of the street I checked behind. No one. Phone in hand, my finger hovered over the number pad. No. I should probably wait until I was a little further away, just in case. Leading my pursuers straight to the Freysons would be unforgivable.

It was a long walk, but it felt good to stride out. I eased into a slow jog, enjoying the physical movement after a day of mental exercise harder than any dojo session. Sweet night air, cool after a late afternoon sprinkle of rain, slipped over my skin. Overhead bats fluttered in the darkness. Rain trees and palms towered over modern, architect-designed statements of money.

Maeve's directions led me to a larger street and the shop. The grocery was small, just one of a set of four little shops in a row. Standard brick and corrugated iron commercial design; single-storey with unbarred, plain glass doors and windows. Must be a good neighbourhood. No graffiti or broken windows. The grocery was promisingly-named "Friendly". I smiled, anticipating the cool interior and a cold drink. My skin was sticky with the humidity.

Outside, I stopped and retrieved my phone and the paper. I dialled Paul's number and waited while it rang.

'Yo,' he answered, laconic and cheerful.

'Paul?'

'Ya. Who's this?' He sounded relaxed.

'It's Meghan. Have you got a minute?'

'Hey! Sure. Hang on.' Something scraped against the phone mike, muffling the sound of his voice. 'I'm back. Sorry. Just telling the driver where to go. Where've you been? Anna said you've been sick? Y'ok?'

'Yeah,' I replied. 'Hey, I wanted to catch up.' I studied the quiet suburban street, orientating myself. If I was right, the Freyson's safehouse wasn't very far from Paul's place.

'Sure. Where?'

'D'you know the store on the corner of Marti Street?'

'Course. It's our local.'

'I'm there now. Can you meet me?'

'Uh…' He covered the mouthpiece again then came back. 'Done. Be there in five. You ok? You sound a bit stressed.'

'Just tired. See you in a sec.' I hung up, my heart pounding. Hopefully I was right and his phone wasn't wired. If it was, I could be in serious trouble in five minutes. And I could be putting Paul in danger.

For eight long minutes I paced in the shadows, peering down each of the four streets, checking for black fourbys. Nothing.

When at last a sleek black BMW pulled over, I froze against the building, waiting in the darkness. The back door opened and Paul Eisen climbed out. I stepped into a streetlamp's orange cone of light.

'Meghan? Hey, beautiful, we must stop meeting like this! Whatcha doing so far from home?' He leaned back into the car and said something to the driver, then shut the door. The car accelerated away, leaving Paul walking beside me.

He threw a companionable arm around my shoulder and fell into step. 'What'd you do to your hair?' He tweaked an auburn curl. 'I like it. Almost didn't recognise you.'

I wormed my way out from under his arm and put a space between us, kicking myself for leaving the house without remembering my wig. How stupidly complacent.

'You got here fast.'

He opened his arms expansively. 'Our house is up the hill. Just on my way home for dinner. I'm supposed to bring some special bubbly we've run out of. There's a bottle shop down the road.' He peered at my face. 'Enough about me. You ok now? Y'look ok. Coming to school tomorrow?' His eyes widened. 'Hey. You weren't just hiding out and avoiding me or anything, were you? I mean, you don't have to go to extremes. I can take rejection, I promise.'

In spite of my discomfort, I had to laugh at his expression of comic dejection. 'No, just migraines again.' The truth was the easiest lie to remember.

'So...what?' He surveyed the opulent suburban street. 'You're in a hospital somewhere here? I didn't know there was one out this way.'

'No, I...'

Maeve's words about information getting to the wrong people gave me pause. Insane though the whole thing was, I couldn't put Maeve, Jennifer and Logan in possible danger by blithely revealing where they lived.

'I'm staying with a friend for a while. Having treatments to help the headaches. It's just quieter here than in our city apartment.'

'Fair enough.' He shrugged. 'When do you come back to the land of the living?'

A musical jangling interrupted his question. He pulled out his phone and pressed it to his ear before I could reply. With a wry shrug and raised eyebrows, he spoke into the device, still holding eye contact.

'Hey, Dad. Just had to stop for wine, remember? Be a few minutes.' He listened for a second and I moved off a little in an attempt to give him some privacy. Difficult to do when he had a booming voice and we stood in an open area. I inspected my shoes.

'Hey!' He grinned at me and, sensing what he was about to say, I shook my head emphatically. He gave me a non-comprehending frown and shrugged. 'Guess who I just ran into? Meghan! Yep. Corner shop. Shall I ask her over for dinner?' He waggled his eyebrows enthusiastically at me. I shook my head again, waving my hands in negation. He nodded. 'Great. I'll drag her if I have to. See ya.'

Thumbing the End button he spread his hands wide, clearly pleased with himself. 'Can't refuse, now, can you? Anna's there. It's fate. You need to come over.'

I glared at him and folded my arms across my chest, thinking fast. 'Actually, I can refuse and I damned well will, Paul.' I plucked at my creased, green linen pants. 'For one I'm not dressed for it and I'm also expected back in the next few minutes.'

'Call and tell 'em you'll be late. You said you wanted to catch up.' He shrugged. Inspecting me critically he added, 'Anna'll have some spare clothes at Dad's place you can borrow.'

I gaped at him as an appalling thought struck me: if my mother was watched and monitored as closely as I believed then so was Michael. Which meant, thanks to Paul's big mouth, they probably now knew exactly where I was. All I'd wanted was to talk with Anna, and now she, Paul, Michael and I were all in danger.

TWENTY-ONE

<She's gone to the shop. When she returns, play it carefully, Logan. She's not stupid.>

Stay out of it, Maeve. I can handle this.

Paul threw his arm over my shoulder again and walked me to the shop. 'So how about it? You get what you came for. My driver's getting the wine. When he gets back we can head on over.'

The doors swooshed open and I found myself inside the shop, unable to think of a polite way to say no.

And in breaking news...

The TV in the top corner of the shop caught my attention. Paul inspected the array of chocolate bars, apparently not noticing the screen.

Police today boarded a cruise liner searching for a missing woman, but she wasn't amongst the passengers. Her burnt out car was found abandoned near Smithfield. A tipoff led police to believe that this *woman...*

A clear photo of myself – taken from the driver's licence I'd used to buy my car two weeks before – flashed up on the screen. It was under a different name, of course, but the image was recognisably me. I grabbed Paul's face, my hands conveniently covering his ears. His eyes widened as I planted a kiss on his mouth and dragged him to the door. Away from too much information. He went willingly. His arms slid around my waist and he carried me outside.

There, he backed me up against a wall and kissed me in earnest, his hands sliding under my shirt to caress my back. I was already on edge with the tension between Logan and I. Even though Paul wasn't Logan, I couldn't help reacting. It was almost impossible to keep my mind on the reason for the distraction. I had to stop this before things got out of hand. More out of hand.

I broke the kiss and leaned away. A quick check through the shop window showed a different news story on the screen and an interested shop assistant watching us.

Paul smiled down at me, eyes glittering and heart beating hard against my palms. His salacious surface thoughts, all revolving around his obvious intent and desire, effectively switched off my own instinctive responses.

I shuddered.

Pushing memory aside before it could overwhelm sense, I forced a smile and stepped away. If I'd made it to the news, it was past time to get the hell out of the country, regardless of what else was going on. I couldn't dodge police *and* the Mors Ferrum. And that meant I had to take Anna with me. If Anna and Michael were watched or bugged, and someone knew I wasn't on the ship, then it was only a matter of time before they came after Anna to draw me out of hiding. There was no time to waste. I had to get her to safety right now.

'Well, how about we do this, Paul?' I briskly straightened my shirt. 'I'll zip back to my room and get changed and I'll come past for dinner in about half an hour. Sound good?'

He blinked at me.

'Uh...' He cleared his throat, audibly getting his derailed thinking back on track. 'Sure, I guess.' He pulled out a piece of paper and jotted an address on it. 'Here's the address, in case you didn't see it the other day. I'll make sure they hold dinner for you. Maybe after we can go out for a drink...or something?'

'Sure.' I leaned in to kiss him swiftly, turning a hip to prevent him drawing me close again. 'Sounds great. I'll see you then. Oh, do me a favour?' He raised his eyebrows at me. 'When you get into your car, call your dad and tell him you couldn't get me to come. That way it'll be a nice surprise for Anna when I do arrive. Here's your car.'

As if by magic, his beemer appeared and I hustled him into it, tucking the address into my pocket as the car disappeared into the darkness. My attempt to deceive anyone who might be listening in to Michael's phone conversation may or may not work. Probably not. It was a long shot and Paul was just as likely to ignore it. Which meant I had little time to get what I needed from the house and get over there.

'Shit.' I turned and, with a swift check for witnesses, kicked into high speed and sprinted back up the hill.

As I approached the Freyson's house, I slowed both my feet and my thoughts. I needed to think this through and make sure I had my mental shields firmly in place, otherwise Maeve would know instantly I planned to leave. There wasn't much I wanted, just my passports, karambit, throwing knives and lockpicks – things hard to replace. I'd left them in the dojo so I needn't even go into the house.

At least there was no way anyone listening to Paul's phone call could find me fast enough to follow me from the shop to here, so the Freysons should be safe.

Or should I tell them? Should I ask Logan for help?

No. I took several long, slow breaths and calmed my tumultuous thoughts. This wasn't their problem and I couldn't ask their help any more. I'd imposed enough. I'd blown my chance to destroy this branch of the Mors Ferrum. And staying with the Freysons would jeopardise their plans as well. As much as it burned, I had to run again. Now I just needed to be quick and get to Anna before anyone else did.

The side gate was too tall to climb over, but had a security code pad with a flashing red light. I punched in the override code Logan had given me and the light went off. The gate opened silently.

Easing along the side of the house, I found the back garden in unoccupied darkness. Each plant exuded that silver-green non-light aura, adding a kind of extra vision that made negotiating easy. How had I never seen this before?

Inside the dojo I slid sideways through the doorway, into the shadows and paused, listening and watching. Unease slipped down my spine.

I wasn't alone.

Warm golden lights flooded the building, blinding me. I deflected a punch aimed at my face. I grabbed the extended wrist, yanked and jabbed an elbow over the top.

I pulled the strike at the last second.

Logan.

He shoved my elbow away with lighting reflexes and twisted aside. He leapt back, circling outside my reach with almost feral movements that hinted at some strong emotion hidden behind his smooth mental signature. His face was unreadable; blank and cold.

What was going on?

Whatever it was, I had no time for it. Anna's safety was paramount. The Freysons could take care of themselves. Anna couldn't.

I backed away, waiting. I didn't want to fight him and I didn't have time for whatever games he played. He stood between me and my backpack, or I would have walked out.

He slanted me a narrow look and held out a hand, palm up. I hesitated, still not sure what was happening. He turned away, picked up a small towel and threw it to me. I rubbed it over skin damp from the run back to the house.

Outside crickets chirruped in the soft evening, competing with the frogs' warning of another storm to come. I glanced surreptitiously at my watch. Off to one side of the room, on a window ledge, lay my backpack containing knives and passports.

I tossed the towel back.

Logan caught it. He seemed about to speak then shut his mouth, turned away and threw the towel into a corner with uncharacteristic vehemence.

'The Mors cell here is more dangerous than you realise,' he said flatly. He moved over to the window and stared into the darkness. 'My cousin, Jonathan, was a Hunter. Over a hundred, experienced and well trained. His whole purpose was Hunting the Mors. He disappeared. Here.'

He plucked my gear off the windowsill and turned the bag over. He zipped it shut and flicked it to me.

'Were you looking for this?'

I caught the bag, along with flashes of pure, unadulterated fury that slipped through his barriers. I almost dropped the bag. My first instinct was to ask, to soothe, to reassure, to calm. I liked him and it hurt to have him angry at me. I could, of course, guess why. He'd either seen me with Paul or I'd let something through my shields he'd misunderstood. But even as the words of assurance were on my lips, I stalled them.

Wasn't my aim here to get away? To take my mother and get the hell out of the country as fast as I could? How was reconciling with Logan going to help that? He and Maeve had a different agenda. One they hadn't seen fit to share with me. Quite frankly, I'd had my fill of the intrigue and secrets.

Protecting Anna was clearcut and something I could control. My feelings for Logan couldn't be allowed to hold me here. He didn't need me and any relationship started now, while I felt so uncertain and insecure, would end in disaster. I would cling to him like some pathetic romance heroine waiting to be rescued. Feelings like that would doom anything.

No, I needed to find myself and my own limitations without having a backup net in the form of a partner. I had to know I could rely on myself with these new skills just as I could my physical abilities. Most of all, I needed to know I could manage the darkness inside my head. Once I had that under control, I could focus on getting the Mors off my back. After that I'd be free to bring something solid to a relationship.

So I closed my mouth and turned away. He'd get over the anger. And, if I got out now, my vision for his death would not come true. That was the best way to protect him. Incentive enough not to mend fences.

'Red?'

'What?' I kept my back to him.

'You could try trusting me. It wouldn't kill you.'

I glanced over my shoulder at him. His jaw was sharp, his face hard and uncompromising.

'Maybe,' I said, 'but it might kill you.'

I walked out.

TWENTY-TWO

<She's gone?>

Yes.

<Why do you sound surprised? You know her first loyalty is to her mother.>

I just thought…

<What, that she'd fall into your arms and beg for your help? She doesn't want it, Logan. She told you she doesn't want to help us, either. She's angry and dangerous. Let her go.>

Yes.

<Now, you go.>

Slipping into the house, I changed into soft linen pants and a loose, grey silk blouse lent to me by Maeve, tucked a few more things into my bag and slid out again without seeing my hostess or Jennifer. I left everything else behind, including the possibility of knowing who I was and how to control my gifts. I'd work it out.

Ten minutes later I stepped out of a cab in front of Michael Eisen's mansion.

'R-Meghan! You made it!' My mother's voice made me look up from navigating the root-broken sidewalk up to the front gate.

The gate slid open and I smiled as Anna engulfed me in an enthusiastic hug. It was such a massive relief to find her ok. Tears spilled. I wiped them hastily away.

She peered into my face. 'What's wrong? Everything ok?'

'No.' I gripped her wrists. 'We have to get out. You're in danger. There's been three attempts to kidnap me. They're watching you.'

Anna gasped, blood leaving her cheeks. 'Rowan!'

'And,' I added quickly, 'whoever's after me has tapped your phone and probably Michael's. They'll know I'm here. We need to go. Now. Have you got your passport?'

Anna pressed her lips together but nodded. 'Always…well, back at the apartment, anyway. But I can't leave. If Mick's being watched then I need to warn him. I...' She flushed, her gaze drifting over my shoulder. Michael stood not far away, framed in the front door, talking with Paul.

I groaned. 'I'm sorry. I'm so sorry. We don't have much time. I know he's important to you and I don't want to make you choose. I also don't want to lose you or to have you be used as a hostage against me. Will you come?'

Chewing on her lower lip, Anna looked again at Michael. 'Yes, of course. But I need to get my things and at least say goodbye. Come in for a minute while I try and mend fences with Mick. Maybe I can come back.'

Before I could reply with more than a nod, Michael called my mother's name. Anna sent me a quick, worried look and put on her best social face.

'Mick.' Anna put out her hands. 'Look who's here.'

He took them and smiled at me. 'Lovely to see you again, Meghan. I'm so glad Paul bumped into you.' His smile held something of Paul's carefree character but with an underlying vein of condescension I found annoying.

Paul strode up, all teeth, tailored shirt and good looks - acting like a puppy with a toy. He stopped and openly admired me.

'Man! You are gorgeous, girl!' He slid an arm around my waist.

Ignoring my subtle attempt to slide out from his embrace he pulled me closer and planted a kiss on my cheek. I pushed away with a smile to soothe any hurt.

'Shall we go up to dinner ladies? Anna?' Michael extended his arm, elbow crooked like an old-fashioned courtier. She hooked her hand inside his elbow and glanced quickly at me, nodding and holding up one finger to indicate she'd speak with him in a minute.

I ground my teeth.

Paul extended his arm and clicked his heels together on a bow. I smiled but my heart wasn't in it. I didn't want to sit through dinner. I wanted to get my mother and get out before the damned black fourbys turned up and trashed Michael's expensive house.

As we stepped inside, I was diverted to utter amazement. I'd gone in through the side door last time and hadn't seen much of the place. The front entrance was a whole different ball game. The foyer ranked as ridiculously opulent - gilt and marble, red velvet curtains and Persian carpets were only the beginning. Some Italian designer had gone mad with an open bank account and dumped every classical decorative item and architectural feature possible into one building.

Paul led me up an impressive flight of pink marble stairs, perfectly designed to be swept down by a debutante in a ball dress. At the top we emerged into an impressive indoor-outdoor living space, complete with chandelier, sparkling expensively in the discrete light.

Soft jazz music played from some hidden source. In one corner, behind a timber-topped bar, Michael poured a cocktail for a serious-faced Anna as she spoke earnestly to him.

I scrubbed sweaty palms on my pants. A now-familiar foreboding prickled, making me restless and antsy. How was I going to extract my mother politely from this? The longer we stayed, the more chance there was of collateral damage if, no *when,* the black fourbys showed up guns blazing. I couldn't be responsible for the deaths of innocent people. The Eisens weren't part of this, but the men who came for me wouldn't care about that.

Paul appeared at my side again. I hadn't noticed him leave. He passed me a drink. I regarded its red and orange hues and bright pink umbrella dubiously. Raising an eyebrow at him brought a chuckle and flicker of his boyish smirk.

'It's a tequila sunrise.' He slurped at his. 'Dad's own mix. Let's have some fun.'

I hesitated then took a small sip. It was cool and refreshing but I wasn't prepared to let my guard down, so one was the limit.

'Ah, there you are.' Michael's cheerful voice drew my attention.

He and my mother joined us. We sat on white leather sofas around a pink marble coffee table. He gestured to a man standing discreetly a few feet away; a man who bore all the hallmarks of a paid security detail: the bulge under one arm of his tailored black suit; the watchful wariness. He handed Michael an attaché case. Michael rummaged inside it, then produced two small, giftwrapped packages and passed one to me and one to my mother.

'But Mick,' Anna protested, 'it's not my birthday yet and I've just told you I have to go! Please don't.'

He laughed, white teeth flashing in the soft lighting. 'Don't be silly. I wanted to give you this at the party, so you could wear it. And Meghan's getting one because I understand we already missed your birthday.'

Paul's face lit up. He nodded at me and at the small, gold-wrapped parcel in my palm.

Having no idea how to politely refuse, I murmured a thank you, picking at the wrappings without enthusiasm.

Ever eager, my mother had hers open in a flurry of torn paper. She gasped, holding up a sparkling confectionery of diamonds, sapphires and gold.

'Oh, Mick, I can't accept this!' Anna said, but her expression showed conflict.

Michael said nothing, he simply took it from her and clasped it onto her neck. The jewels lay against her white skin like a thousand tiny dewdrops, glistening with every movement. She kissed him on the cheek and whispered something in his ear that made him smile. I looked away, embarrassed.

'Your turn.' Anna fingered the jewels at her throat.

Apprehension twisted in my stomach as I pulled the wrapping paper off. My fingers shook as I opened the small jewellery box inside. I could only stare in horror at the exquisite bracelet, gleaming in the red velvet case.

Before I could close it, my mother plucked the bracelet free. She clasped it around my wrist and turned my arm to admire the green and gold shimmer of the emeralds. It was the bracelet from my vision.

'I...I can't...' I stammered, trying to undo the clasp.

The parrot-clasp was too tiny and awkward to open left-handed. Michael's warm fingers wrapped over mine, his blue eyes sympathetic and amused.

'You'll have to, my dear,' he replied. 'I won't take No for an answer.'

I couldn't break free without hurting him. Instead I nodded and murmured my reluctant thanks. He let go and returned my drink.

'Drink up, ladies.' He stood and twitched his jacket back into place. 'Paul, please take care of them. I must check on something but I'll be back to escort you both home. We'll just have to have dinner when you get back from your trip, Anna.' He bowed and she beamed at him as he strode away.

I shot to my feet and gave my empty glass to Paul. 'I need to go to the ladies. Anna?' I scowled at my mother. She got the message and joined me.

Once inside the ridiculously oversized, gilt-and-black marble restroom, Anna opened her mouth. I shook my head and tapped my ear. I had no idea how much of Michael's house, if any, was bugged by whoever watched Anna. Somehow I had to get rid of this bracelet and convince my mother to leave immediately, all without saying anything meaningful.

I focussed on settling my raging heartbeat until my fingers were steady.

'Anna.' I searched for the right words, even as my nails worked at the clasp on the bracelet, 'We need to go. Now.'

'I know.' Anna touched the necklace at her throat, her eyes troubled. 'I've told Mick we've had a family emergency and we have to go back to Ireland. He won't come away with me, though.'

I let go a frustrated breath, still scrabbling at the bracelet. Why wouldn't it release? Dammit!

'I'm sorry. Do what you can to convince him but we have to go even if he doesn't. And soon.'

Anna nodded. 'Just give me a minute to get my bag and a change of clothes. We'll have to stop at the apartment for my passport.'

I hugged her and, after Anna left, turned my attention back to the bracelet. My vision showed me wearing this bracelet therefore without it the image of Logan's death couldn't possibly come true. I yanked at the gold chain. It didn't break. I turned the chain over. Woven into the chain was a thin, silvery filament of something not gold. Something I couldn't break, even though I pulled so hard the metal bit into my wrist.

Real worry crept into my enforced calm. I sought reassurance from my own reflection then closed my eyes when all I saw in myself was fear. Fear was just my imagination telling stories. I was anxious and my fingers weren't working properly. I'd get it off later. Right now my focus had to be on getting Anna away. That was more important.

Leaving the bathroom, I emerged to an empty room. Where was Anna? Paul lounged against a nearby wall.

'There you are! Thought you musta been sick or something.' He held out a hand.

I took it, not knowing what else to do. 'Where's Anna?'

'C'mon, they're outside on the roof. Dinner's on. You may as well eat here as at the airport. Food'll be better here, I guarantee it.' He towed me out through enormous concertina glass doors onto a massive rooftop garden and entertaining area.

Michael and Anna stood, with their arms around each other, near a buffet table laden with enough food for ten people. Behind that was a covered spa, a luxurious pagoda and daybed area, awash with shining silks and overlooked by an enormous statue of the Buddha. Surrounding it was a glorious tropical garden, rich with deep greens and vibrant reds, glistening in the spotlights.

I glanced down.

Fake grass.

Had I just walked into the very scene I'd forecast? No. Logan had no idea where I was. Yet my internal uneasiness ramped up. Sweat trickled down my spine. Darkness stirred. Dammit.

'You look worried, my dear.' Michael's deep voice startled me and I backed involuntarily away from his closeness.

I stopped and faced him squarely. 'Look, I...'

How did I say it without sounding ridiculous? I could hardly just come out with a wild story about being chased by anonymous badguys in black fourwheelers. It would sound insane.

'I'm just not feeling all that well.' I snatched at the excuse. 'I thought I'd be ok but I think I'll need to go home. We have to pack and catch a plane tonight anyway.'

'Oh?' He raised his brows at me. 'I'm sorry to hear that. Can I get you something? A drink. What time does your plane leave?' He waved the bartender over and plucked a softdrink off the tray.

'Thankyou.' I was hot so I took it and swallowed a big, cool mouthful, screwing up my nose at the over-sweetness of it. 'I just need to go home and pack and lie down awhile. The flight goes just after midnight. I'm sorry to drag Anna away but it's important.'

Michael quirked a charming grin. 'Yes, that family emergency. I understand. This is a large house, you know. I'm quite sure the staff can find you an empty room. I can send my staff to pack for both of you.' He winked conspiratorially. 'Part of the perks of being rich. People at your beck and call.'

Taking my hand, he gazed earnestly into my eyes. I tightened my mental shields to prevent any visions bleeding through.

'Please. I'll only have this short evening with Anna and she's not sure how long you'll be away. She's just gone to get her bag but I'm hoping I can convince you to stay a little longer. Don't spoil this evening for us.'

I gave him a quick, troubled smile, torn between wanting Anna's happiness and wanting her safety. And what if he was still in danger even after we left? Could I get him out of the way as well, even if just for awhile?

'How about we do this?' I said brightly. 'We'll head over to our apartment and start packing. You and Paul join us at the airport for a drink in the lounge before we go. We've only got…' I checked my watch. '…six hours until the flight goes anyway. We need to go.'

'No, I think I insist you stay a little longer.' His ice blue eyes held amused understanding. 'Even just a few minutes. I have something special I'd like you to be part of. Please, it's quite important to both Anna and me. After all, if you miss your flight, I've got a jet of my own.'

'What?' I stepped back, not wanting to absorb the implications of what he'd said.

Slack-jawed, I stood frozen as he walked away. Was he going to make some sort of announcement about him and my *mother?* Oh God. Could this get any worse? If that went public it would make him vulnerable as a hostage for Anna, and hence for me. Even Paul would be in danger. No amount of security could protect them well enough.

Then again... I put a lid on my spiralling fears. Maybe I was just being paranoid and nothing bad was going to happen. Michael would announce some important breakthrough at work. Maybe the bracelet was just simply a good quality bracelet I couldn't get my clumsy fingers to open. Maybe I had just caught paranoia from Maeve and Logan and this whole thing was a figment of my imagination.

But the feeling of an impending storm built thunderheads in my body and the taste of lightning in my mouth. I took a long sip of my drink to steady myself then held the cool glass against my heated cheek. No, I wasn't wrong. Something bad was coming. Soon. I had to get Anna out and had to warn Michael and Paul somehow.

TWENTY-THREE

Maeve, it's time.

Unspecified urgency pushed my feet towards my mother when she reappeared in the doorway. Paul intercepted, sauntering over and wrapping an arm around my waist. Michael, with his arm firmly around Anna's shoulders, smiled urbanely.

'I know you need to go, Meghan, but there's just one more thing to take care of first. John?' He glanced over his shoulder at his security shadow, who nodded without speaking and vanished through a side door.

'What is it, Mick? You're being very mysterious.' My mother laughed, but her blue eyes caught mine in mutual worry. 'We have to get home and pack.'

He smiled down at her and squeezed her against his side. 'Just one more gift for your daughter, my dear.'

Anna cast me a confused look. 'A gift for Meghan? Why?'

Michael winked. 'Because I know what a very special young lady she is.' He turned and picked up a glass of champagne, handing it to my mother. 'Let's drink to our very special families, shall we?' He clinked a glass with her and they both drank, Anna smiling faintly, him watching her.

All the vague uneasiness of the evening congealed into real, sharp fear in my gut. A thousand tiny pinpricks under my skin. Any second would bring the squeal of brakes and slam of doors at the front of the house. Paul shifted next to me, his grip on my shoulder relaxing. I tugged free, eyeing my surroundings with a view to escape routes and weapons. I palmed a throwing knife out of my bag.

Michael still held Anna under his arm and continued to watch both of us with amusement. Paul slouched over to the buffet and picked at the untouched array food.

'I don't...feel...' Anna swayed on her feet.

Eisen curled an arm around her waist and she sagged against him. I ran to her side and helped him lay her down on a nearby couch.

'What's wrong with her?' Anna's pulse beat slow but steady. 'She was ok a second ago.'

Michael lowered his voice. 'She'll be fine. Just a little too much to drink, I'm sure. She'd already had a couple before you got here. And she's been working very long hours.'

His phone beeped. He read the screen, smiled and raised his voice. 'Ah, good. Paul?'

'Yep?' Paul left the table and strolled over to his father's side. 'She ok?'

'Would you please take Anna home to her place? She's had a little too much. On your way out you'll find a gentleman in the foyer. Please direct him up here. I'm expecting him. You can come back and escort Meghan home.'

'Uh... you sure?' Paul flicked a quick frown at me. 'Now? You said she's—'

'Yes! Do as I ask,' Eisen snapped, his urbanity slipping in the face of his son's hesitation.

None of this made any sense. I needed to go with Anna; to get her away and out of the country. I rubbed at my forehead, struggling to hang onto a train of thought I knew was important somehow. My thinking blurred, like wet paint bleeding on a wet canvas: nothing sharp or coherent. What the hell was wrong with me? I needed to get out of here, that much was clear.

'I'll come with you, Paul.'

'Unfortunately, there's no room in Paul's Porsche.' Michael smiled regretfully. 'You'd best wait here. He'll be back soon.'

Paul, with an apologetic shrug and a quick, bewildered look at me, picked my mother up and carried her to the elevator. My heart leapt to my throat. No, this was wrong. I had to go with them. So why was I struggling to voice that opinion? Uncertainty wasn't my thing. Somehow Michael had taken control and left me powerless to take it back.

The doors closed behind Paul and my mother.

Another door opened and two men entered.

'Ah, John, you're back. Please just put them down on the couch right behind me.' Michael gestured to his men. They came in, baseball caps low over their faces, each carrying a large, blanket-wrapped item; one smaller than the other. The parcels looked like people, cocooned. But that was crazy.

A blanket slipped open, revealing Maeve's serene countenance. Her long hair trailed to the ground.

I covered an involuntary gasp of horror. The men laid the two bundles down and pulled back the second blanket to show Jennifer's beautiful young face, eyes closed and still. Were they dead? Horrified disbelief hijacked my sluggish thinking.

'Where did you find them? Why did you bring them here? Are… are they...?' I found my voice but it was shaky and broken.

'They're alive – for the moment. They're here because I wanted them here.' Michael dismissed my questions with a flick of his hand. 'As to why, well, it doesn't really matter, does it?' He raised his glass to me and sipped.

The habit of running moved my feet towards the door. Movement of his other hand halted me. Shock congealed doubt into appalling certainty.

Michael held a gun, trained squarely on me. I was too far away to take it from him. The blade lay heavy in my palm but even I wasn't fast enough to beat a bullet.

The last few days' events snapped into bleak perspective.

How had I been so oblivious?

We stayed in that tableau for an uncountable time. My heart pounded blood into my ears, deafening me.

The door opened again.

Logan strode into the scene and, for me anyway, the dynamic changed. How had he found me? His fists were clenched, jaw sharp with tension. He walked in a lithe, controlled way that spoke of awareness. He knew exactly what was going on – more so than I did.

His steel eyes caught mine, fury in their icy depths. Hope crashed into despair. He'd come for his family, not me.

And everything was now set up for the vision of the future I had tried to avoid.

'Now…' Michael's voice was cold.

This had never been some sort of pleasure party. The whole thing was a setup, using my mother as bait to get to me and then the Freysons all in one place. Michael Eisen had scoured the world to find my mother and had undoubtedly seduced her in order to get to me. He'd known who I was the whole time. I had walked right into it. Worse, I had dragged in Logan, Jennifer and Maeve.

Eisen had probably planned this for Wednesday night at Anna's birthday party but had brought his plans forward when Paul invited me tonight.

'Now,' Michael repeated, 'if you would please stand over there, Mr Litson, or should I say Freyson?'

He knew? Who was this about, me or them?

Or both?

Michael stepped behind the couches where Maeve and Jennifer lay. He pointed the pistol at Jennifer's head.

'No!' I took a step and stopped when he cocked the pistol and pressed it against her temple.

I glanced helplessly at Logan who returned a long, steady look. He tilted his head slightly, his expression shifting to puzzled concentration.

He must be trying to contact me. Opening a 'window' in my mental shield, I reached out and encountered…nothing. Not just no connection to him, but none to the *sianfath* either. For the second time since I'd found out who I was, I was alone inside my own head; reduced, isolated and missing something vital to my very being.

What was wrong? Without telepathy there was no way of planning an escape.

We were at Michael's mercy.

Panic shortened my breath.

Why hadn't I seen any of this coming? If I hadn't shielded myself from visions when Eisen held my hand tonight, I might have. Despair strangled hope in my heart and I turned my eyes away from Logan's.

This was all my fault.

TWENTY-FOUR

Rowan?

...

Shit.

'Yes, I can see you're starting to get the idea.' Michael smiled.

One of his men moved behind and to one side of Logan, a gun in his hand; well out of reach.

Michael jerked his chin at me. 'Throw your bag down and take the gun from Connor.'

I turned. Connor Blake stood behind me, a pistol in each hand. One barrel he pointed at me, the other he put on the ground and kicked across. His lips split into a mirthless, mocking smile. I shook my head. He clicked the safety off his gun and sharpened his focus to a point between my eyes.

He stayed a careful distance away.

I dropped my bag but slid my knife into a pocket. The opportunity to use it might present itself. Unable to think of an alternative, I snatched the gun from the turf. Angry and reckless, I pointed it back at Connor's nose, safety off. He had everything and everyone I cared about at his mercy. I had nothing left to lose. His eyes widened, then his expression settled back into slightly amused scorn.

'Oh well done, my dear.' Michael drawled. 'That's more like what I expected from your kind.'

'My kind?' I slid my gaze to his, vowing not to show any more fear in front of this madman.

The gaping muzzle of the Connor's pistol stayed unwaveringly pointed at my head, making it hard to concentrate. Michael's smug expression made me want to pull the trigger. The barrel aimed at Jennifer stopped me. I couldn't be responsible for her death by killing a mere henchman in a moment of stupid anger.

'The sidhe.' Michael spat the words, his face twisting in disgust. 'I'm hunting you down, one by one. We know all about your people. You've been trying to control humanity for thousands of years. And my family have been slaughtering you for a very long time.'

'I think you have me confused with someone else, Mr Eisen,' I said, trying to suppress the tremor in my voice. 'Do you know how ridiculous you sound? You're hunting fairies? If you have some problem with me, then I'll do whatever you want. Just let the others go. They are nothing to do with this.'

He laughed shortly. 'I know you'll do whatever I want, but not if I let them go. No, I have plans for all of you. None of them involve letting anyone go. First, you'll tell me where the *ocair* is. Then you, my dear, are going to follow in your father's footsteps.'

'What?' I dropped my arm in shock. 'What the hell do you know about my father? He's dead. What does he have to do with you or anything? What *is* an *ocair*? Your men asked me about it five years ago and I still have no idea what you're talking about.'

Michael's face settled into cold calm. There was tension in Logan's lean form; balanced on the balls of his feet, ready for action. But now was not the time. Not yet.

If only I could contact him.

Michael waved a languorous hand at me. 'Your father, dear girl, was responsible for the death of my parents, thirty years ago. I've hunted him since I was eighteen years old. The Mors Ferrum – of which I'm a small cog – have been after him for far longer.'

'So *that's* what this is?' I indicated the scene. 'Revenge on me for something my father did before I was even born?'

'Oh, not entirely. That would be plain crazy.' He gave a soft laugh. 'Money has a lot to do with it, too. And power.' He picked up a drink from the nearby table and threw it back. 'As for your father…I was not impressed to find him already dead. It took me years to find out he had a wife and child. I almost had you in that cathedral in New Zealand. And again, in Japan, two years ago. You must tell me how you got away from my man, by the way.' Michael eyed me with detached interest. 'After you escaped he didn't live long enough to do so.'

I covered my mouth with a hand, sickened.

'Did she tell you?' His question was directed at Logan, who remained silent and calm. 'My man…had…her.' Michael drawled the phrase into a deliberate double-entendre and smiled as Logan's fingers fisted. 'Then, just as he was about to bring her to me, she escaped and he died. So irritating.'

I wanted to tell Logan; to explain. I'd been sixteen. Afraid if I protected myself a vision would come true and I'd kill him. So, I'd submitted; let him start to touch me, but couldn't go through with it. And now the memories haunted me. His hands, his gasping, dying breaths, his blazing life pouring into me.

I shoved the thoughts aside and tore my eyes from Logan's stony countenance. Michael was just trying to get inside my head. I needed to concentrate. There had to be a way out of this.

'Now.' Michael smiled bleakly. 'You'll suffer as I did. You and your kind are a cancer inside humanity – destroying us from the inside. I intend to wipe you all out, starting with these three.'

'You're mad!' I whispered, horrified. 'I'm not my father and Jennifer is just a child. She doesn't deserve to die. You can't kill her.'

He barked a laugh. 'I'm not going to, you will. Then I'll see to it you're tried for triple-murder and put away for life as a lunatic – and we both know how long your life will be.' He bowed. 'I will, of course, use all my medical research department to analyse your brain physiology to try and find a "cure" for your insanity. After all, mankind should benefit from your abilities and I should benefit from them as well. Yes, you *will* suffer for a very long time and you *will* tell me where the *ocair* is.'

'What possible motive would I have for shooting my friends? No-one will believe you.'

He indicated his men. 'There will be three reliable witnesses to tell how you went insane like your father and shot them in cold blood. I'll be convincing, I assure you.'

My heart stopped for a second as the horrible plausibility of his story sank home. My father's death was a matter of public record. After my conversation with Paul earlier, he would reveal I'd received treatments for headaches. Maeve was a psychiatrist and my mother would never know any different, since I had withheld any other information.

I looked to Logan for inspiration. He regarded me steadily, giving me nothing. I tried again to reach him telepathically but again failed. What was wrong with me?

The drink.

Michael had slipped something into my drink to block psychic abilities. That had to be why my brain was mush.

'Now.' Michael's tone became brisk and businesslike. 'It's time. There's just one bullet in that gun. You'll shoot Freyson first. Then I'll load another two and you'll shoot the women.'

'I won't do it,' I said. 'You can't make me.'

Eisen sent me a pitying look. 'Have you forgotten your mother? She's safe as long as you do what you're told. If you refuse or try to escape, she'll die.'

'Oh my...' The enormity of his obsession broke over me and my knees sagged with the weight.

To save my mother I had to sacrifice Logan and his family and even my own future.

No. There had to be another way out. My heart lodged in my throat and strangled me. Head spinning, I sucked at the thick, damp night air. What could I do? How could I save them?

But there was no other option.

I looked at the gun I held.

Darkness roared in my head, fogged and vague, thrashing like a chained dragon. I wanted to release it, but the drug held it in check.

'Red.' Logan's deep voice caught my attention, drawing me back from the morass.

He indicated my gun. 'It's ok.' His voice was calm. 'Do what you need. Save Anna.' With a faint smile he patted himself over the heart. 'Just do me a favour and shoot straight, please. I'd rather not die slowly.'

I hesitated. A certain tone to his voice filtered through my fear. What if I got it wrong? Did he really have that much trust in me?

I pointed the gun at Logan's heart. The emerald and gold bracelet on my wrist glittered. And so my vision came to fruition.

Logan had to die so I could save Anna, Maeve and Jennifer.

Swallowing nausea and fear, I held his gaze one last time.

'I'm sorry, Logan.'

He nodded, his face impassive, body tensed. It wouldn't help him against what I had to do.

I held my breath, took careful aim... and squeezed the trigger.

TWENTY-FIVE

The flash, roar and jerk of the gun tore through the thick air. Logan's body jerked. He fell backward and onto his side, landing exactly as I'd foreseen. Blood poured scarlet onto the glossy green turf. His eyes closed, fingers loosely curled, mouth opened.

I dropped my arm and took a step in his direction, only to be restrained by my personal thug. It took a massive amount of self-control not to break Connor's hold and his neck. But this insane plan was only half-complete. I couldn't stop now.

Michael's laugh rang out, exultant and loud in the shocking silence.

'My God, girl, I didn't think you had it in you.' He gestured to his flunkey. 'Check he's dead. Then we'll set up the others.'

'No. Logan!' I twisted out of Connor's hold and ran towards Logan's prone form. It took both of the men to restrain me. They dragged me, fighting all the way, to where Michael still held a gun to Jennifer. Connor dumped me on the ground and plucked the gun from my hand. He wore gloves.

Panting and half-sobbing, I raised my head to look at Michael Eisen, hating him with all my heart. Where was the darkness within me when I needed it? I would drain him with pleasure.

He regarded me coldly. 'Now you're starting to know what it feels like, aren't you? Don't worry. It'll get worse. You've killed your boyfriend, now you're about to kill his family.'

Calmly he picked out one more bullet from his pocket.

I had all of them close enough now. I had to push through the drugs and use my new skills, otherwise what was the point of having them? I reached into the untrained healing power and pictured burning the drugs from my blood. Perhaps it was my imagination, but my whole body warmed, my mind cleared a little. Encouraged, I stretched outward, seeking to draw energy to speed the healing process. I ignored the sharp pain behind my eyes that came from working around the last block.

Connor and the other man went about setting up the murder scene to Michael's satisfaction. They unwrapped the Freyson women and placed them side by side, slumped on the bench. Next they injected both with some sort of fluid that must be to counteract the sedative. Otherwise, in an autopsy, questions would be asked.

Hope spurted. If I could delay things long enough, Maeve would wake and use her skills. Could her telekinesis handle three weapons and three men at once? One of them would get off a shot before I could do anything with a single knife. Maeve could do more. I just had to give her time.

I had to try.

My connection to the *sianfath* returned, but too slowly. I couldn't separate Michael's signature from Maeve and Jennifer's. The other men, I could distinguish. They pulled me upright and dragged me aside. Michael raised his arm, the barrel pointed at Jennifer. His finger curled.

Now or never.

I pulled the dirty-orange life-force from Connor and John. But the process was painfully slow – too slow. It was like dragging my arm through thick, wet molasses. My brain was on fire. The men weakened but not fast enough. Michael's shoulders shifted as he steadied his arm.

I released the mental concentration and went back to something I knew better. The men held my arms...perfect. I dropped my weight. They gripped tighter. Even better. John grunted. Michael turned his head. I took a small step forward, dropped to one knee and flicked my arms. Near perfect double throw on the two guards. John let go and tripped over his own feet. Connor rolled into the back of Michael's knees and took him to the ground in a flurry of arms and legs.

A gun went off. I could only hope it hadn't been aimed at Maeve or Jennifer.

Maeve stirred slightly; eyelids fluttering. Only a few more seconds and she could help, surely.

John regained his feet, swaying. Perhaps the after effects of my attempt to take energy from him. Michael and Connor began to disentangle themselves, swearing and shouting. Three at once? With guns? My technique wasn't that good. My heart plummeted. I should have taken at least one out with the knife already.

Hesitation had cost me the advantage.

I ran at John. He raised his head. My palm cupped his chin and carried him up, back and down. His skull hit the turf with sickening hollowness. I couldn't afford to stop and check him.

Where was Michael?

Arms wrapped around me from behind – Connor.

I dropped my hips lower and tried to raise my arms to break the hold. He dropped with me and tightened his grip. My ribs ground against each other. Gasping for breath I tried to headbutt, to shin-kick – anything. He held on.

Panic rose as Michael appeared in front of me. He cast me a disdainful sneer and brushed himself down.

'You aren't worth this much trouble, girl. I'll get the location of the *ocair* from Anna.' He jerked his chin. 'Throw her over the edge.

We can say she killed the adults then suicided. We'll keep the youngest for our experiments.'

Fury sleeted through me and I struggled anew. I was stronger than this idiot. No. Whatever was in that drink weakened me physically as well as mentally.

Michael watched, smiling, as Connor dragged me to the edge.

Out of the darkness a body flew into Michael's. The pair crashed to the ground. I couldn't see who landed on top. I was more focussed on not being thrown over the edge of a three-story building. The weakness in my limbs terrified me. I couldn't think or move fast enough.

Was this what being purely human was like?

I kicked back and found a kneecap. Connor grunted. I dropped my weight and tried to slide out. He tightened his grip around my chest. He adjusted to re-pin my arms, but not quite quickly enough. I scrabbled for the knife in my pocket. It tore straight through the thin material. I jammed the blade up to the hilt in his thigh.

He yelped and his arms relaxed. I slipped free, grabbing one hand and twisting as I turned. I snatched the gun from him. I had him in a wristlock. He wrenched back with a countermove that spoke of serious training. My arm twisted to breaking point. I shoved the gun into his stomach and squeezed the trigger. He turned and deflected my arm. The shot went wild, shattering glass somewhere in the house.

Connor backed me up against the parapet. My feet flew off the ground. My wrist smacked into the concrete and the gun fell. The knife still protruded from his thigh but I couldn't reach it. His mouth stretched into a snarl of white-hot rage and he pushed me further over the void.

Another shot rang out, Connor gasped and jerked. Blood slid down his cheek. He collapsed forward. His momentum tipped me past my balance point.

I fell.

I clutched at the edge of the wall, clinging by fingertips made strong by fear and adrenalin.

Someone grabbed my wrist just as I looked down.

It was remarkably silent this high up – apart from the faint whistling of a warm tropical breeze that stole my breath; breath rushing harshly from my lips. My heart was oddly slow, as though it hadn't yet realised the danger I was in. Wind, breath and the slow, steady pulse of blood in my veins. That's all I could hear. Oh…and the sound of soft, triumphant laughter from the man holding my arm so tightly.

Man? Was it a man, or some sort of ghost? I wasn't sure now. Not sure if he'd keep holding on, or if he'd let go. I craned my neck to try and see his face but it was shadowed. All I glimpsed was the gleam of a pale eye and the white-tipped fingers of a tanned, strong hand.

I glanced down and regretted it. The ground was a long, long way below. Could I survive? I looked up again and the man holding my arm raised his face. The silver glow of moonlight caught his strained, teeth-bared expression.

Logan.

An almost hysterical sob of relief escaped my aching lungs.

He was alive.

It had worked.

'Can't hold on all day, Red.' He grunted. 'Either lose some weight or get yourself back up here.'

I scrabbled against the concrete wall with my toes, trying to find purchase. Pulling against his weight, I got my knees beneath me and inched my way up the wall. This was not as easy as it seemed in the movies.

I was almost level with the railing. Logan gasped. His expression twisted into fear and regret. Then his grip relaxed and he collapsed over the railing.

The handle of my knife, protruded from his neck.

Windows flashed by and the ground rushed closer. With absolute and utter clarity, I knew I would die in a few seconds.

My recurring dream had come true.

Blackness surged; raging and burning out of the depths of my mind.

TWENTY-SIX

<LOGAN!>

Some uncountable time later, I staggered into the front door. My knees and hands shook uncontrollably. My mind burned in unspeakable agony. What had happened? One second I was falling, the next I stood at the front door, unharmed.

Was Logan alive? And Maeve and Jennifer? Was Michael still up there?

I wavered. My mother. If I went back to help the Freysons I might lose the chance to save Anna.

Then, faintly, the sound of someone crying drifted through the still night air. Someone female. Jennifer? I couldn't abandon them.

I took the stairs two at a time. Each jump jarred my skull.

The oak door to the top floor stood open. I crouched down to peer quickly around the frame. Tears of pain blurred my vision. I wiped them away. There was no-one in sight. I crept out. Still nothing.

Outside, a car roared, wheels spinning as it took off down the driveway and into the dark street.

Shit.

The roof garden looked like a riot had taken place. A large pool of blood congealed where Logan had fallen from my shot. The food table lay overturned, plates and rich foods scattered in glistening, colourful piles. Michael and Connor had both vanished. The third man, John, lay on the ground, eyes open. Blood blackened the grass beneath him.

Next to the wall where I'd fallen, Maeve and Jennifer knelt over a still figure. My heart jumped and stole the breath from my lungs. I hurried forward, my vision solely on Logan. After all this, he could not be dead.

'Rowan!' Maeve gaped at me. Her grey top and white pants were spattered with bright red blood. 'But you fell!'

'Later,' I said curtly, gritting my teeth and swallowing nausea. 'Is he...?'

'No.' Maeve bit her lip. 'But we'll lose him if we don't do something fast.'

I dropped as my knees gave way.

Struggling to find my voice through the torture in my head, I whispered, 'Can you heal him?'

'No,' she said. 'There's not enough here for me to draw from. The *sianfath* is too tenuous here. Most of this garden is fake plants. Here.' Her cool fingers brushed my temple and took away the fire.

'Thank you. Hospital?' I couldn't lose him now. He'd tried to save me, now it was my turn. There had to be a way.

'Too far, and we can't risk it.'

Jennifer sobbed uncontrollably nearby, curled into a miserable heap with her arms wrapped around her knees and her face hidden.

'OK.' I closed my eyes. 'I think *I* can do this. I don't need the forest, but you'll have to guide me. Let me show you.' Quickly I flashed Maeve a mental image of what I wanted to do.

Her eyes widened, narrowed in thought and firmed into decision. She nodded.

'It's our only chance. Jennifer!' At Maeve's sharp tone Jennifer's head snapped up, her lower lip trembling, and eyes reddened. 'We need your help. Pull yourself together. Press here. Keep pressure on this. Now!'

Shaking, Jennifer sniffed, wiped her eyes and took over staunching the sluggish flow of blood from the knife wound. Her tears dripped onto Logan's pale face. He didn't move.

The knife must have missed his jugular but only just. The amount of blood suggested some damage to a major artery or vein. Fear threatened to overcome my thinking again.

Maeve touched my arm, leaving bloody prints. 'You can do this, Rowan. I trust you. Here's what you have to do. But you must release the energy correctly. Too fast and it will kill him.' She touched my forehead, Gifting the entire healing process, then quickly draining away the resulting pain.

I rocked back, absorbing it then nodding my understanding.

'I should take that last block down before you try.' Maeve's worry loomed large in her grey eyes.

'There's no time.' I reached for Logan.

Maeve gripped my wrists hard. 'It could kill you. This much psi work and this much pain. Your mind may not be able to handle it. You could burn out.'

'That doesn't change the fact that Logan *will* die if I don't try.' Maeve didn't let go and I shook her roughly off. 'It's *my* fault you're all here. My fault he's like this. Let me fix it.' I wiped the back of a hand across my eyes, ignoring Maeve's shocked, troubled look. 'Jen, use your telekinesis. Try to keep his heart going. If it stops, keep his blood moving and his lungs working. Keep oxygen to his brain. Can you do that?'

The girl nodded, eyes huge in a pale face. I took Maeve's hand and laid my other over the top of Jennifer's, touching both her skin and Logan's. It was the only way I could be certain to clearly distinguish their energies from every other living thing.

My ability to draw life from animals and people had to be closely akin to the standard ability to heal by drawing energy from the trees. Mine simply encompassed all living things, which gave me access to more energy than Maeve could draw on.

My head felt remarkably clear now. Closing my eyes, I opened myself to the world. There: glimmerings of the tiny lives of ants, mice, the rooftop plants, other people in the buildings around. Extending myself outward I touched the energy of hundreds of people in nearby houses.

With a source at my metaphorical fingertips, I drew a fraction of energy from each and every life form – enough to make them a little tired perhaps but no more. The energy flowed into me on invisible threads, pouring orange, and silver-green, power into my frail body until I could barely contain its sizzling potential.

Then I turned my gaze inward and dived into the wound in Logan's neck. It was messy and one quick inspection was enough to show I had neither the skill nor the experience to heal it correctly, even with the Gifting.

Maeve. I didn't bother knocking on the woman's smooth mental shield, there wasn't time. Logan was close to death. I simply created a new door in the imaginary blankness and opened it – from my side.

Ignoring Maeve's horrified astonishment, I showed what I'd seen inside Logan.

I can't do it, I said tersely, holding the power in my body by force, fighting the pain growing with it. I had to let it go soon or I would explode. *I don't have the skill to control the flow of energy that delicately. I'll feed you the power, you do the work.*

Maeve flicked me one more worried look, then turned to work on Logan. Her hand trembled as she moved Jennifer's out of the way.

Using my own arm as a channel, I fed power into Maeve slowly. The urge to pour it in like water in the hopes it would fix him faster was almost irresistible. But that would kill both of them and possibly Jennifer too.

The agony in my head blossomed into anguish. Darkness shivered and shifted but, because the threat wasn't to me, it stayed in its cage.

Energy trickled from myself into Maeve, who directed it; mended, stitched muscle, bone and artery back together. Then, when it was done, I pulled back, almost drained, blinded and nauseated, my brain on fire.

No. Maeve's weariness softened her mental voice to a whisper. *His heart stopped. I need one last shock to restart it. You'll have to do it directly, though.*

Willingly, I pushed through the wall of black pain. I gathered stored energy into an imaginary ball and threw it into Logan. His body jerked and stilled. With a sob I pulled the last of my reserves and shocked him again. I slumped forward, so tired and disorientated with pain I was unable to even reach out for more.

His body jerked... and he sucked a shallow, shuddering breath... and another.

The rooftop garden spun as blackness enveloped me and I passed into oblivion.

TWENTY-SEVEN

'Prithee Kieran, no! 'Tis too dangerous.' A woman's anxious face swam into view; beautiful, frightened, distracted. She glanced over her shoulder.

'We must, my love, recall thy promise and thy warning. We dursn't leave the child in with strangers, bereft of knowledge of his heritage.' This came from a man, his face hidden in shadow. He stroked the woman's face.

She nodded, reluctantly. Leaning down, she kissed the child's forehead and he wrapped his pudgy arms around her neck, squeezing. When she withdrew, tears stained her face.

She stood and used the hem of her long skirt of mop her cheeks. 'Very well. 'Tis done. Now do your part. But make it hold fast for at least a decade. 'Twill be too much to deal with 'til he's of an age to understand. And perchance we may be able to return before...' She looked at Kieran. Hiding a sob in her hands she ran from the room.

Kieran sighed and picked the child up gently. The boy giggled and tugged on the man's long hair. A flash of teeth in the shadows gave the impression of a smile. Kieran set the boy down on a bed of rough sacking. Holding the child's face between his hands he stared into the grey eyes. Then he stood and left the room without a backward look.

Alone in a small, dark room that smelled of dirt and animals, fear stepped in. Where were they? No one came. The boy cried in the dark but still no-one came for him.

Willingly, I floated up from darkness and distress into awareness. Someone called my name, urgently, with more than a touch of fear in their tone. Awake, I kept my eyes closed. In every kidnapping movie the idiot opened their eyes too soon. I extended my other senses. I lay in an awkward position: my neck bent, legs tucked up. A low-level thrum and sickening movement gave a clue to location – the back seat of a car. My head on someone's leg. Logan's leg. The Freysons' car, then.

The events of the evening slammed into me and I sat upright with a gasp, clutching at the door armrest. Warm hands held me up and I squinted into Logan's concerned face. His bloodied shirt was torn, revealing the silvery vest beneath. His eyes were shadowed and strained, but he lived. The car lurched around a corner and he gathered me into a hug that, for some weird reason, made me want to cry. Pressed against his chest, my face tucked into his neck, a knot of tension dissolved.

He was alright.

Yes. His mental voice sounded amused. *Thanks to you. I would like some explanations, though. I'll apologise properly later, when we're alone.*

'Apologise?' I leaned back so I could see him in the flickering orange half-light of passing streetlamps.

Maeve clicked the windscreen wipers on as a faint fall of rain misted the glass. Thunder rumbled.

He nodded gravely. 'I let you fall and I promised you I wouldn't. You saved my life but I let you down – literally.'

'I did shoot you.' I pointed at the blood.

'I told you to.'

'The blood packs and vest under your shirt were a nice touch, by the way.' I gave a shaky laugh and touched the warm, flexible metal. 'Pretty big risk, though.'

He picked my hand off his chest and cradled it to his cheek, leaving a smear of half-dried blood. I shivered. The memory of shooting him was difficult to erase, even though I'd been reasonably sure of his safety at the time.

But that left one question still unanswered. I pulled free and leaned away again in order to better see his reaction.

'What the hell were you doing there, anyway? How did you know where I was? Did you follow me?'

Logan smiled slightly, though it was mirthless and his grey eyes hardened. 'When I saw you with Paul Eisen I could hardly think straight. I thought you'd betrayed me…us.'

'No.' I scrubbed my stained palms on my pants. 'We met at the shop. I just wanted to pass a message to Anna, to make sure she was safe. Then I was on the news and I had to distract him.'

'Yes.' He nodded slowly. 'I worked that out. Your shields aren't perfect yet. I knew, then, where you were going, and why. I'm sorry, Rowan. I let you walk into a trap.'

I grimaced, about to wave away his apology, then stopped as the import of his words hit home. Staring blankly at him, I reviewed the evening and the last few days. *Let* me walk into a trap? That implied he not only knew where I was going, but that he knew it *was* a trap, even before I'd left him in the dojo. A slow burn grew in my belly.

Of course he had. He knew the person hunting me was Michael Eisen. How else had Logan thought to wear the vest? He'd let me go because I was perfect bait. I'd been right to suspect his apparent altruism. There was none.

'You knew.' I shifted away on the seat, watching Logan, wanting him to deny it. 'You'd already worked out who was killing your people. You knew it was Michael when you met me, didn't you? Or was it before you met me?'

He said nothing, his face set, mind-shield smooth and hard as glass.

I shoved across to the other side of the car, sickness growing alongside the anger. In front, Maeve half-turned her head but didn't speak. Jennifer cast her eyes down, fiddling with something on her lap.

'Oh my God. I've been such an idiot. You've known all along, haven't you?' I ran a hand over my face, reassessing everything the Freysons had said and done. 'Was meeting me planned or just dumb luck? Ha!' The laugh was sarcasm rather than humour. 'You weren't even enrolled at Cairns High were, you? You read that in my thoughts when we met and hacked yourself into the student database so I could contact you.' I eyed him with growing disgust. 'The idea to contact you wasn't even mine, was it? You planted it. *That's* why I didn't cut and leave town like I should have.'

He didn't reply, his face pale in the flickering orange streetlights. Maeve pressed her lips together.

'So how long did it take you to work out that I'd make the perfect little fish for Michael? Seconds after we met or did you deliberate for as much as five minutes?' I enjoyed the flinch and grimace that evoked. 'And going out with Paul, that wasn't my idea, either, was it? I should have guessed. Nice bit of reverse psychology there. I'll bet Maeve was proud of that.'

He flicked a look at the back of Maeve's head, sealing any doubts I'd had about who ran this show.

'Oh!' I glared at Maeve in the mirror. 'And tonight. When I suddenly thought to call Paul. That was you, wasn't it. I'd never do something that stupid.'

She said nothing, her eyes fixed on the road.

'Both of you.' I pressed on. 'You knew it was wrong and you still let me go tonight because it was too good a chance to pass up. You endangered my mother's life and mine just to get yourself close to Michael in the *hopes* you could kill him.'

I curled a lip. 'You thought using a helpless human woman and keeping me ignorant was a good way to further your high and mighty, noble cause? Wow. That gives me *such* a good feeling about working with you.' I turned to stare at Maeve. 'And was letting yourself be kidnapped and drugged part of the plan? Or was that just stupidity? Because from where I sit, it looks remarkably like you screwed up.'

There was a long silence.

'No, of course we didn't plan for Anna to be involved or for Jen to be taken.' Logan replied at last, his voice low and strained. 'Eisen's men backtracked your taxi. You'd disarmed the security on the side gate. They snuck in and darted Maeve and Jen.'

I refused to succumb to the twinge of guilt that followed his words. This situation was *not* of my making; at least, not entirely.

'And yes, we suspected it was him, but we weren't certain,' he agreed, his expression grave. 'We had it narrowed down to a few possibilities. Eventually, Eisen's pursuit of you – Anna and Calain's daughter – gave him away.' Logan scrubbed at his face, exhaustion showing for the first time. 'He clearly sees himself as some sort of chivalric defender of the purity of the human race.'

'I don't give a damn, and that's crap.' I cut across, anger boiling over. 'He's not some crazed, revenge-seeking, racist psychopath. He may be working with the Mors Ferrum, but he's more about money than purity. He has his own agenda. He was very keen to use me as a medical guinea pig. Anna told me his labs are running studies on anti-aging proteins. I can guess where they source them from.'

'Rowan—' Maeve's soft voice interrupted.

'No.' I snapped. 'Don't even start, Maeve. I do *not* care what noble reasons you had – and revenge for your son's death, by the way, is *not* noble. There were any number of points when you could've treated me as a person you cared about, and told me. Even asked me for help. And I would have, willingly, if I'd understood.'

'I wanted—' Logan began.

'I came *back* for you,' I snarled at him. 'I could have gone after my mother, but I trusted you. Felt like I owed you, so I came back. I saved your *goddamned* life and you betrayed me.'

TWENTY-EIGHT

What the hell do I say?

<There's nothing you can say. Let her be.>

Dammit, Maeve. This is our fault. Anna—

<Every war has casualties, Logan. You have to separate yourself emotionally.>

Well, you'd know, wouldn't you?

Logan said nothing, his expression hooded, his eyes meeting Maeve's in the rear view for one, brief, troubled moment.

I sent him a bleak look. 'I'm done. You blew it. Stop the car. I'm getting out here.' I grabbed my bag from the floor and stared out the window. The car slid into a side street and stopped. The door lever was turning under my hand when Logan spoke again.

'What about Anna? What about Michael?'

'What do you mean? Didn't Paul take her home? Is he in this too?'

'I can't tell how much *he* knows, but Michael got away,' Logan said. He pointed out the front window. 'We were taking you home to try and get to her before he did. Michael wants this *ocair* thing and he thinks you or Anna has it. You don't think he'll just give up, do you?'

'Dammit!' I slid back and rebuckled. 'Drive, Maeve.' When Logan opened his mouth I cut him off. 'Don't even think about speaking to me.'

A quick phone call to our home phone produced nothing but Anna's cheerful voicemail message. A second one, to her cellphone, got the same result.

I turned my face to the window and hardened my mental shields. I should have known better than to trust anyone. Hadn't that been my life's lesson? It had kept me and Anna alive for years. And now it was clear what my father tried to protect me from – not just the Ferrum but my own kind; his kind.

It took several minutes to redirect my thoughts into something more useful. Betrayal was a difficult feeling to release. All I could do for now was bury it. The darkness in me fed on it.

The rest of the short drive played out in stony silence. I chose not to listen to the fast subtext flying between the others. Whatever they planned they could do without me. I needed none of their help.

When the car halted, half a block away from the entrance to our apartment complex, I turned to Logan. I kept my tone low and reasonable, but couldn't bring myself to meet his eyes.

'Go. I don't need your help.'

Logan ignored me, climbing out and walking around to my side. 'You don't know who's up there. Don't be a fool.'

Slamming the car door and shouldering my pack, I sent him a scathing glare. 'I've already been a fool for trusting you once, Logan. I won't make the same mistake twice. Get out of my way.'

A long silence followed, during which a two-way conversation went on behind his hard expression. He stepped aside. I strode towards the building, trying not to let the sound of a car door closing and the rev of an engine accelerating away have any affect.

I failed. It hurt, in spite of everything.

Bitter anger burned in my throat. Anger at both myself and the Freysons, Michael, Paul, and even at Anna for being stupid enough to fall for a con-artist.

I approached the entrance cautiously. The after-hours reception desk was empty, which was unusual. The secured apartment block hired a twenty-four-hour concierge-guard.

A quick look over the desk gave the answer. I gulped, dropped to the floor and put my back to the wall. Judging by the amount of blood pooling on the floor under the body, calling the paramedics was a waste of time. I palmed a throwing knife, wishing for a gun.

I closed my eyes, listening. Nothing. A quick peek around the corner showed nothing in the hallway to the elevators. I'd have to risk it. I ran the ten steps to the elevators, half-expecting a bullet. The doors swooshed open at a touch of the button.

Empty.

Inside, I pressed for the fourth floor and rode it up. A plan that didn't involve putting both myself and my mother at risk again would be nice. Nothing sprang to mind.

On the fourth floor, I checked the hall then slid out of the elevator. The modern, white-and-grey decorated corridor was empty. I didn't expect anyone to be waiting. Our apartment was on the fifth. Soft carpet underfoot absorbed any stray footfalls as I darted into the fire escape. With the door closed carefully behind, I peered upward.

Nothing.

Five long jumps brought me to the fifth-floor door. I punched the security code for entrance then eased the handle and opened the door a crack. Our door was in sight, and unguarded.

Keeping out of the scope of the peephole, I pressed an ear to the wood. Nothing. I relaxed the tight control on my new skills. Tentatively, I extended one tiny tendril of self into the room, trying to gauge the presence of humans inside.

Pain flashed a warning. I retreated, biting my lip against an involuntary groan. There were at least two people inside. I couldn't tell who, though. If I was lucky, it was Paul and Anna and this would be a quick and easy rescue. At the very least, the attempt showed I couldn't use all of my newfound abilities without an incapacitating level of pain. Which made them pointless, as far as I was concerned. Back to basics, then.

I headed for the roof exit. Our place was on the top floor and my code gave access to the roof deck. The front door was likely to be watched but it was out of sight of the roof entrance.

Outside, the seemingly ever-present threat of summer storms made good and the sky opened on me. Rain tumbled down, fat and cool on my hot skin. I vaulted over the token rail separating our outdoor area from the rest of the roof and crouched behind a chair. I peered through the downpour, into the brilliantly lit apartment.

Disorder and chaos. We were always a little messy, but this was more than normal. Someone had upended every drawer and emptied every cupboard in search of something. The *ocair?*

So where were they? The main living area, with its brilliant blue and green cushions shredded and scattered on the floor and couches overturned, was empty. In the kitchen, the fridge and cupboards stood open, contents smashed or strewn on the floor. Every picture was stripped from the wall and tossed aside. Shards of glass glittered on the white tiles.

Throwing knife in hand, I tried the balcony door and slipped inside when it gave easily. I left my backpack tucked behind a couch then stepped carefully amongst the broken glass and paused at the hall entrance. No guard at the front door. My room opened off the hall. It appeared to be empty. All my scant wardrobe lay scattered across the floor, my boxes shredded.

Avoiding an overturned lamp and a pile of broken crockery, I picked up the phone handset on the wall. Silence. No wonder it had gone to voicemail. The line was cut. I didn't bother checking the odds and ends drawer in the kitchen. The gun my mother kept wouldn't be there. Knives it was. I collected a kitchen utility knife on the way past and slid it into my leather belt with the others I'd pulled from my bag. It wasn't exactly a throwing knife but at least gave me four blades instead of just three.

As ready as I'd ever be, I glided towards the main bedroom. Crashing of cupboard doors and a male voice swearing attested to a search in there as well.

No sound of Anna, but she would still be sedated, anyway.

Three steps from the door, I took a long slow breath to steady my nerves and hefted my first throwing knife. The second rested in my other hand, ready. Hopefully it wouldn't be needed. Hopefully it would be one knife, one throw. If the second person wasn't Anna then things could get tricky. I had no easy cover, in this bare, narrow hall. Nowhere to retreat if there were more men inside. Knives were slower than bullets.

I slipped in, found my target and threw. The knife sank squarely into an exposed back. The man straightened, his astonished gaze catching mine in the wall mirror. He gargled and collapsed to the floor. A second man stood next to him.

Damn!

Unless she was in the ensuite, Anna was not there. I'd felt only two people. Michael had already taken her.

TWENTY-NINE

We have to help her.

<No, Logan, we don't. She's made it abundantly clear and we can't prioritise an individual over our people's wellbeing.>

Dammit, Maeve. We caused this. Her mother's in danger because of us. She saved my life twice. We owe her.

<Logan...it's not safe to be near her now. Can't you feel how angry and afraid she is? There's something in her that responds to that. She can't control it. If it's released, she could—>

I know. That's why we have to help. She's spent her whole life not trusting anyone. She trusted us and we betrayed that. She won't be able to control what she's so afraid of on her own. She won't admit it, but she needs my help.

<If she won't admit it, then she won't let you help. You'll die, along with everyone else in that building.>

I know. I have to try.

The second man turned, his gun coming into view.

I threw my second knife.

The man brought his gun up. He shifted. The knife caught him in the arm instead of the body. He yelped, dropped the gun and swore inventively. He yanked the blade out and flicked it inexpertly back at me. I had ample time to dodge. I used the movement to gain ground. If I could grab him before he regathered the gun... The knife hit the wall and ricocheted into the hall, tinkling across the tiles.

A dark figure emerged from the ensuite.

A third man.

Silhouetted in brilliant light, was the distinctive shape of a gun. I changed direction in mid-stride and dived to the floor behind the bed. The *phut* of a silenced shot hit the wall. The bed was all that stood between me and another bullet.

The odds were not fabulous. I needed to even them somehow. Spinning on my back, I placed both feet against the bed base. I dug my fingers into the pile carpet and shoved.

The base rolled and I rolled with it, keeping out of view. It hit something. A strangled yell and a thump said someone else was down. Last throwing knife in hand, I peered through the narrow gap beneath the bed.

There. Two bodies. Where was the third man?

'Enough.' A smooth voice, full of scorn and superiority, sounded from above me. 'Drop it.'

Connor towered over me, gun pointed squarely at my head. He stood just too far away. He could get a shot off before I could reach him with hand, foot or knife. Icy realisation solidified rage into fear in the pit of my stomach. I let the knife slide to the carpet.

Shit. Shit. Shit.

I turned, slowly, to gather my feet beneath me. How could I get closer?

'No.' He gestured with the muzzle. 'Stay down. I know how fast you are.' His gaunt face and deepset dark eyes betrayed only professional interest. The gun stayed solidly on my head. A red-stained bandage on his thigh didn't seem to bother him. Nor did the sluggish trickle of blood down the side of his head from Logan's shot.

I obeyed; numb, vulnerable and exposed. The handle of the kitchen knife pressed into the small of my back, hidden but inaccessible.

This was my own fault. If I'd let Logan come it would have evened the odds. My arrogance, distrust and anger had got me into this. There was no one to get me out. Steeling myself for the bullet, I tried to calm the sick fluttering in my belly.

'I dropped you off a building,' Connor said, tugging at the cuff on his sleeve. 'I'd be quite interested to know how you survived.'

'Just lucky, I guess. What now?'

'I very much doubt luck had anything to do with it.' Connor smiled thinly, the gun muzzle unwavering. 'Mr Eisen and Mr Dyson will be *most* interested to hear of your survival. Mr Eisen was *so* looking forward to dissecting you. And Mr Dyson – the head of the Mors Ferrum, you know – will be keen to study you. I believe this trip was worthwhile after all.' He touched a finger to the blood on his cheek and inspected it without changing expression.

'Where's Anna?' At least I didn't sound frightened. That was some comfort. Not much.

'Long since gone to the airport.' Connor pulled a second weapon out from his waistband and checked the clip. 'By this time, she'll be on an MJE jet for Brisbane.'

A curious mixture of relief and horror washed through me. Anna was alive but still in Michael's custody; still oblivious to what was going on and who was responsible. I thrust the knowledge aside.

If there was a future, getting Anna back lay there, not here. Here and now I had to find a way out of this. Connor was not the sort of man to underestimate me again. He was a professional and probably harbouring a grudge for the taser and the knife to the thigh.

'So, what are you going to do with me?' I did my best to ignore the narrow black hole aiming death at me.

He smiled a little more broadly. 'Well…' He pointed the second weapon at my body. A dart gun. 'First you're going to tell me where Anna keeps the *ocair*. Then we'll take the second jet to Brisbane to meet up with Mr Eisen.' He raised thin brows. 'His facility there is well-established and will be overjoyed to have you as their…guest.'

'Why the hell would I tell you anything?' I allowed scorn to colour my voice. 'Besides, as I told Michael, I don't even know what an *ocair* is, let alone where to find it.'

'Ah.' He inspected me thoughtfully. 'I think I believe you. I'd already come to the conclusion it wasn't here, anyway. Thank you for making it so easy. Now we can get on with stage two.' He pulled the dart-gun trigger. The dart slapped into my thigh and the familiar, warm lassitude spread through the muscle. He threw the dartgun aside and re-trained the nine millimetre between my eyes. His lips twitched into a patient, condescending smile.

There had to be something I could do. I couldn't just lie here on the floor, waiting to be taken captive and studied like some animal. I had to save Anna.

Desperation and anger makes me do dumb things.

I'd observed Maeve's work. I knew what to do. I turned inward and contemplated that last block in my mind. I couldn't remove it, but I saw how to open it temporarily – enough to release the bonds holding the shadows fast.

If I did it, what would come out? What would I do? Who was I, really?

Connor slid his phone out of his pocket and thumbed the screen. No. If he told Michael I lived I'd lose any element of surprise.

The choice was made. I would live with the consequences. Or not. I opened the door.

Darkness surged, exploding out of hiding, encompassing the world in its fiery arms, burning away the drug…

…And I stood behind Connor, disorientated but fully alive to the danger he still posed. I grabbed his right arm and levered it across my forearm. The bone snapped at the elbow with a sickening crack.

He shrieked and dropped to his knees. Snatching at the fallen gun, he rolled and came up with the weapon in his left hand.

He pulled the trigger.

Something thumped into my body. The mirror behind me shattered, showering silver onto the cream carpet.

Blackness roared again, smashing seals and barriers, blinding me with pain and power. Stretched, enveloped, besieged in both body and mind, I watched my hand reach towards Connor. His eyes jumped to my stomach. Real fear flickered in him. Something warm slid down my leg. He raised the gun, his arm shaking.

Connecting to the *sianfath* was surprisingly easy this time. I simply extended myself to include him and the two men still lying, half alive, on the floor behind the bed. Then beyond to touch the life force of everyone else in the building. I was simultaneously three hundred or more people. Three hundred lives at my mercy. It was a curious feeling and I was tempted to explore; to see exactly how far I could stretch.

A faint sound from the floor brought my attention back. Connor gaped at me, his eyes stark. What did he see in my face to make him look so? His finger tightened on the trigger. I swayed to one side and something punched my left arm.

I ignored it.

He pulled the trigger once more. I withdrew everything he was: his life, his energy, his essence. An empty husk collapsed bonelessly to the floor. His angular face slackened. Dark eyes stared blankly at the ceiling. The gun fell to the carpet. The bright ball of Connor's life-energy flared inside me.

One of the other men groaned from behind the bed and I walked around to stand over him. Somewhere I registered pain; wounds that should be addressed. A mind within my own, broken and drowning in agony and horror. I ignored it. Pain was illusory. I was bigger than mere body and mind now.

I was the world and it was mine.

I extended a hand towards the men lying behind the bed. Their life-lights were bright and compelling. They would heal me. Their lives were nothing.

'Red, stop.'

Something in that voice gave me pause. Someone familiar stood in the doorway. Logan. The name came to me as though shouted down a tunnel. Friend. No: betrayer of trust. I eyed him calmly. His mental touch brushed my mind. I swatted it aside. He flinched. His eyes widened as Connor's had.

Was he afraid, too? Good. It was time someone feared me, rather than the reverse. I'd spent too many years running and hiding; centuries of being hunted. Now I had the means to change that. Time the world saw what I could do.

'Who are you?' His soft, incredulous question fell into the silence.

I stretched the mouth I owned into a smile. 'I'm Ruadhán. I am what the *Daoine sidhe* are meant to be. I am one with the *sianfath* and…' I reached out to pull his mind into mine. 'I'm everything she was afraid of. I'm what the world needs. What the *Daoine* need to overcome the Mors Ferrum. Join me. Be one with me.'

'Stop it.' Logan backed away, holding his shields firm. 'Whoever you are, you're not her. Red wouldn't do *this.* ' He pointed to the shell of Connor, twisted on the floor.

A hollow laugh emerged from my lips. 'Then you don't know her. Why do you think she keeps running? Not because she's afraid of these fools.' I drained the life-force of one Michael's men with no more thought than drinking water. The burning brightness filled me. 'It's because she's afraid of *herself* and what she's done.'

Logan pursed his lips. 'We've all done things we regret to survive. She said she'd never intentionally—'

My lips twisted into a smirk. 'No. She's afraid because she *doesn't* regret them. And now, I think, she's almost ready. Once I take that last block down we'll be able to—'

Something slapped into my thigh, two of the faintest mosquito bites compared to the pain held at bay elsewhere. I plucked the darts free and tossed them aside, sneering contemptuously at the man on the floor who'd dared to shoot.

'A bullet couldn't stop me, you idiot, so this won't either.' I laughed at him, draining his life-force in a millisecond and smiling as he slumped. 'I will simply—'

The room spun and the body sagged under the drug's influence. Logan appeared at my side, holding me up. Staring hard into my eyes, searching my soul, he spoke,

'Red, hold on. I know you're in there. Fight him. Let me help you. Trust me. Just this once. You have to trust me. Please!'

He kissed me.

The room darkened. Pain, held at bay, exploded in every neurone of my body. Weakened and horror-struck I lacked the strength to bind the shadows away again. I clung to Logan. To the feel of his mouth on mine, the fierce power of his mind, helping me fight back against myself.

I hesitated, afraid to let him in. I'd been betrayed too often. Did he just want this power for himself?

No, this time I needed help. Without it the monster would be unleashed on the world. With my abilities, nothing would stand against it...me.

I had to take the risk and trust him.

I opened my shields and thoughts to him.

Together we waged war.

The strength of Logan's mind augmented mine. His skill directed my power. I stood against that which was, and was not, both me and my father. I battled myself and Calain, fought my hate and his, my fear and his, my blackest impulses…and his.

And, together, Logan and I forced my will upon the darkness that was Calain's memories, embedded in my mind. I screamed my self-loathing defiance into the faceless morass of my soul and thrust his dark presence back into its prison. He retreated into the darkest corner of my mind, locked away again in the dungeon of Lothien; hidden, waiting.

Smaller, lost, horrified, self-aware at last, I touched my stomach. Blood ran freely, pumping with my heart's every erratic beat. I looked to Logan, whispering his name. The edges of my vision yellowed into unconsciousness.

He caught me as I fell.

'Stay with me, Red,' were the last words I heard.

THIRTY

She's waking up.

<I know>

Is it just her?

<Yes>

What do we tell her?

<Only what we must. We still need to get to Michael.>

Dammit, Maeve. When will this stop? You can't keep using her this way.

<I can and I shall, Logan. If you don't approve of my methods, leave. There are more important things at risk than one girl, especially one this dangerous.>

She's not—

<She is, and you know it.>

Lethargy pinned my limbs to the bed and held my eyelids closed. Even my lungs felt heavy in my chest, each breath a struggle. Fighting against the dregs of sleep, I opened my eyes to a ceiling that had no place in my life. The bed beneath felt unfamiliar, the sheets new and crisp, mattress too soft, threatening to suck me back into darkness.

I shied away from the thought. Darkness. There was something…It had taken over, evicted me from my own mind, empowered and terrified, killed without regret. Oh my God. What was I?

'You are Rowan Gilmore, nothing more,' stated a no-nonsense voice from the half-lit room.

'Maeve?' I cleared my throat and tried again when the word emerged broken. 'What happened?' Under the blankets, I prodded at my stomach and found only a small, raised scar where blood had poured forth only…How long ago?

'It's healed. You're fine.'

A rustle of cloth and a dark shape moved closer. I flinched away, memories of the night closing my throat with self-hatred.

'No.' I struggled from beneath the suffocating blankets. 'I'm not fine. I don't know what I am, but fine isn't it.'

The window curtains twitched aside, allowing pre-dawn pink to softly illuminate the room. Maeve returned to sit on the bed, her face drawn and shadowed by more than the absence of light. I held her gaze in silence. She glanced at the door. It opened and Logan entered. He moved soundlessly across the wooden floor and perched on the end of the bed.

'How long was I out?' I frowned at them both. 'What day is it?'

'Only the next morning,' Maeve replied, her eyes troubled. 'Do you…remember what happened?'

I looked away, slid across Logan's impassive expression and caught sight of my own face in a mirror. Lingering horror limned my eyes. Of course I remembered. How could I forget losing control of my own mind to someone…thing else? The heady lure of limitless potential. Easy death. The satisfying taste of energy drawn from the lives of others. I shivered and touched my face, half-expecting to feel someone else's jaw.

'I was…Calain, and…everything...everyone, all at once. I…he...we killed Connor and those other men.' I studied my palm wonderingly. 'It was so easy and I…he did it without caring, without even thinking. What was he, my father, some sort of psychopath?'

Tears glimmered in Maeve's eyes. 'No, and neither are you.'

'So what am I?' I pulled the sheet up, feeling the need for protection, though from what I wasn't sure. 'What was he? Could he do what I did?'

'He was a half-breed, and no, he couldn't.'

I turned to Logan. 'I thought you said he was full-blood sidhe?'

'Yes,' Maeve agreed, 'but half Light and half Dark. He would never reveal to me his parentage, only that he believed he'd inherited the Dark from his father. I know he was concerned it would overcome him.'

'What? Aren't Light and Dark just a way of distinguishing between two warring factions.' I glanced between the two. 'Is it more than that?'

Logan nodded, speaking for the first time, his voice tight with some unidentifiable emotion. 'It's a gene affecting brain chemistry. In the best cases it causes mild depression and anxiety. In the worst, megalomania, paranoia and insanity. Of course, we only know this now because of Maeve's research. Before we just knew it ran in families.'

'Insanity...' I ran a hand through my hair and inspected my reflection again. My father's grey eyes stared back. 'Can you test me for the gene?'

'Of course,' Maeve assured me, 'but I don't have any laboratory facilities here and I can't send your bloodwork to a pathology lab.'

'But he couldn't do what I did, could he? So what happened? What did I do?' Sick realisation settled in my stomach. If Calain's presence hadn't been responsible for Connor's death, then it meant some part of *me* was that ruthless, unemotional, uncaring.

'In the old language, it's called *skath sheel*.' There was a tremor in Maeve's voice that, in anyone else, I would label as fear.

'Shadow-thought,' I translated aloud. It didn't help.

'The last I heard of who had the skill,' Maeve said quietly, 'was Aeona Silverblade. The most powerful sidhe ever recorded. She disappeared in the early fifteenth century during a battle in Wales and no one knows what happened to her.'

'What could she do?' I whispered, afraid of the answer.

'What Logan said you did,' she returned matter-of-factly. 'She could attenuate her whole self into the *sianfath*, leaving her body behind if she wanted. She could also absorb power from any living thing. Channel it through herself into others. It's similar to our ability. But we can only draw from plants and let that power flow through in small quantities to others. She could take from humans as well. And store it in vast amounts before releasing it.'

'That's it.' Hope faded. 'That's what I can do.'

This time there was no mistaking the naked flash of fear in Maeve's eyes, although she hid it behind a brisk, schoolteacherish front. 'I suspected as much when we healed Logan. There's always a price to pay for great power, dear. If you join completely with the *sianfath* your heart will stop and your body will die. It's imperative you always leave a little of yourself in your body.'

She wrapped her arms around her waist. 'In the case the other part of the gift, it is a matter of kill or be killed.'

A shiver sleeted across my skin. 'What does that mean?'

'From what little I know of Aeona's ability, it means,' Maeve said, 'that if she drew enough power to kill, she had to expel it or the energy would extinguish her life instead. Given the status of women in that era, her fate was to be the pawn of kings who used her skill against their enemies. They held her infant hostage to force her co-operation. Rumour was she died attempting to obliterate an army. I, personally, hope she took her child and walked out because she couldn't stand the killing any longer. We'll never know, I suppose.'

A cold stone of horror settled in the pit of my stomach. 'Why aren't I dead then? I drew Connor's life from him, and those other two. I held them inside myself. Why didn't it kill me?'

Maeve slanted me a sideways look and pursed her lips, preventing speech.

I took firm hold of myself. 'What aren't you telling me, Maeve?'

The older woman stood. 'You healed yourself. That's where the energy went. You used the lives of others to heal yourself.' There was condemnation in her tone.

'Maeve!' Logan's interjection earned him a haughty glare. '*You* don't get to judge her.'

I buried a flash of hurt under a harsh laugh. 'She's right, though. Even if I don't remember, it's still the truth.'

'To be fair...' Maeve slowly brushed down her skirt. '...you would've died within minutes. I don't know how you did it, either. Logan says you were unconscious. All we know is that, by the time I arrived, you were healed. Logan hadn't had time to do more than catch you.' She looked down her nose at me. 'If I had to guess, I'd say Calain did it.'

She stepped away from the bed, then paused. 'How did you survive the fall off Michael's roof?'

I searched my memories and came up with nothing – just black fury. 'I honestly don't know. It's...there's a gap.' I gave up, frustrated. 'I just found myself standing at the front door.'

Maeve chewed at her lower lip. 'Has anything similar occurred previously? A memory loss, I mean?'

I nodded slowly. 'Twice. Both times when I was in trouble. Two years ago, in Japan, when I was a passenger in a car accident. Somehow I ended up outside the car. The accident was a setup. Michael's men were waiting for me. They took me when I was still disorientated. Knocked me unconscious.' I shuddered at the memory: the abduction; what I'd done to survive and escape; the fallout; the hurried, secretive departure.

I turned the thoughts aside. 'And once, when I was thirteen, in a cathedral during an earthquake. I was there on a school trip when two men cornered me. The roof fell in and I ended up ten metres away. It crushed them.'

'And you have no recollection of what you did or how you did it?' Maeve leaned forward, her grey eyes intent. 'Well, if I had to guess, I'd say Calain helped you there, too, bizarre as that sounds. I think he's left a part of himself in your mind. More than just memories. A sort of protection mechanism behind that last block. Whenever you're in danger he…takes over.'

'But how, exactly?'

Maeve let out a sigh. 'I don't know. I'd like to take down that last block and find out, though.'

'No!' I stood, mastering unexpected weakness in my knees, and moved to put a chair between us. Purely symbolic, but there was no way I was letting Maeve mess about in my head again.

'No, I'm not ready. There's too much of him in there. I don't think I could hold onto myself if I open that.' I clung to the chair. 'I promised, after Japan, that I wouldn't…kill… anyone again. Now…Calain…' I pressed cold fingers to my mouth to stop the sob bottled in my throat from escaping. 'If that last block comes down there'll be nothing to stop him from using me like that again.'

'It's ok.' Logan walked over and gripped my shoulder. 'She won't do anything you don't want. I promise. Relax, Red.'

I sank into the chair as my knees gave way. Logan crouched before me, peering into my face.

'Do you remember anything else from last night?'

I shied away from the memory, not wanting to relive it yet fully aware it would haunt me for the rest of my life. 'No.' I closed my eyes. 'Wait, yes. Michael and Connor both said something about the *ocair*. Connor was searching for it in Anna's apartment.'

'Did they say what it was?' Maeve said, her gaze abstracted.

'No. Logan said it means 'key', but key to what?'

'Yes, it does. But I don't know what the context is,' Maeve said thoughtfully. 'Why is Michael looking for it?'

'I don't know,' I insisted, folding my arms over my chest, 'but it has to be important. They first asked me about it five years ago, in the cathedral. They obviously think it's something small. What is it a key *to*? It must have been something Calain owned. They think Anna has it.'

Maeve joined Logan, kneeling gracefully in front of me. She put her fingers under my chin and raised my face. Her expression was troubled.

'The answer is probably locked away behind that last block,' she said quietly. 'I can help you find out.'

'I said, No,' I returned, slapping her arm away. 'You are *not* getting inside my head again. And the fact you're so eager to makes me wonder what this *ocair* is and why it's important. I haven't forgotten how you used me, Maeve.'

'I know you have no reason to trust me, but I do want to help.' She pressed her lips together. 'I'm sorry for the way I handled the situation. You must remember I've been fighting this war for longer than either you or Logan have been alive.' Deep sadness coloured her tone and dimmed the luminosity of her eyes. 'I've lost many, many family and friends to the Mors Ferrum. I've done a number of things of which I'm ashamed, Rowan. Using you to get to Michael is one of them. But I *will not* lose Jennifer and Logan.' Tears slid down her cheeks.

I leaned forward and pinned her with a strait look. 'I understand that, Maeve.' I glanced at Logan, then back to Maeve. 'That's exactly why I don't trust you. I'm not family and you're frightened of what I can do. You'll always be willing to sacrifice me to protect them.' I rubbed my arms.

Something was missing. The bracelet. I caught Logan's eye and tapped my wrist. He nodded and made scissor motions with his fingers. Relief surged. He'd cut it off, so Michael Eisen wouldn't be able to track me, if that's what it had been.

Maeve rose and walked to the window to stare out. 'Very well. I can understand your hesitancy. We haven't the luxury of debating our worth to each other now, anyway.' She glanced coolly back over her shoulder. 'Logan, is the aeroplane ready?'

'Plane?' I raised my brows at him. The rest of the events of the night leapt back into my mind and I clutched at the chair arms, struggling to my feet.

'My mother! Michael took her to Brisbane. From there they could go anywhere.' My knees weakened again and only sheer force of will kept me upright.

Maeve's expression was cool. 'Yes, we were just planning what to do next. Michael took Anna and flew out to Brisbane only an hour after you fell from his roof. Her passport was missing from the apartment.' She grimaced. 'By the time we'd finished wet cleaning the rooms, disposing of the bodies and erasing security tapes, he'd landed in Brisbane and gone. We don't know if he's still there or has already left the country.'

'Connor said they had a facility there,' I said.

'Well, we are pursuing him. You may, of course, accompany us.' She swept from the room without looking back.

Stunned, I sank back into the chair, turning in bewilderment to Logan. I couldn't make myself think. My brain seized up. How could I trust them? Wasn't chasing after Michael just helping them with their agenda? What if I wasn't of any use any longer? What would they do?

That bastard had my mother. What choice did I have?

Logan knelt again in front of my chair. He turned his steady gaze on me, taking both my hands in his, thumbs gently caressing the backs of mine.

'Red,' he said, his voice low and intense. 'I know you don't trust me and I won't ask you to, not yet. You're scared, you're worried about Anna – and justifiably. All I ask is that you let me help get her back.' He grimaced. 'I am still after Michael. He has more to answer for than ever. So we're on the same side. I can't speak for Maeve's motivations, but I can for mine. I won't lie to you again. Please, let me help.'

I pulled free and rose, pacing the room in agitation, angry at my own weakness and fear. What other options did I have? Given Michael's vast resources, and the limitations imposed on me by that last mental block, I could hardly take him on by myself. I was afraid to – afraid that if I met him I'd lose control and become... whatever it was Calain turned me into when he took over.

'That's why you hate me, isn't it?' I looked back at him. 'Because I'm part Dark and one of them killed your mother.' I laughed. 'And the irony is that my father named me "light" in our language. Man, that must have burned you. That's why you started calling me "Red" instead of Ruadhán or Rowan, isn't it?'

He flushed, his eyes darkening with old pain and coloured by confusion. 'Yes. No, I don't... Dammit. You're potentially the most dangerous person on this planet, Re...Rowan. What you can do, coupled with who you are...might be...' He stopped. 'It scares the crap out of me. But I—'

'Good.' I didn't want to hear any exceptions. 'Keep thinking that way. Don't *let* yourself feel anything else for me. It's not safe.'

He frowned, taking a step towards me.

I backed off. 'No, Logan. I know we're going to need everything in me to even have a hope of defeating Michael. But I don't think I'll ever be able to control Calain and I don't know what he wants. So I want someone…someone to do what's needed if the time comes. *That*, at least, I trust you to do.'

His eyes widened. His hand dropped to his side and he swallowed.

'I see.' He sighed. *Alright. I don't believe it will ever be necessary, but if that's what it takes to get you to trust me even a little, then I'll promise. I won't let you become a monster. I give you my word.*

Good. Let's go, then.

For years I've hidden from the stories in my head. The stories that told me I was something different, something special. Hoping they were wrong.

Now, it seems, they're true.

So, what happens next? I'm not sure I want to find out.

But I don't seem to have a choice.

I am Light in which Shadows have awoken.

THE END

Other books
by Aiki Flinthart

Discover other titles by Aiki Flinthart at:
www.aikiflinthart.com

The 80AD series (YA Adventure/Fantasy)
80AD Book 1: *The Jewel of Asgard*
80AD Book 2: *The Hammer of Thor*
80AD Book 3: *The Tekhen of Anuket*
80AD Book 4: *The Sudarshana*
80AD Book 5: *The Yu Dragon*

The Kalima Chronicles (YA Adventure/Fantasy)
IRON – Book one in the Kalima Chronicles

Sold! (Contemporary Romance/Adventure)

Short Story Anthologies
Return
Like a Woman

Connect with me on Facebook
Twitter: @aikiflinthart
Instagram: Aikiflinthart

Shadows Bane

A taste of things to come…

Whatever happens, Rowan, keep a lid on it. We're here to observe, only.

Logan's terse instruction slid in my head as we commando-crawled our way to the tree line.

Will you take your own advice? I returned irony, which he ignored. I needed to remember to close the "window" in my mental shields that let him talk to me whenever he felt like it. It had been comforting, at first. Now it felt more like I had a constant watchdog, ready to put a leash on the minute I even looked like losing control…well maybe he had a point.

I settled onto my stomach behind a large eucalypt trunk and eased one eye around its smooth silvery bark. Beneath me, dead leaves and curls of long-dried bark crackled and poked through the thin cotton of my black shirt. Wet leaves stuck to my elbows. The pungent smell of damp earth and crushed leaves soothed my tight-wound senses. A night bird hooted in the distance. To the north, the city's vast glow lit the night sky a dirty orange, dimming the stars and lending a dramatic backdrop to the buildings huddled before us.

Almost-automatically, I extended filaments of my mind into the *sianfath* and tested the immediate area. Lots of eucalypts, a few possums watching us, sleeping birds, a myriad of lizards, snakes, tiny insects and spiders. The usual gamut of Australian scary, bitey things. Nothing else. No people, except myself and Logan. Pain in my head flared a warning and I pulled back. Whatever else happened, I needed to find a way to get my father's corrupted memories out of my brain. What was the point of having powers if using them could destroy every human on the Earth?

I caught Logan's eye, sliding a thought into his mind.

There's no-one close by. I pointed at the fenced compound twenty metres away, past open ground stripped of cover. *The closest human is that guard doing the perimeter run. I'd rather not push myself out further, though. I'm risking a major brain-fry as it is. Can you check?*

Logan's eyes unfocussed and I left him to it, watching instead for physical threats. The guard continued his slow stroll around the compound. He yawned and adjusted the belt-holster of his gun. The tap-tap of his boots on concrete slapped back a fraction later off the concrete walls around him. Car headlights swept past, illuminating him for a second. He froze, one hand on his weapon, until the lights vanished. The swish of tyres on wet road, and burr of the engine dwindled away along the dark street.

An ant bit my arm. I swore, pressing at the sharp burn. That *stung!* Dammit, being half-sidhe and connecting to the *sianfath* was supposed to put me at one with the natural world now. Things weren't supposed to bite me, were they? I crushed the brittle exoskeleton, regretting the action as its tiny life faded.

Logan tapped me and pointed at a pair of guards and their dogs, dawdling around one corner of the buildings. They acknowledged the solitary guard as they passed, but didn't speak. Apart from the guards, a three metre mesh fence, topped with rolls of barbed wire, stood between us and the buildings. Security lights and cameras covered every square metre of space between the treeline and the buildings inside the fence. From where we lay, only three of the five concrete monoliths making up the MJE Laboratory facility were visible.

If there was a way to get in unobserved, I couldn't see it.

But we needed to get in. Maybe not right now, but soon. In one of them, we believed, my mother was held hostage by Michael Eisen, MJE's CEO. No, not hostage, for that implied the possibility of a negotiated release; and communication with someone for that negotiation. As far as Eisen was concerned, I was dead, so he had no one to negotiate with. Anna was his prisoner. To do with as he pleased.

I shuddered, imagining the worst. And I already had a fair idea of what the worst might be.

Logan shot me a warning glare. I sucked a slow breath and calmed my racing heart. I needed to be logical; to come up with some new angle. But I'd been over this a thousand times in the last two weeks. There was no conceivable reason why Michael Eisen should keep Anna this long. He wanted information about the *ocair* from her, but she had no idea what an *ocair* was. Beyond knowing it translated to 'key' in the sidhe language, I had no idea either. And key to what? Eisen wanted it, but why?

And Anna wasn't trained to resist torture so why was he keeping her alive – assuming she was still alive – here in his Brisbane lab facility? Not being sidhe, or even half-sidhe like me, she wasn't any use to his genetics research. Could he have real feelings for her? Was it possible their liaison in Cairns hadn't been just a pretence to lure me out of hiding?

There were far more questions than answers, none of which were any help. They only served to wind up my fears of losing her, and increase the risk of me ruining the whole exercise. I forced my heart to slow and the dark-chaos in the back of my mind to settle.

Right now, we were scoping out the MJE facility with a view to getting into it. It had taken us two weeks to find out where my mother was being held. I could wait a few more minutes so Logan could find that out. That and things internet Streetview and satellite images couldn't show us. Like how many people worked there at night and where Anna was being held. How much of the state electricity grid went into lighting up the compound like a prison yard. A lot, was the answer to that.

Finding that out was Logan's job, too. The risk to me – to everyone else - was too great if I tried. I shifted, resenting the need for anyone else, even Logan. But him I trusted, to a limited extent. Myself, I didn't.

If I lost control, things could end catastrophically.

A deep furrow creased his brows. His dark-rimmed, grey eyes skimmed the compound as he used telepathy to search beyond the visible, into the building interiors. His lean form tensed, fingers whitening where they pressed against the ground. Dark leather strained across his broad shoulders.

I followed his line of sight.

Five figures emerged from a steel door, set into the closest building's blank concrete south wall. Two were dressed in black, with helmets and night-vision goggles. They carried automatic rifles of some sort. I didn't know enough about guns to be able to tell what kind from a distance. Weren't they illegal in Australia?

A third also wore black, but sans helmet, goggles and weapon. He carried himself relaxed and loose, his arms easy by his sides, dark hair pulled back into a low, short ponytail. White teeth flashed as he exchanged words with the armed men. He reached behind his waist and metal gleamed dully. A gun or a knife? Hard to tell.

The other two wore dark business suits, even though the evening air was thick with heat and humidity. The taller had his back to us, his dark head and wide shoulders almost obscuring the blond man. The blond I recognised, even from afar: Michael Eisen.

Adrenalin flashed fire into my blood. I placed my palms flat on the leaf-littered ground. Logan's fingers snapped like steel bands around my upper arm. Flesh pressed against bone as he restrained me.

Don't be stupid, Rowan. There's nothing we can do right now.

I twisted free and glared at him. He was right, though. Physically I probably couldn't do anything but get myself captured or killed. That wouldn't help Anna.

There was one thing I could do, though: I could end this, here and now. I could drain Eisen's life as I had his men in Cairns. He deserved it even more. There was no reason why I should play the nice guy.

I focussed my newly-acquired psychic skills on the group.

In the depths of my mind, the caged beast rattled its chains. Shadows stirred, hungry. A flash of pain warned me the psychic block holding them back was being tested. I steadied myself, shoving the darkness deep down. I had to control it. But could I, and still use this particular skill?

Gritting my teeth, I ignored both pain and Logan's attempts to get my attention. I reached through the *sianfath,* the connection my people had with all living things, searching for Michael's unique energy signature.

There: his scent. His aura was a clean, orange-red non-colour. He tasted…angry; frustrated. Why? No, it didn't matter. A few seconds and he would be dead and all this would be over. Pain flared higher. I pushed through it. Even if this killed me, it would be worth it to rid the world of him and make Anna and Logan safe.

I had him; tasted the sour-sweetness of his life-energy; revelled in his vulnerability. He was defenceless; his life was mine.

Shadows Bane will be released in mid 2018